The last thing she wanted was to be indebted to this arrogant man.

She did not want to cause him or his family any more inconvenience than she already had. Nor did she want to remain in such close proximity to him. He disturbed her too much.

"If word gets about that you have been under my roof unchaperoned, the pressure will be brought to bear on me to make a respectable woman of you."

"What?" Her voice rose in earnest. "Make a respectable woman out of me?" Her shoulders straightened. "I may not remember who I am, but I know what I am. I am a respectable woman already, whether *your* reputation is compromised or not."

Georgina Devon has a Bachelor of Arts degree in Social Sciences with a concentration in History. Her interest in England began when the United States Air Force stationed her at RAF Woodbridge, near Ipswich in East Anglia. This is also where she met her husband, who flew fighter aircraft for the United States. She began writing when she left the Air Force. Her husband's military career moved the family every two to three years and she wanted a career she could take with her anywhere in the world. Today, she and her husband live in Tucson, Arizona, with their teenage daughter, two dogs and a cockatiel.

Recent titles by the same author:

THE RAKE*
THE REBEL*
THE ROGUE'S SEDUCTION*

*novels have linking characters

THE LORD AND THE MYSTERY LADY

Georgina Devon

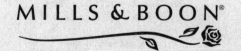

MILLS & BOON®

*First published in Great Britain 2003
Harlequin Mills & Boon Limited,
Eton House, 18-24 Paradise Road, Richmond, Surrey TW9 1SR*

© Alison J. Hentges 2003

ISBN 0 263 83534 0

*Set in Times Roman 10½ on 12 pt.
04-1203-77723*

*Printed and bound in Spain
by Litografía Rosés S.A., Barcelona*

THE LORD AND THE
MYSTERY LADY

Prologue

"Ah, chatting over the daily mutton," Dominic Mandrake Chillings drawled as he took a seat opposite his sister and on the right of his brother.

Guy William Chillings, Seventh Viscount Chillings, raised one black brow. "Witty as usual, Dominic." He took a bite of his well-prepared lamb, topped with a French sauce made by his very French chef, and chewed slowly. "I am glad you could make your way here while the Season is still in full panoply."

Dominic made a mocking half-bow. "The wishes of the head of the family are my marching orders."

"Hah!" Annabell Fenwick-Clyde, Dowager Lady Fenwick-Clyde, said. "You came only because you are curious, Dominic. Nothing more."

Dominic shrugged and cut into the mutton the butler had just set in front of him.

"Enough," Guy said, setting down his fork and rising. "I asked both of you here to discuss my betrothal."

"I beg your pardon?" Dominic said, standing, his food forgotten, his chair pushed back so abruptly that it nearly toppled. "Becoming leg-shackled? About time."

Annabell, a tall, elegant woman in her early thirties with gray, almost silver, hair and black brows like her twin, the Viscount, eyed her brother. "Dominic, I vow, you are being overly dramatic." She turned to her twin and smiled. "Whom do you intend to wed, Guy? Hopefully not one of those bits of muslin you and Dominic insist on enjoying."

Guy tsked. "Sarcasm does not become you, Bell."

He returned her smile to take the sting from his words. He knew his sister disapproved of men keeping mistresses, and she knew he would do as he pleased.

Dominic grinned. "They are not for marrying, Bell. They are for sowing one's wild oats."

Annabell set down her knife and fork. "The both of you use them."

"And pay them well," Dominic said, a small frown drawing his coal-black brows together.

"Enough," Guy said, moving from the table. "I did not invite you here to discuss my proclivities. Although, Dominic is right. The ladies are well paid and more than willing to enter into the bargain. They know the lay of the land very well."

Annabell snorted. "As though they had any choice." She rose as well. "I gather the two of you will not stay here and drink your…whisky."

Dominic stood, his blue, nearly black eyes twinkling. "You make us sound so heathen, Bell. I swear you malign us."

"I merely state the obvious," she said.

He grinned. "Not that you have much leeway in calling us uncivilized. We may not drink port till we slip under the table—"

"No," she interrupted, "you drink unfashionable Scotch whisky."

"But," he continued, "you travel to all parts of the world known and unknown. And usually with only your maid."

She eyed him. "None of my male relatives will accompany me. So I go alone."

He gave a mock shudder. "I've no wish to travel to the places you go, Bell. If you went to the Continent, that would be one thing. But I like my comforts. A tent in the heat and sand are not my idea of comfort."

"Then you have nothing to say about what I do."

She turned and marched to the door before either man could say anything more. Guy exchanged a glance with his younger brother. Both shook their heads.

"She is a widowed bluestocking, and glad of it," Guy said. "I suppose outbursts on women's right to equality are to be expected. Goodness knows she's never let being a female keep her from doing as she damn well pleased."

"Not since Fenwick-Clyde stuck his spoon in the wall."

They followed their sister into the library, where Guy crossed to the burl-walnut desk and poured two glasses of the unfashionable Scotch whisky. He handed one to Dominic and drank the second in two long swallows and poured another. Then Guy raised his glass. "Here's to the future." He downed the contents in one long gulp.

Dominic did the same, saying, "Here's to a life of wine, women and song—or something along those lines."

Annabell grimaced.

A soft knock on the door preceded the butler's arrival with the tea tray, which he set on a small kidney table near the front windows. Annabell smiled at Oswald and thanked him. The butler, his short, lean frame impeccably groomed, smiled back.

"Do either of you wish for tea?" she enquired, knowing the answer, but asking anyway. It was one of the small ways she nettled them.

Both men looked aghast at her while Guy picked up the decanter and poured each of them another generous portion. He sauntered to one of the chairs grouped around the window that looked out on to Grosvenor Square and beside the table where the tea tray sat. A fashionable phaeton driven by an even more fashionable dandy passed by. Several young ladies, followed by footmen carrying parcels, strolled along the pavement. The Season was in full swing. He sat and stretched his legs out.

"As I started to tell you, I am engaged."

"To whom?" Annabell interjected. She sat by the tea table and across from her brother.

"Miss Emily Duckworth," he said flatly.

"No, Guy," Annabell said. "She is not up to your weight."

"I never," Dominic said in disgust. He paced the room, his energy needing an outlet. "You will get no pleasure from her, I vow."

"You are both wrong," Guy drawled. "The lady is very aware of the bargain we strike and more than willing to fulfil her duty. I need an heir and she wants a husband."

"Cold, Guy," Annabell said. "You are as cold as…as…"

"Let me help you," Dominic said. "Cold as a witch's—"

"Thank you very much," Annabell interrupted before he could finish the saying.

"You are both wrong," Guy said, swirling the amber liquid in its cut-crystal glass. "I am pragmatic. I need an heir. Miss Duckworth will provide one. She needs a husband to protect her and to give her the wealth and caché to make a splash in Society. She has an impeccable lineage, but her brother is finishing what her father started by gambling away what is left of the family funds." He finished the liquor. "I, not to be too vulgar, am as rich as Golden Ball. In short, we are perfectly suited."

Annabell muttered something unladylike under her breath. "Cold as Siberia."

Dominic laughed, but it was more bitter than humourous. "So apropos. Women only marry where they see advantage. Give me the ladies of the night. They, at least, are honest in their dealings."

"You are jaded, Dominic," Guy said, setting down his empty glass.

"And what are you?" Annabell asked. "Bright-eyed and bushy-tailed?"

"Neither," Guy said, beginning to get bored with the conversation. "As I said, this is a practical arrangement. Nothing more."

"It could be worse," Dominic said. "It could be a love match, as your first marriage was." He crossed to the desk and poured himself another glass, thus missing the dark look that crossed his brother's countenance. "Care for another?" he asked.

"Just bring the decanter over here," Guy said.

"Ah," Annabell murmured, having seen the flash of pain on her twin's face. "You are doing this because

Suzanne died in childbirth and the babe with her. No more emotional risks for you.''

"That was ten years ago," Guy said, his voice flat. "I am past that. But I am thirty-three. I need an heir." He eyed his siblings through narrowed lids. "Unless one of you intends to provide me with one, since the title can pass to Dominic and then you, Bell.''

"Don't look to me," Dominic said. "I have no need of an heir, so I don't need to marry—for convenience or love.''

"And I cannot inherit while there is a male heir, Guy, so don't be ridiculous," Annabell said tartly.

"Just so," Guy murmured. "Hence my upcoming marriage.''

"To your nuptials," Dominic said, lifting his glass as he continued to pace.

Guy raised one black brow. "Must you make a nuisance of yourself with constant movement?''

Annabell smiled. "He never could sit still. Not even in the nursery, when his reward for not moving for ten minutes was cake. You cannot expect him to have changed, Guy." She added, "Particularly considering what you just told us.''

Dominic stopped momentarily and grinned. "She's right, you know.''

Guy shrugged and turned his attention to the portrait of the three of them, which hung over the mantel. It had been painted when he and Bell were twenty and Dominic sixteen. Before Suzanne.

Suzanne was a subject he found hard to discuss. They had been childhood friends who married. He had been happy with her, had thought he loved her. Then she had died trying to give him an heir and the baby with her. It was only in the past couple of years that he had come to terms with the guilt he felt over her death. If he had not got her pregnant she would be alive. But that was the way of their world.

He took a deep breath, intending to speak and instead stood. He felt as pent up as Dominic looked. He poured himself another full glass of whisky, not offering any to Dominic. He downed the drink as he had the previous ones. Then poured another.

"No sense drinking yourself into oblivion," Annabell said, taking a sip of tea. "Do you even like Miss Duckworth, Guy?"

Guy smiled. "You always could change subjects faster than anyone I know. As for Miss Duckworth, I don't know her well enough to like or dislike her." Which was fine with him. She was to have his heir. Nothing more.

"Going a bit too far," Dominic said. He stopped his pacing and came to stand beside them. "Ramshackle as I am, I would not marry a woman I didn't at least like."

"He has a point, Guy," Annabell said gently.

"For him, perhaps," Guy said. "But then he does not have to marry. He can afford to do as he pleases."

Both Annabell and Dominic nodded.

Dominic said sardonically, "It is tough being the oldest. All that blunt, not to mention the title." He raised one hand to forestall comments when Annabell opened her mouth. "Not that I want the title. No, not me. Having too much fun being the black sheep of the family."

"Is that why you aren't married?" Annabell arched one dark brow.

Dominic's swarthy face darkened. "Tease me all

you like, Bell. I don't intend to marry. Besides, no respectable woman would have me.''

Dominic had been wild as a boy. As a man he was nearly a reprobate and decidedly a libertine.

Guy interrupted Bell's quizzing of Dominic, who was beginning to look harassed. ''I think we have discussed everything. Shall we go on to Prinny's gathering at Covent Garden?''

Annabell shuddered. ''Not me, thank you. There are some things I need to research before we start seriously uncovering the Roman villa we have just found on Sir Hugo Fitzsimmon's Kent estate.''

''Fitzsimmon?'' Guy said, concern entering his voice. ''He is a worse libertine than Dominic. And he makes me look like a boy still in leading strings.''

She shrugged. ''He is in Paris with Wellington. I shall never even meet him.''

''Hope not, Bell,'' Dominic said. ''He has led me down a long, dark night before. You would not like him in the least.''

''And I shall not meet him, brothers,'' she said pointedly. ''I learned more about debauchery than any woman needs to know from Fenwick-Clyde.''

A barely suppressed shudder sped through her body. Her marriage had been arranged and not happy.

Guy regretted what had happened to Bell, but he had not been Viscount then, and their parents had believed in marriages of convenience. Theirs had been one and a very happy one. Both had died in a boating accident shortly after Annabell wed and they therefore did not live to see her unhappiness.

''Well, I am going to Prinny's little get-together,'' Guy said pointedly. ''The two of you are welcome to do as you please.''

"Getting as much enjoyment from life as you can before walking down the aisle?" Dominic teased.

"Leave him be," Annabell said.

"A man has to do what he has to do, Dominic," Guy said darkly. "Some day you will learn that." He turned back to them, his lips twisted sardonically. "Wish me luck."

Chapter One

Six months later...

Guy spurred his gelding on. The sleet and wind billowed out his many-caped greatcoat and laid a layer of frost on his moustache and beard, both a fashionable *faux pas*. He did not care. He had decided long ago to do as he pleased. And if he wished to have facial hair, then he would.

The weather had trapped him in The Folly for the last week, making him irritable. He had decided this morning to visit the nearest town, where his current mistress, a widow of good standing, lived. Their arrangement was for mutual convenience. He provided the money and she provided the sexual relief. The situation suited him and he intended to enjoy it as much as possible. When he married Miss Duckworth in the coming spring, he would feel honour bound to terminate this liaison. He was not looking forward to that time. Jane was very skilled in many things.

He slowed his horse to cross a small, rock bridge that spanned a rapidly running stream. The animal slipped on the ice. Man and beast swayed. Then they were safely across the bridge and on to hard-packed earth that was fast turning to mud.

Guy leaned forward and patted his gelding on the neck. "Good boy, Dante."

The horse whickered and tossed its head in regal acceptance. Guy laughed.

They cantered up the hill until the valley spread below them. A light sprinkling of snow blanketed the moor. Gorse, a deep grey-green, was everywhere Guy looked. The wind grabbed at the muffler wrapped around his face and pulled it away. He caught the woollen scarf at the last instant.

He stopped, the muffler safe in his right hand. Below him, where a larger road ran, was a turned-over coach. The axle had broken. The horses did not look hurt from here. A man, whom guy took to be the driver, walked the animals in an attempt to keep them from cooling too rapidly. The accident must have happened recently.

Guy spurred Dante forward until they came abreast of the wreck. He reined in his mount and leapt lightly to the ground, his Hessians crunching rock and ice. "Is anyone hurt?"

The coachman paused only long enough to give Guy a quick once-over, then jerked his head towards a small outcropping of rock. "Her."

A woman lay on the cold ground, a black cape wrapped around her recumbent body. Her eyes were closed and her skin was deathly pale. Wisps of chestnut-coloured hair strayed around her face. Her lips were blue tinged.

Guy's heart skipped a beat.

He crossed the ground and squatted by her. Her chest

rose and fell in rapid, shallow breaths. Relief was sharper than he liked.

"Madam?" he asked softly.

When she did not respond, he took one of her hands. Her fingers were like ice through the black kid of her gloves. She had to be moved to a warm location. Soon.

"How long has she been like this?" he asked, never taking his eyes from her.

"Since I pulled her from the carriage," came the laconic answer.

The man's curt answer told him nothing. Impatience twisted Guy's gut. "How long ago was that?" he asked, biting off each word.

"Thirty, sixty minutes. Don't rightly know for sure."

Guy swallowed a scathing retort. Berating the man would not help the woman.

Letting go of the woman's hand, he slid his arms under her back and thighs and lifted her. She settled against his chest, curling automatically into him. The hood of her cape fell back, and her hair loosened and tumbled down until it nearly touched the ground. Guy paused instinctively, not wanting to tread on the silken strands.

She had beautiful hair. The weak winter sunlight made the thick ripples flash like diamonds tossed into copper. The weight of it pulled her head back, exposing the slim column of her neck. A pulse, weak and quick, beat like a bird's wings. She was delicate and sensual all at once.

And she was hurt.

Guy took a deep breath and looked away from her. The closest place was The Folly. His housekeeper could look after this woman better than the town's apothecary. The nearest doctor was in Newcastle, several hours away.

He whistled and Dante came. There was no way to lift her gently without help. "You, sir," Guy said to the man, who was finally slowing down the horses, "come give me a hand."

The man scowled, his brown brows forming an uninterrupted bar across his forehead. But he came.

Guy handed the woman to him. "Hand her up to me once I'm mounted."

The man hesitated before taking her. "Who'm you be?"

Totally unused to having someone ask his identity, Guy paused in the act of swinging his leg over the saddle. "Viscount Chillings."

"How'm I ter know that?"

A sardonic smile curved Guy's thin lips. "Because I say so. Besides, man, you have no choice. She cannot remain here on the ground in the cold. I am taking her to my home. I will send a groom to help you." The man still did not hand the woman up. "You may count on it." Guy said softly, his eyes narrowing.

Something in the look swayed the man for he finally lifted the woman up. Guy caught her under the arms, her cape initially keeping him from getting a good grip. Finally, after much shifting, she lay precariously in front of him, her back against his chest with his arms around her. He had tucked her glorious hair into the hood of her cape. It was a less than perfect place for such heavy and unbound curls, but it would have to do.

He urged Dante slowly forward. The last thing he or the woman needed was to take a fall. He heard the man return to the horses as he guided Dante to the track that led home. Jane would have to wait until he got this woman situated.

Guy looked down at her. Close to his chest, with his body shielding her from the wind, her face was regaining some colour. Peach blossomed on her high cheekbones, a striking contrast to the rich chestnut of her lashes that lay like a slash against the paleness of her eyelids. Her lips had relaxed into a full, plump pout that must be natural rather than caused by dissatisfaction. Her hair tangled around her face in waves before falling into the folds of her cape.

He realized with an unpleasant start that he wanted her. There was nothing logical about it, only pure desire. He never responded like this to a woman—any woman.

He told himself it was because he had been anticipating his visit to Jane. He had not been with his mistress for long enough that his body was behaving toward this woman like a boy with his first encounter, which was out of character. Guy made it a point not to let himself get carried away by his desires; being aroused by a woman he did not even know and who lay limply in his arms would be getting carried away.

Still, the occasional hint of lavender that wafted from her was enough to make him tighten. Once she stirred and he thought she would waken. She didn't.

They covered ground slowly, giving Guy more than enough time to think. Who was she? Quality from her dress. Where was she bound and why was she alone? He would find out soon enough when she woke. Patience was a virtue he had cultivated while he waited agonizingly for Suzanne to finish her unusually long labour and present him with his heir. Only she had been dying and taking their son with her. Ever since then he had waited for nothing. An event or object was either his for the taking or he walked away.

He roused from his thoughts when The Folly came into view. Without being directed, Dante turned on to the circular drive that passed by the front door and stopped when they reached the steps.

Like the superbly trained butler he was, Oswald was down the marble steps before Guy could summon him. ''My lord, let me help.''

The butler reached for the still-unconscious woman, and Guy gave her over. The day's cold hit him in the chest and groin, tightening his muscles. It was an uncomfortable reaction.

''Have Mrs Drummond see to her.'' He turned Dante around and headed for the stables without a backward glance. He would check on the woman and then, if the weather did not worsen, he would go to the village and finish what he had started out to do.

Guy entered the foyer and stamped the ice off his boots. The frozen water turned into puddles on the black-and-white marble squares.

''Tsk, my lord. You know how you dislike any imperfection in The Folly and dirty water is an imperfection,'' a woman said.

Already irritated with the entire situation, Guy rounded on the speaker. ''Mrs Drummond, you are a favoured servant, but even you may only go so far.''

She drew herself up to a very imposing height. She was a veritable Hera, her greying hair pulled back into a severe bun, her brown eyes still full of spirit. In her youth she had been Guy's nanny.

''Yes, my lord.'' She made him a deep curtsy.

Guy sighed and scratched at his beard. "Yes, Mrs Drummond," he said, his tone back to the indulgent one he normally used with her. "Fortunately you hold a spot in my heart."

The smile she always had for him came out. "Yes, my lord, and you in mine. Now, about the girl."

"What about her? She will have to stay here until she is able to travel."

It was not the answer he wanted to give, but there was no other. It boded no good for anyone that she aroused him even when she was unconscious, but he still could not throw her out. He would just have to resist the urgings of his body, something he was more than capable of doing.

"Just as I thought." The older woman eyed the man who had once run to her with every hurt. "I will be chaperon enough, I believe. For now, and for as long as none of your friends realize she is here."

His eyes clouded. He had been so focused on his reaction to the strange woman that he had forgotten about the proprieties. The last thing he wanted to do was compromise a woman of Quality, and he suspected that his unwelcome guest was just that. Then he would have to pay the piper with his freedom. Or, worse still, seduce her.

He had reconciled himself back in June to marrying for convenience. He needed an heir before all else since Dominic was giving no indication of ever marrying. But he intended to marry Miss Duckworth, not some strange woman whose name he did not even know simply because of the proprieties.

"She should not be here long. She did not appear to have injuries," he said, confident of his ability to avoid compromise. "Otherwise, I will need someone besides you for appearance's sake."

"She will be here as long as she needs," Mrs Drummond said, her voice a shade sharp. "She has a head injury. There is a bump the size of a hen's egg on the back of her head. That is very likely why she has not regained consciousness." Mrs Drummond shook her head. "Remember when Miss Annabell fell out of that tree, and she didn't wake up for a day? Like to scare ten years off my life."

Guy remembered only too well. That was only one of his sister's more punishing adventures. Bell had been a hellion. She was still more independent than was acceptable.

But Bell was his sister and that had been a long time ago. The last thing he wanted was for this woman to be confined under his roof for more than a couple of hours, a couple of days at the outside.

"Do you think that is what this woman will do?"

Mrs Drummond shrugged. "Only time will tell. Will you be checking on her?"

He did not need to go near his unwelcome guest any more than he needed to stick his hand in a basket of adders. But it was his duty to see that she was cared for. That meant, to him, looking in on her himself. He trusted his servants, but he was ultimately responsible.

"Later," he said, irritated at the tiny spurt of interest that held him. "After you have seen to her comfort."

Already this woman was causing him trouble. She had prevented his trip to Jane and now she was going to be a burden until she left. Heaven help her if her presence compromised his engagement to Miss Duckworth.

* * *

Hours later, Guy entered the Sylph Room where his unwelcome guest slept. Aqua and jewel-tone shades of green and blue made the chamber seem like an underwater grotto. Mahogany and rosewood furniture mixed like elegant tropical fish. Gossamer curtains done in ever-shifting shades of blue and green framed the high four-poster bed that held the woman.

By the light of the fire, he noticed a young serving girl seated in a corner, her fingers busy darning a stocking. "You may go now, Mary," he told her.

She jumped up and bobbed a curtsy. "Yes, my lord. I dinna know you were here, my lord." Even as the words left her mouth, she skittered to the door.

Guy smiled. She had only been here a fortnight or so. Given time, she would learn that none of his servants feared him. They respected him and he respected them. He found that to be a mutually satisfying arrangement. His parents had taught him the benefits and the burdens of *noblesse oblige*.

He crossed to get the servant's forgotten candle before going to the bed. His guest lay pale as the frost that rimed the windows. Her skin stretched taut and translucent over elegantly formed cheekbones and a pointed chin. Dark circles accentuated her wide-set eyes and drew attention to high arched brows and a thick sweep of lashes. Her lips were still full, pink and pouty. But it was her hair, a gloriously tumbled mess, which caught and held him. The urge to touch the silken strands, to run his fingers through their length, was nearly overwhelming.

He stepped abruptly back. The last thing he needed was to intimately touch this woman. She was alone and under his protection. She was also a woman he would

be obligated to marry if he compromised her. Both
were arguments that should help him keep his distance.

To hell with her hair.

He took a deep, calming breath and studied the rest
of her. The cover was pulled up over her small breasts
and tucked around her. Mrs Drummond had found a
nightshirt that buttoned up the woman's long, elegant
neck, completely hiding the vulnerable pulse he had
seen when she had lain in his arms.

The scent of lavender was stronger now. Was it her
hair or coming from the clothing Mrs Drummond had
dressed her in? Possibly both.

A shift, a moan, and he found himself looking into
hazel eyes, ringed in gold. He took a step back.

Her mouth opened and her tongue peeked out. His
loins tightened in a response so automatic, so strong,
that Guy cursed under his breath.

"Who are you?" His voice was harsher than he had
intended.

She blinked. "I…" She closed her eyes and took a
deep breath. "Could I please have a drink of water?"

Nonplussed but ever the courteous host, he picked
up the jug by the bed and poured her a glass. "Of
course." He held out the water. "Can you drink it on
your own?"

She watched him with an intensity he found disturbing. "I think so. Thank you."

She edged up in bed and reached for the glass he
still held. With a mental expletive at his own awk-
wardness, he moved closer to the bed so that she could
grasp the glass. Her fingers, long and slim, touched his
briefly as she took the drink. Her arm trembled but she
said nothing, only put the liquid to her lips and drank

until it was gone. He took the glass from her just as she sank back into the pillows.

"Thank you," she murmured, her voice low and weak.

"You are welcome," he answered formally, setting the empty container aside. Without asking her permission, he pulled a chair up and sat down so that his face was level with hers. "Now, who are you?"

He knew it was impossible for her to pale more, but it appeared as though she did. Perhaps it was the way she seemed to shrink into the bed.

For long seconds she looked at him before shifting slightly and staring at the fire. Impatience began to gnaw at him, but Guy kept quiet. Finally, she turned back to him.

"I…" She licked her lips. "I don't—can't…" Her eyes widened and their brilliance dimmed. "I don't know." Her voice lowered until he could barely hear her. "I don't know who I am."

He scowled. "The hit on the head." When she turned her bewildered face to him, he repeated, "You hit your head. That probably made you forget who you are. It happened to my sister, but she regained her memory the following day."

Her mouth opened in a soft circle, but she said nothing. It was as though her power of speech was gone along with her memory loss.

He instinctively took her hand and held it between his palms, regretted it as electricity sparked up his arm. Still he did not release her.

"Don't worry. This will not last long."

He smiled even though irritation and worry battled in his gut. The last thing he needed was a lady of Quality in his home, let alone one with no memory and one he was inexplicably drawn to—to put his reaction to her mildly. Yet there was nothing he could do. Until she regained her memory, he could not send her away because no one knew where her way led. And it might take minutes or weeks before she remembered.

She did not return his smile. Her hand lay flaccid in his as though with her memory went not only speech but all sensation.

"It will be all right," he said again. "These things happen."

Her eyes closed and he would swear she cried softly, the tears seeping like crystals from the corners of her eyes. But she made no sound and the light was too weak for him to be sure of what he saw. He waited.

Suzanne had not cried much, but when she had she had wanted him to hold her and just let her cry. It was a painful jolt to remember that now, under these circumstances. He no longer thought about Suzanne as much as he had. Ten years had gone a long way to easing his grief. But he still remembered the pain of losing her and the babe.

Finally the woman opened her eyes. "Thank you," she said softly. "Thank you for your patience."

She was so frail. Much as he wanted to question her further, he knew she needed a rest. He would talk to the man who had driven her coach and see what he knew.

Guy released her hand and stood. "I will send my housekeeper to you. You need to sleep. Really sleep to regain your strength. And in all likelihood when you waken your memory will have returned."

She smiled wanly at him. "Like your sister?" she said softly.

He had not yet reached the door when it opened and

Mrs Drummond bustled in. She glanced at him, saw he was fine and turned her attention and energies on the invalid.

"You poor dear. You must have the headache to end all headaches. The lump on the back of your head is as big as my fist."

The woman's smile widened slightly, but tiredness etched lines around her mouth and eyes. "It does hurt a little."

Mrs Drummond shook her head. "I dare say it hurts more than that. A good dose of laudanum will go far in easing the discomfort."

Suiting action to words, she picked up a small bottle that sat beside the jug, opened it and measured out a dose into the nearby glass. She added water, mixed the concoction and put the glass to the woman's lips.

Guy left.

She drank the opium willingly, unsure which hurt more, her head or the emptiness that filled her. Mrs Drummond smiled at her and took the empty glass from her shaking hands.

"You will feel better when this takes effect," the housekeeper said kindly.

She forced herself to smile at the older woman. "Thank you."

"You rest now," Mrs Drummond said, snuffing the candle by the bed.

She watched the housekeeper leave. She knew the laudanum would ease the pain. Her mouth twisted bitterly. But she did not know her own name and despair welled up in her.

Who was she? Why had she been travelling alone? She did not think women did that. She sighed and closed her eyes. But maybe they did. If she could not remember who she was, how could she trust the memories she did have?

And that man. Viscount Chillings. Heat flushed her cheeks. He had been so arrogant and demanding…and her heart had skipped a beat when she first saw him. Tall, slim and elegant, with eyes so dark a blue they were nearly black. His face was long and thin, aristocratic, with a nose that had the hint of a hook and a mouth that had sent shivers of awareness down her spine. She had hoped he was someone in her life, a lover or husband. But no. He had put paid to that fleeting thought.

He had made it abundantly clear that she was not welcome and would be seen out the door as soon as her memory returned. Yet, he had also been kind when she had given way to emotion and cried. She knew that most men would have lost their patience, although she did not know how she knew that.

She sighed and shifted, trying to get more comfortable. The way her senses had reacted to him, it would be to the better if she left right now. Especially if he was going to be even a little bit caring. But she could not.

The drowsy, floating sensation of the drug began to take hold. With the medication came a sense of emotional ease, the anguish of not knowing who she was fading as sleep claimed her.

She welcomed it.

Chapter Two

The coachman stood before Guy, hat in hand, finally awed by the personage who had rescued them. Behind Guy, the library windows looked out on gardens covered in a light drift of snow. The coachman shifted from scuffed boot to scuffed boot as Guy came around to the front of his desk. Hopefully, this man knew who the woman upstairs was. Otherwise she was going to be his guest for a longer time than he liked.

"The lady you were driving has lost her memory," Guy began without preamble. There was no sense in dragging this interview out. "Therefore, I need your help in finding her family. First, what is her name?"

The man grimaced. "Doan' rightly know, my lord. She gave it as Mrs Smith." He shrugged his massive shoulders while his fingers twisted his woollen cap. "Doan' rightly think that could be her name. But mayhap it is."

Guy swallowed an expletive. The man was probably right. Mrs Smith. How unimaginative. "Mrs. Smith?"

"Yes'm, my lord." Now he twisted the brim of his hat in earnest until it was a screw of material.

"You don't work for her, then." It was a flat state-

ment that did more than any show of anger to convey
Guy's growing exasperation.

"No, my lord."

Guy scowled. "You can answer in more than two-
and three-word sentences, my good man."

"Yes'm, my lord."

Guy swallowed a sharp retort. He was going to have
to pull every bit of information from this man. "Where
did she hire you and where was she going?"

"Newcastle-upon-Tyne. London. My lord." The
man's Adam's apple bobbed beneath grey stubble.

"Any other details?" Guy asked, impatience creeping into his tone.

"No, my lord."

"Did she pay you with cash or a bank draft?"

"Coin, my lord."

"I am not a bloody Bow Street Runner out to catch
you for a crime," Guy said, allowing his irritation to
break forth. "There are obviously details that you don't
consider important. I want to know them."

"Yes'm, my lord."

Guy eyed him with dislike. Even the surly lout the
man had been when Guy found them would be pref-
erable to this oaf he had turned into who could not or
would not put effort into his answers. Nothing irritated
Guy more than a man or woman who shirked his duty.
And it was this man's duty to help the woman upstairs.
He had taken her money.

"Did she have much luggage?"

"A portmanteau, my lord."

Not a long stay, then. "Any other luggage?" Most
women of his acquaintance carried more than one
piece.

"A small leather one, my lord. I brought it and the other here."

Guy nodded. "Was anyone with her when she dealt with you?"

"No, my lord."

Guy leaned back on the edge of his desk, arms crossed, and decided he was getting nowhere fast. But he did not know anything else to ask this man. Ah, one last thing.

"Did she come to you in a carriage?"

"Yes'm, my lord."

"Was there any marking on the carriage? And, if so, what colour was it? Were the horses of good quality?"

"No, my lord. It was a plain black carriage. Decent horses. Probably hired." The man's lips lifted in the beginning of a smile.

Guy smiled back, tightly and not entirely satisfied, but the answer was more detailed than he had expected. The man obviously noticed horseflesh and enjoyed talking about them. He would have to be content with that.

"Thank you. That will be all."

The man's feet shuffled faster but he didn't leave. Guy waited him out.

"About my coach, your lordship."

Guy knew what was coming, but said nothing. The woman had paid coin for her journey. Unless the coach was ruined, the money should be enough to fix it. They were not that far from Newcastle that the man's expenses had taken up the compensation.

The man cleared his throat. "I needed to make a profit on this trip, my lord. Fixing the vehicle will take everything I have left from Mrs Smith's payment."

"And why should she or I pay for the repairs? You

did not take her all the way to London, so you don't have those expenses.''

The coachman's brows drew together. ''Because it was 'cause of her that we turned over. She told me to go fast even though I told her the road was bad. She said she had an appointment that she could not miss or be late for.'' His frown intensified. ''She promised me more money if I did as she bade.''

An appointment she could not miss or be late for. Interesting. ''Did she give you the extra money before you sped up?''

''No, my lord. She said she did not have enough on her. I would get it when we reached London.''

The man did have a claim and this was information that might be useful. At the least, it told him more about the woman. And, if it were true, then she was to blame for the man's broken axle. If the man lied, there was no way he could find that out until she regained her memory. There was nothing for it.

''I will have my smith repair your coach.''

The man nodded. ''Thank you, my lord.''

As though realizing he would get no more and had already tried Guy's patience nearly to exhaustion, he hurried from the room.

Guy watched the door close behind the coachman. How much more was this woman going to inconvenience him? The cost of fixing the coach was negligible. It was the time.

He stood and went to stand in front of one of a series of windows that ran the circular outside wall of the room. Outside the grounds were covered with frost. The artificial lake had a sheen of ice that might be thick enough to skate on. He would have to try it later.

Meanwhile, he had to do something. He crossed to

the fireplace and yanked the bell pull that would call Oswald. The butler was quick.

"My lord?" he said.

Guy smiled at him. "You at least have a brain and a will to use it."

Face impassive, Oswald said, "Yes, my lord."

Guy's smile widened as he told his butler about the interview. "As you can see, the man is dimwitted or lazy or both. I want someone to take the lady's luggage to my rooms. Perhaps there is something in them that will tell us who she is."

"Immediately, my lord."

"If there is nothing of note and she does not regain her memory in the next day or two, I shall send a man to Newcastle."

"Tim would be just the man, my lord. He has family there."

"Good."

Guy turned back to the window. Another inconvenience. Tim was the only Englishman the French chef would tolerate. François would raise the roof if he left.

Oswald left with a purposeful stride. Guy knew he could depend on the servant. He thought briefly about having the luggage brought here instead, but somehow the library seemed too public for her private things.

He would answer his correspondence and check with his factor on estate business and then he would go upstairs. Some things he would not put off.

Several hours later he entered the privacy of his rooms. "Jeffries," he called to his valet.

The gentleman's gentleman materialized from the doorway that led to where Guy's clothing was kept. "Yes, my lord?"

The valet was small and wiry, prim and proper. Impeccably clothed, he ensured that Guy was dressed to the nines—when Guy let him.

"I have some personal business to attend to. I will call you when I need you again."

Jeffries cast a glance at the luggage that sat in the middle of the floor. "As you wish, my lord."

Guy watched him take his leave before going to the woman's toiletry case. It was expensive; tooled leather with silver chasing. The bottles and jars inside were cut crystal with silver tops. The comb and brush were both hallmarked silver, each worked with a capital F and A. Possibly her initials. The toothbrush was immaculate. Everything sparkled. He emptied the case and turned it over, his long fingers working along the edges to see if there was a catch or lever that opened a secret compartment. That was where anything of value would be.

"Ah," he murmured as his fingers detected a tiny projection. Seconds later, a small drawer slid open.

A golden glint caught his attention. He picked up a simple band and took it closer to a candle. Winter's gloom had set in early as usual.

He turned the ring so that he could see inside. Often there was writing. As there was this time. He could barely make out the names Felicia and Edmund. Was this a wedding band? It looked like one. But was it hers? And if it was, why wasn't she wearing it? It was too small to be a man's. It could be her mother's.

Guy laid it on the table by the toiletry case and put everything else back where it belonged. He sat down in one of two large, leather wing-backed chairs that angled around the roaring fire.

She was probably married. He should be thankful.

A married woman might be ostracized if it became known that she had spent time in his bachelor establishment, but she would not be ruined like a maiden would. He would not be required to wed this woman no matter what happened.

Perhaps there was something in her portmanteau that would tell him who she was. He got back up and went to the piece, only to pause with both hands on the clasp. Her intimate apparel would be inside. Somehow that was much more disturbing than looking in the toiletry case had been. But he needed more information than Felicia and Edmund engraved on the inside of a wedding band.

With a quick flick of his fingers, he opened the case. The first thing out was a warm black woollen dress with long sleeves and a high neckline. Nothing like the thin muslins women of fashion wore in London. Guy's lips curved. She was not a slave to the current style. He set that aside.

Next was a pair of fine lawn drawers trimmed in Brussels lace. They slid across his hands like the finest silk. Lavender rose from the gossamer material. Without thought, he put the delicate material to his face and breathed deeply. Lavender, a scent as innocent as linens, yet as provocative as a partially clad woman. His loins tightened in a hard, fast reaction. He dropped the underclothing.

Taking a deep breath, he forced himself to relax. She was only a woman and one he did not even know. The last thing he—or she—needed was for him to desire her.

He left the drawers where they had fallen on the floor and reached for the next item of clothing. Stays. Again the scent of lavender clung to them. Again, he could picture all too vividly the rich material cupping below her small breasts.

This was insane.

He dropped the stays as well and paced to the window, which he opened wide to the freezing evening air. Something needed to cool his unwanted ardour for a strange woman who meant nothing to him.

His reaction was absurd. He had never had this uncontrolled reaction to Suzanne or any other woman, for that matter. He had wanted to protect Suzanne and cherish her. He had enjoyed making love to her, but he had never desired her as wantonly as his body did this unknown woman. Never.

A knock on the door interrupted his unacceptable thoughts. ''Come in,'' he said without leaving the window and the bracing cold of the outside.

''My lord,'' Mrs Drummond said. ''The woman is awake.'' Her voice lowered. ''She still does not know who she is.''

Weary and fed up with his unwelcome reactions to the woman, he said, ''I believe her name is Felicia. Or that was her mother's. If it is hers, she is probably married to Edmund. If not, he is likely her father.''

''Oh,'' Mrs Drummond said, entering and making her way to the portmanteau and the dropped underclothing. She picked up the drawers and stays. ''These are expensive.''

''Yes, they are,'' Guy said, turning at last and watching his housekeeper.

Mrs Drummond picked up the dress and turned it inside out. ''Very nicely done. Not the height of fashion as might be seen in London, but top quality.''

''I thought so,'' Guy said drily. A tiny smile tugged

up one corner of his mouth. "It seems she is a lady of means, whoever she is."

"These are all black," Mrs Drummond said. "As was the clothing she had on."

"I know," Guy said solemnly.

"Was there any jewellery?" Mrs Drummond folded the clothes and replaced them in the portmanteau before turning her attention to the toiletry case. She immediately saw the gold band, which lay on the table beside the case. Picking it up, she squinted to see if there was any writing.

Guy took mercy on her older eyes. "Felicia and Edmund are engraved on the inside."

Mrs Drummond raised one grey brow. "Anything about love?"

Guy shook his head, realizing this was the first time it had occurred to him that there might be a term of endearment. "Perhaps it is merely a friendship ring."

"Or a ring given in a marriage of convenience."

"That, too."

Mrs Drummond kept the ring in her hand. "The young lady wishes to speak with you. Take this and show it to her. It might jolt something loose, my lord."

"The sooner she remembers who she is the better." Guy took the ring and left.

Her room was on the floor above. He stopped and knocked on the door, then opened it before she responded.

She lay on the bed, propped up by numerous pillows, her hair spread around her like a fan. A single lit candle provided a golden glow in contrast to the orange flames of the fire. The light caught the ripples of her hair and turned them copper and gold and bronze. He ached to bury his fingers in the thick tresses.

Surely, he was going crazy.

She watched him pace towards her.

Tall, with an arrogant tilt to his long, narrow face, he was an aristocrat from the top of his head to the finely tooled leather slippers on his feet. A short black beard and full moustache softened what she thought was a square jaw. His mouth was wide and well formed, the opposite of thin and pinched.

She paused in her study and wondered where the last thought had come from. Did she know a man whose mouth was thin and pinched, almost cruel in its sparseness?

He passed between her and the fire, throwing his shadow on the bed where she lay. Her attention rushed back to him. From this distance his eyes appeared as dark as his brows, which were drawn into a frown. Yet, his hair was silver. Her senses were on edge from his nearness.

He stopped several feet from the bed and seemed to tower over her. A black satin dressing gown, picked out in a silver pattern that reminded her of chinoiserie, was belted at his narrow waist. A white shirt showed at the V of the robe and black trousers flowed from the robe's hem to his feet. With the exception of his moustache and beard, he was the height of fashion.

She frowned. She knew he was fashionable, yet she did not know her own name or where she was from or where she had been going.

The man—the housekeeper had said he was Guy William Chillings, Seventh Viscount Chillings—pulled a slipper chair covered in ice blue satin up to the bed. She watched him sit down with the grace of a man who was familiar with his own body. A shiver skipped down her spine.

She chided herself. For all she knew, she was married. The thought of marriage made her uncomfortable, as though the idea were repugnant. But there was no other sensation, no remembrance of a man touching her, kissing her. Nothing. A sigh escaped her.

Viscount Chillings leaned forward. "Have you remembered something?"

His voice was a low, smooth baritone, seductive in its beauty. Its elegant tone suited him.

"No," she managed.

"No," he repeated, his voice wrapping around the word and making it seem nearly a term of endearment.

She shook her head in an attempt to clear it of this fancifulness. His voice did unusual things to her, made her think of things better left unsaid and undone. When she had herself under better control, she spoke. "Nothing, really, Lord Chillings."

He crossed one leg over the other. "That is too bad. I had hoped you would be back to normal by now." His eyes narrowed as he held out his hand. "Perhaps this will help."

Gold flashed in the light from the candle. A wedding band rested in the palm of his hand. She stared at it for what seemed like a long time. He continued to hold the piece of jewellery towards her as though he intended her to take it. She did not want to. She had an unreasonable aversion to the ring.

She looked back at him. If he noticed her reluctance, his face did not show that awareness. His eyes, cool and detached in their impersonal perusal, were a deep blue and hooded by heavy lids. Lashes, black and thick as a mink pelt, softened his gaze—but not much.

"Take it," he said, his voice a curt command.

She reached for the ring but, before she touched it,

her hand fell back to her side. "Where did you get it, my lord?"

He lounged back and crossed his right leg over his left knee, the pose so casual they might have been discussing the weather instead of the disaster in her life. A tiny kernel of resentment formed in her.

"From your travelling case."

The kernel blossomed into a knot of irritation. Not even the insane attraction he held for her could stop the sense of having been encroached upon that left her cold.

"You went through my things without my permission? You violated my privacy."

He tossed the ring up and caught it, his gaze never leaving her. "You were asleep so could not give me permission." Her chin notched up and he added, "I do what I must. No one knows who you are or where you are from."

"That does not give you the right to go through my belongings."

"My position gives me the right."

She stiffened. Grateful as she had been before, she could not and would not suppress the anger his trespassing created. He had no right to search her things, no matter what he thought.

"To abuse your guest's privacy?"

He shrugged. "It is not as though you are invited."

"That still—"

"Enough." He leaned forward and thrust the ring at her. "Take it. The last thing I need in my life at the moment is an uninvited woman in my house unchaperoned. Yet, here you are."

She ignored the ring and glared at him. "If I am such a burden, then you should not have taken me in."

His lip curled sardonically. "When I find a woman unconscious in the middle of the road and it is snowing, I do not leave her there to freeze to death."

"Perhaps you should have since you seem to regret it so."

He looked at her, his face hard, and dropped the ring on to the bed. "Put it on and see if it fits. There are two names inscribed on the inside. One might be yours. Felicia."

"Felicia?" she murmured. "No, I don't remember that name." But it felt comfortable. She did not have an aversion to it as she did to the ring. "Perhaps."

He continued to stare down at her, his will implacable. She would have to do his bidding or they would stay like this for ever. Much as she did not want to touch the ring, she disliked this stalemate more.

She took a deep breath and picked the band up, handling it carefully as though it might snap at her. She turned it around, looking at it from all sides. Putting it close to the candle flame, she could just make out the engraving.

He had said two names. She was not sure she wanted to know the second, for surely it was a man's. Yet, this apprehension over a name was silly.

"What is the second name?"

"Edmund."

His deep rich voice clipped the name. She glanced at him, wondering why she sensed animosity in him about the name. Surely she was being fanciful. His dislike was aimed at her for the inconvenience of her being here. Nothing more. Nor did his expression tell her anything other than he was tired of this entire situation and wished it over.

"Edmund," she murmured. "It is no more familiar

than Felicia.'' But she did not feel the same warmth for it as she did for Felicia.

"Put the ring on," he said, impatience making his voice husky. "See if it fits."

"I…" For some unfathomable reason, she felt an aversion to wearing the ring. "Perhaps this is not mine. I don't want to wear it."

She dropped it on to the bed and looked away from it. Why would she feel this way about the ring? Her reactions made no sense.

"It might be your mother's."

She looked at him to see if he might actually think so. As she was beginning to expect, his face showed nothing of what he thought. The irritation of seconds before was gone as though it had never existed. He did stroke his beard, something she had not seen him do before.

She told herself she was being silly. The ring was only an object. If it fitted, then it might be hers, in which case her name would likely be Felicia. Edmund would be her husband. Even should it fit her that did not definitely mean it was hers, only that it was her size. Still, her reluctance to put it on was surprising.

Enough. She grabbed the ring and jammed it on to her wedding finger. The perfect size. She looked up at her reluctant host.

He watched her. "In your travel case there is a brush and comb set with a mirror. The initials F and A are the centre of the design. They are also on the lids of all the vials and bottles. The case is not old. Perhaps several years."

Her mouth dropped. Not in surprise, but anger. "How dare you? Finding the ring was not enough. First you violate my privacy, next you take your own time telling me everything you have found. You knew from the start that this ring very likely was mine and that my name almost assuredly is Felicia.''

The fingers of his right hand drummed on his thigh. ''I wanted to see if the ring would bring any memories before I told you anything else. I did not want to create preconceived ideas in you.''

She glared at him. ''You are the most arrogant and thoughtless man.''

He drew himself up. ''As I told you before, I do what I feel necessary.''

Bitterness welled up inside her. It was sudden and far exceeded what this man had done. It seeped out in her voice. ''Don't all men, regardless of who they hurt in doing so?''

''Someone must do the difficult things in life.''

Another comment like that and she would be hard pressed not to throw something at him. For some reason, she responded more strongly to his arrogant assumption that he could do with her and her belongings as he saw fit than she had responded to the ring or the initials…or even her loss of memory.

Strange. She did not think she was an unreasonable woman, but then she did not know who she was. Her chest tightened. If he had not been here, she knew she would cry. She would cry from fear and anger and… and loss.

Instead, she sank back into the multitude of pillows, the anger seeping from her to be replaced by exhaustion. ''Is there anything else, Lord Chillings, that you know about me from snooping in my belongings? Something that I, perhaps, should know as well?''

His eyes narrowed, but he made no comment on her sarcasm. ''One other thing, yes.''

When he did not come out and say what it was, she said, "I suppose you will tell me when you are good and ready. Perhaps tomorrow?"

He studied her for long minutes. "That might be better."

His voice was low and without a hint of snideness or even coldness. She could almost think he was considering her vulnerability and trying to protect her from something that would be even more trying than what had just transpired. But she would have none of that.

"Tell me now. In for a penny, in for a pound, as the saying goes. Nothing can be worse than losing my memory and being an unwelcome guest in a strange man's home."

"You think not?" he murmured, his deep baritone sounding like a beautiful dirge. "I hope so, for your sake."

His mouth, which had been a straight line of disapproval, softened, showing sensual curves and a fullness she had not expected. She could almost think he felt sorry for her.

"Well?" she prompted.

"Don't you think you have gone through enough for one day?"

His sudden compassion and the words he used set off alarm bells. Her pulse quickened.

"Been in a wrecked carriage and lost my memory. Is there something worse?"

He stood and put the chair back in its place. "Perhaps."

"You are making this harder."

He turned to her. "I suppose I am, and I had not intended to do so. Fortunately, you seem to be a strong woman."

There was nothing to say to that. She did not know if she was strong. She did not know if she wasn't.

"All your clothes are black," he said softly. "Unrelieved."

"Mourning," she murmured. "I must have lost someone close to me and within the last year."

He nodded.

Somehow, she knew that to be true. There was a sense of emptiness that rushed in on her. She had not noticed it before in her preoccupation with her memory loss. Now that void loomed like a chasm ready for her to fall into. His words must have triggered her response. But whom had she lost?

The tightness that had caught her chest earlier returned. Her stomach clenched. She turned her face from his gaze. This grief, for someone she did not even remember, was too private for him to witness.

"Please. Please go," she said, holding back tears by sheer strength of will.

"I will send Mrs Drummond to you," he said quietly.

"No. Please. No one." She took a deep breath. "Not yet."

The housekeeper would want to give her laudanum. Laudanum would numb her pain and her emotions. She did not want that. Not yet. Hurtful as this was, it might jar her memory. She could hope.

"Are you sure?" he persisted.

"Yes," she whispered.

She could not look at him. She did not want him to see the hurt she knew was in her eyes. Her vulnerability. Or the tears that were flowing now in spite of her determination that they not start until he was gone. It was as though something inside her had broken.

''As you wish.''

Relief flooded her at his agreement. She heard the door close and knew he was gone. She felt a sudden and inexplicable sense of terrible aloneness. At least while he was with her, there was the chance of human warmth and kindness. Never mind that he had shown neither—this time.

Drat the man. Drat him for invading her privacy. Drat him for telling her she was in deep mourning and opening this abyss of grief. And drat him for leaving her to suffer through this alone.

Then she was lost. She fell into the dark chasm of grief over a loss she could put no name to, but sensed was immense. Tears flowed. Her chest rose and fell in gasping little sobs. Her hands twisted the sheets and she burrowed her face into the pillows, not wanting to see the world.

Her heart knew what her mind did not. Whatever it had been, her loss had been devastating.

Guy stayed outside her door to insure that no servant intruded on her and listened to her sob as though her heart was breaking. More than anything, he wanted to go back in and comfort her. He wanted to hold her and stroke his hands down the thick fall of hair that seemed heavier than her delicate neck could hold. He wanted…

He wanted things that he should not even think about, let alone desire.

Her crying lessened, jogging him from his unwelcome thoughts. He had not known he was so attuned to her that he would realize she had quieted.

He should have been gentler with her, but she had goaded him with her anger over what he had done. Then she had called him arrogant. Suzanne had often called him that, and high-handed, and many other things that all meant the same thing. This woman saying the nearly exact words had made him uncomfortable.

Yes, he was autocratic.

Silence came from the room at last. The urge was strong to go back in and make sure she was okay. But it would do no good and probably harm. He reacted to her in ways that might provoke him to do more than he wanted.

He crossed the hall to where a sconce held a flickering candle. He plucked the light free and headed to his own room.

Chapter Three

She woke with a sigh. She still remembered nothing, not even her name. Mrs Drummond came in as she was getting up, and helped her to dress.

She glanced at the bottle of laudanum sitting on the table by her bed. Yesterday she had been grateful for its numbing of her pain, both physical and emotional. But yesterday was gone and she needed to move on. Somehow, she had to discover who she was.

Still, her head hurt with a dull throb that made it hard to think. The opium would be welcome, although she knew it would dull her concentration as well as the pain.

But no. She did not like being dependent on the drug. She sighed. Had she been this way before her accident? Was she always loath to take medication? Or just laudanum? She did not know.

To take her mind off the discomfort, she turned back to study herself in the full-length mirror, framed in mahogany inlaid with rosewood. She looked like a crow. Black shrouded her from top to bottom. Her hair was scraped back and knotted at the nape of her neck into a thick chignon. Even so, tendrils escaped. She was paste white and dark circles under her eyes made her look sick. Black did not become her.

Mrs Drummond hovered in the background, tsking. "You must be in deep, deep mourning, ma'am. Everything in your portmanteau is solid black. Nothing in white and black stripes for half-mourning."

She continued staring at herself. "This is not a becoming colour, but somehow it seems familiar. I think I have been dressed like this for a long time."

Mrs Drummond shook her head. "If only we knew. His lordship was talking to Oswald, the butler, only this morn. Seems he is going to send someone to Newcastle-upon-Tyne." At the younger woman's raised brow, she added, "The coachman you hired said you started there."

"I did?" She turned from her unbecoming reflection. "The only thing that comes to mind about the city is that it produces a large quantity of coal. But anyone would know that."

Mrs Drummond pursed her lips. "Perhaps. I know that, but I've lived my entire life here. His lordship probably knows."

She shrugged. "Well, that is all I can think of about the place."

She reached for a black wool shawl trimmed in black tassels. Mrs Drummond helped her drape it over her shoulders. The heavy weave would keep her comfortable. As modern as this house seemed, this room was large and even the state-of-the-art fireplace did not send its heat to all the corners.

"His lordship is in the breakfast room, ma'am. I will show you the way."

"I am sure you are much too busy to be spending time with me like this."

Mrs Drummond smiled. "I am busy. But his lord-ship has instructed me to see that you are well taken care of. A lady needs a lady's maid, but none of the young girls have the skills. As for escorting you to his lordship, I could leave that to a footman, but I wish to show you myself."

She returned the older woman's smile. Mrs Drum-mond was obviously a loved and respected servant who did her job well and then did as she pleased. Fortu-nately for the Viscount, anything the housekeeper wanted to do would only benefit him.

"As you wish, Mrs Drummond."

Instead of going to the door where the housekeeper stood, she moved to the dressing stand where her toi-letry case sat. As though from long practice, her hand went to the lever that opened the hidden drawer. The compartment slid out and the gleam of gold caught her eye.

She had returned the ring last night after she had woken from her grief-induced sleep. Silly as it seemed now, in the morning light, she had not wanted the thing on her finger.

"There is no doubt the case is yours, ma'am," Mrs Drummond said. "You know your way around it like his lordship does this house."

Momentarily distracted, she paused in the act of reaching for the piece of jewellery. But her attention came instantly back to the ring. The case was hers. The clothes she wore fitted her as though they had been made for her so they had to be hers. The ring also fitted her perfectly.

Her fingers brushed the gold, but stopped short of picking it up. She shook her head. What was the matter with her? Putting the clothes on had saddened her, but when they were on she had felt right about wearing them. But the ring had never felt right. Why?

Overreacting. She was overreacting. Nothing more. She picked up the plain band and slipped it on her left ring finger, where a wedding ring should be. A shudder ran bone deep through her. This ring had to hold unhappy memories for her.

Very likely she was a widow, hence the deep mourning and this sense of great loss. That had to be it. She removed the ring from her left hand and shifted it to her right.

She hastened to the door and through it, eager to be somewhere else now that she had made a decision. She strode into the hallway where elaborately chased silver sconces each held two lit candles. Walnut panelling rose to midway on the walls where it was met by sage green watered damask that went to the high ceiling. She marvelled at the wealth needed to create this beauty.

"This way, ma'am."

Mrs Drummond's summons and stately figure led her down a long corridor to a set of curving stairs. A silver banister, designed like ivy, led the way to a small foyer floored in creamy marble. Mrs Drummond continued across this area and into a hall, which formed a half-moon until the apogee where it spilled into a sumptuously furnished games room done in shades of blue. A billiard table held pride of place. They passed around the table and through the room to where the hall continued its half-moon course. Windows stood every ten feet, framing what she knew must be a very lovely garden during the spring and summer. Right now, the lawn and shrubs were dusted with snow. The trees stood bare, their gnarled limbs in stark relief against the grey winter sky.

They walked into the main entrance and she gasped. The ceiling was three storeys above them where a circular stained-glass window fashioned into a coat of arms formed the dome. The weak winter sun sent pale beams of blue and green light drifting to the white marble under their feet. It was like being in an underwater grotto.

"Did Viscount Chillings build this place?" she asked in awe when Mrs Drummond paused. "It seems very modern."

"His lordship's father, the Sixth Viscount, started The Folly, but the current Viscount finished it." Her face glowed with pride. "He was such a mischievous boy and accomplished young man."

Some of her former animosity toward Viscount Chillings faded in light of the other woman's emotion. "You must love him very much."

Mrs Drummond nodded. "I raised him and would do anything for him."

"How very fortunate for him," she said sincerely in spite of her own opinion about the man.

She could not help but smile warmly at the older woman. Mrs Drummond radiated love and devotion. There must be more to the Viscount than the one act of kindness buried in among the actions of aggression that he had shown her yesterday.

"The door across the foyer is the breakfast room," Mrs Drummond said. "Where the footman is standing."

"Thank you very much for your help," she said.

Mrs Drummond gave her a brief curtsy and left. She looked across the open expanse to the footman. He was young and attractive in his suit of sage green piped with silver. His white stockings were pristine.

She crossed to the young man, her slippered feet making no sound. He bowed deeply when she stopped in front of him.

"His lordship is expecting you."

She nodded and smiled at him.

He opened the door, and announced, "Madam Felicia."

She gave him a startled glance. *Madam Felicia?* Then she gave a mental shrug. There was nothing else to call her. She was obviously the Felicia of the ring and must have been married and now widowed. There was no other explanation she could think of.

She nodded to the footman as she passed him. The room was delightful, light and airy even though it was winter. French doors opened on to an orangery and the green growth lent the warmth of living things. The walls were done in sage green, as so much of the house seemed to be. It must be his family colour.

Viscount Chillings stood by the table, monogrammed linen napkin in hand, and waited for her. She made him a brief curtsy.

"Your lordship."

He nodded. "Call me Chillings."

"As you wish."

"Please have a seat. Oswald will bring anything you wish." He waited till she sat before resuming his place.

The butler was at her side immediately. He was as short and round as Mrs Drummond was tall and slim. His sparse grey hair was combed from one side to the other and smoothed down with a pomander. A twinkle lurked in the back of his grey eyes.

"What may I get you, ma'am?"

She smiled. "Toast and tea, please."

"Kippers, eggs, kidneys, chocolate?" he recited the list.

"No, thank you. I am not a large breakfast eater." No sooner were the words out of her mouth, than Felicia paused. "How can I know that—for I do—when I don't even know my name?"

Chillings took a sip of black coffee. "How indeed? I believe the human brain is a cipher." He cut a piece of kidney and ate it slowly, his attention never leaving her. "Have you remembered anything else?"

"No. Or if I have, I don't realize it yet."

Oswald appeared with her tea and toast. She put a generous helping of sugar and cream into the beverage. Then spread marmalade on a triangular wedge of toast.

"It is delightful to have something solid to eat." She swallowed the toast and followed with a sip of tea.

"You tire of sickroom food."

The cynical gleam in his eyes made her realize how ungrateful she must sound. "Mrs Drummond was perfectly right to feed me calve's-foot jelly and weak tea, but surely you will agree that those are nothing compared with what you are eating now."

"True." The ghost of a smile lifted one corner of his mouth, softening the harshness of his face. "I remember eating that particular diet many times. She swore it would make me feel better." His smile became a grin, showing strong white teeth. "Perhaps she was right. I always got better."

Felicia laughed. "Perhaps you would have got better anyway."

"Perhaps, but I would never have suggested that. I would have got my ears boxed."

"I doubt she would have gone so far as to do that."

"Mrs Drummond would go as far as she deemed necessary to keep my brother, sister and myself on the path of health and honour."

He finished his kidneys and drank the last of his coffee, the hard angles of his face no longer the arrogant slashes Felicia remembered so well from the previous night. He was a totally different man from the one who had questioned her so unmercifully.

She found herself smiling broadly at him before she realized what she was doing. His sharing this bit of his childhood with her, and doing so with humour, charmed her.

As she waited for him to continue talking, he leaned back in his chair and templed his fingertips. The amusement left his countenance. Seeing the change come over him, Felicia's sense of ease fled.

"I have started some inquiries about you." His baritone was flat, the music gone, as though the sharing of moments before had never happened. She was back to being the strange, unwelcome woman to whom he was a reluctant host. "Or they will start as soon as my man gets to Newcastle-upon-Tyne."

"Newcastle-upon-Tyne?" she echoed him. "Mrs Drummond said the coachman had brought me from there, but I don't remember the place or seem to know much about it."

"Nothing?" The cynicism she remembered so well from the night before crept back into his tone.

"Nothing much. As I told her, I know that it is a large coal centre."

"Most people know that." He took a drink of fresh coffee. "Most educated people, that is, with an awareness of the world outside their own village or home."

"I realize that." Exasperation made it easy to be

curt. "Perhaps you have forgotten that I have lost my memory?"

He set his cup down with a clink. "No, I have not."

"So, as I said before, why there?"

"It is the most logical place to start. The man whose coach you were in said that is where you hired him to take you to London as quickly as possible." He stopped a moment. "He blames your haste for the accident."

She drew herself up. "That is all very convenient since I cannot gainsay him."

Ill use over the entire situation welled up in her. No memory, and now some strange man was blaming her for an expensive wreck that might have killed them both, and she could say nothing in her own support. And he might very well be correct.

"Did he say why I wanted to go to London in such a hurry?"

"You have or had an urgent appointment and you paid him handsomely."

Her brows drew together. "Where did I get the money?"

Chillings's mouth curled sardonically. "From your dress and travelling case, I would say you are not a woman in poverty."

"But am I wealthy enough to hire a private coach to take me all the way to London?"

"It would seem that way. Although, it appears not wealthy enough to have a travelling chaise of your own."

She sighed. "Another piece of the puzzle, and like the others it does me no good."

"Yet." He stood. "With luck, someone in Newcastle will know who you are."

"And how will you find that out?" She stood so that he would not tower over her. The resultant feeling of being overwhelmed was not one she wanted to repeat.

"My man will put an advertisement into the papers. Farfetched, but a start. He will also visit solicitors. If you are a woman of means, you will have a solicitor."

She nodded her understanding. Much as she was not sure she even liked him, she had to give the devil his due. "Very smart of you, my lord. I am not sure I would have thought of those things."

He looked down at her, his eyes inscrutable. "I am sure you would have eventually." To ruin the compliment, he added, "You are not a stupid woman."

She clamped her mouth closed to keep from making a scathing comment. She looked around the room, searching for something to discuss other than how he annoyed her. She found it in a portrait over the fireplace's pink marble mantel. She had noticed it earlier, but before she could comment on it, she had seen him waiting for her. All else had fled from her mind. Much as he irritated her, he drew her. Not a good thing. Even now, determined as she was to change the topic of conversation, just thinking of him made her lose her thread of thought. She forced herself to study the portrait.

A young woman sat in fashionable dishabille, her pale blonde hair falling around her shoulders like fine lace. Large blue, almost grey, eyes looked out on the world with confidence. Her mouth was a red cupid's bow. The white gown she wore draped a full bosom and hinted at a tiny waist. She was a Beauty.

Felicia looked from the Beauty to her host and saw him looking at the portrait. There was a stillness about him that she had not seen before. Who was this woman?

As though he heard her unspoken question, Chillings said flatly, his voice barely audible, ''My wife.''

The tension in him made Felicia incredibly uncomfortable. But if she was honest with herself, and she thought that she normally was, she must admit to a twinge of something very like jealousy. Surely not. How could she be jealous of a woman in a portrait and over a man she did not even know and was not even sure she liked?

She wished she had not even looked at the portrait. She wished she had left and gone to the boredom and safety of her chamber. But it was too late.

She had to say something now. ''She is lovely.'' Her words were inadequate to describe his wife, but Felicia wanted nothing more than a change of topic.

''Was,'' he said softly.

Felicia gasped in dismay. Chillings had suffered a loss as great as her own. Sympathy for the man, and a sense of connection with him, overwhelmed her. She reached a hand to his arm, only to draw it abruptly back. She did not know him well enough to touch him, and she sensed that he would not welcome her compassion.

Instead, she settled for more inadequate words. ''I am so sorry.''

He looked at her now, his face grim. ''It was a long time ago.''

She nodded, helpless to ease his pain or the tension that was so thick it could be cut with the proverbial knife. Of all the things Mrs Drummond had talked about, Felicia wished strongly that this had been one of them.

The need to comfort, and knowing she could not, knotted her stomach. Desperate to change the subject, she said, "I would like to speak with the coachman I hired. I don't wish to impose on your hospitality longer. It is time I continued to London."

He turned to face her. Emotions moved across his face, the most prominent being anger. "Are you always so difficult?"

She took a step back, not having expected his attack. "I beg your pardon, Lord Chillings. I am trying to do the right thing. You have been more than plain about the inconvenience of my staying here, not to mention the impropriety."

He pivoted on his heel and stalked to the door. "A woman on her own, with no memory of who she is or where she is going or why, should not be on the road alone. I would have thought you intelligent enough to realize that."

The knot in her stomach tightened. His hurtful words put up her back. "Not when you are constantly reminding me of how unwanted I am. I have no wish to further discommode you. Please summon the coachman for me."

"He left. Yesterday." He bit the words off.

She gaped. "You let him leave? After I had paid him to take me to London and without asking me? You are very high-handed."

He gripped the doorknob with enough strength to turn his knuckles white. "I did what I thought best. You were in no condition to travel. Furthermore, where would you go in London? You did not even know you were headed there."

She tossed her head and to her chagrin one of the pins holding the thick roll of hair secured to her nape flew out and landed on the carpet. A strand fell to her shoulder, and with it, she was sure, fell her dignity. Instinctively, her hands lifted to tuck the errant piece back in. She stopped herself. Let it be.

"No, I did not, but now I do. Surely I also told him where I wished to go in London."

"No, you did not. Evidently you planned on telling him when you arrived."

She frowned. "Why was I so secretive?"

He released the doorknob and took a step toward her. "I've no idea, but you have certainly made it difficult for us to find out who you are."

She drew herself up, refusing to let him intimidate her with his approach. "Whatever I was doing, it must have been extremely important to me and I obviously did not want anyone to know I was doing it. Perhaps if I saw the coachman I would remember something. Surely I would not entrust myself to a man I could not depend on not to harm me."

"One would hope," he said, his lip curling. "But that is neither here nor there. He is gone. If you continue to London, I or one of my people will escort you."

This was becoming more and more surreal. "You most certainly will not. I am not your responsibility."

He took another step towards her. "Much as I dislike it, you became my responsibility the minute I picked you up from the snow unconscious."

"You put far too great an importance on your rescue."

"Do I?"

His voice was dangerously low. His eyes seemed to devour her, his gaze lingering on the strand of hair that tumbled down her shoulder. She tried desperately to ignore the tremors running through her body, but it was nearly impossible. She was not afraid of him. No, never that.

"Yes, you do. Anyone could have found me and brought me to their home." Her voice rose the tiniest bit. "I am obviously able to care for myself. And I must be a woman alone and used to being so, otherwise a man, or at the very least a maid, would have accompanied me."

"You are certainly foolhardy. A maid should have accompanied you regardless of whether or not you have male relatives."

He was right and she could not refute it. Her memory of who she was might be gone, but she knew well enough what propriety demanded. Why had she travelled without a maid? She shook her head and some of her bravado dissipated.

"Yes, I should have had a maid."

A glint of something that might be humour entered his dark blue eyes. The tension that had radiated from his body seconds before lessened. Against her better judgment, she was disappointed.

"Capitulation?" he asked, his rich voice low.

"Agreement."

"Ah."

He was so smug. She notched her chin up. "But that does not excuse your high-handed dismissal of the coachman. How am I to get to London now?" He opened his mouth, but she forestalled him. "And do not say you or one of your people will take me, for I won't allow it. I am not your concern."

"I will not argue the point with you any more. My sister, Lady Annabell Fenwick-Clyde, will be here in several days."

"Not for my sake," she blurted out. "I shall be gone by then."

He took another step towards her. She took a step back. The last thing she wanted was to be more indebted to this arrogant man. She did not want to cause him or his family any more inconvenience than she already had. Nor did she want to remain in such close proximity to him. He disturbed her too much.

"Not for your sake, ma'am. Mine."

"Yours? Whatever do you mean?"

"Exactly that. Mine. If word gets about that you have been under my roof unchaperoned, the pressure will be brought to bear on me to make a respectable woman of you."

"What?" Her voice rose in earnest. "Make a respectable woman of me?" Her shoulders straightened. "I may not remember who I am, but I know what I am. I am a respectable woman already, whether *your* reputation is compromised or not. Nor would I marry you."

She stopped in full tirade. Her eyes widened as she realized what she had said. He took another step toward her, bringing him much too close. She could almost feel the heat radiating from his lithe body. She was a fool twice over.

"I could not marry you, even should we both wish it." She raised one white hand to forestall the comment she knew was on the tip of his tongue. "I am a widow of recent bereavement."

All her bravado and energy seeped from her. It was an effort not to sit back down and put her face into her hands. She fought the urge, remained standing and looked him square in the eye.

"Yes, you are. And I am engaged. Totally out of the

question, no matter what anyone might say." His voice had a husky quality that made her think of loss and something else she could not, would not, name. "Consequently, my sister is coming as soon as possible."

She nodded, all words gone. *He was engaged.* Of course he was. And she was a recent widow. Silly to have imagined anything else.

His gaze remained on her. "If you will excuse me, ma'am. I have work to do."

She nodded again, her emotions numb. Too much was happening, too fast. He strode from the room without a backward glance at her.

She turned back to the portrait.

Chapter Four

Being lonely was not a good enough reason for accepting Viscount Chillings's invitation to dinner, Felicia decided. This was her seventh day here and she had long ago decided she was far too attracted to him—and he was engaged to another woman. This was refined torture. Nor did it do her any good to tell herself that she was a widow. She did not feel like a widow, she felt like a woman sitting far too close to a man she found exciting.

She was on his right side at a beautiful satinwood-inlaid walnut table that went the length of the large dining room. Behind her, ceiling-to-floor windows, draped in cream and sage velvet curtains, looked on to the grounds and could be opened in warmer weather for access to the terrace. Across from her, the fireplace filled nearly one-third of the wall. Above the imported Italian marble of the mantel, and flanked by gilt candelabra that were at least four feet tall, hung a portrait.

The late Viscountess Chillings.

This time her pose was formal. Her dress was high-waisted and pale pink silk over a white muslin under-skirt. The style was from years before when Grecian simplicity was the height of fashion. Her hair was cut short and curled around her face, accentuating her wide-set eyes and full, red cupid's bow mouth. Her complexion was the traditional roses and cream. If anything, she was more beautiful in this portrait than in the one in the breakfast room.

Yet, as lovely as her face was and as perfectly formed as her figure was, it was the necklace that held Felicia's attention. A triple strand of large, perfectly matched white pearls circled the Viscountess's slender neck. They were caught at the base of her throat by a magnificent emerald that had to be the size of a goose's egg. That gem was surrounded by diamonds. A piece of jewellery one would never forget. A piece of jewellery that would pay to feed a thousand or more people for their entire lives.

She had known from the estate that Viscount Chillings was wealthy. This necklace told her he was rich as Golden Ball. No wonder he worried about women trying to trap him into matrimony. He must be the most eligible bachelor in England or, if not that, close.

The butler set a bowl of turtle soup in front of her, making her look away from the portrait. "Thank you, Oswald." She smiled at him.

His mouth curved in the hint of a returned smile. "You are very welcome, ma'am."

She looked at the array of cutlery set before her and marvelled that she knew which one was the soup spoon. She had no personal knowledge of herself, but she seemed to know everything pertinent to the world around her.

She took a sip of soup. "Your cook is excellent, Chillings."

He nodded. "François is French. Returned with me from Paris."

"Paris? Were you there after Waterloo?" She took another sip while Oswald poured her white wine.

She sensed rather than saw Chillings tense. His face flushed a deeper tan. But when he spoke there was no sign of emotion in his voice, other than that of polite conversation.

"Yes. I was one of the Duke's aide-de-camps. I went with him to Paris when he left Brussels."

She longed to ask him for stories of his travels, but sensed that this, like the topic of his wife, was not one he wanted to dwell on. She was surprised when he continued on his own.

"I enjoyed Paris very much. It seemed that the entire British aristocracy went there with Wellington. Parties went on round the clock, given by us and the French aristocrats who had been restored to their lands and titles." He laughed. "The things that were done in the name of entertainment."

She watched animation ease the lines at his mouth and decided that she must have been mistaken earlier when she thought the topic bothered him.

"I had heard that everyone was giddy with victory."

His eyes narrowed and he watched her carefully over the rim of his wine glass. "You had? From whom?"

Nonplussed, she stopped eating. "I…" She shook her head. It was as though a wisp of memory came to her only to disappear like fog on a hot morning. Frustration was like a cord around her throat, choking her. "I don't recall. Only that I heard such."

As though he realized her discomfort, he finished his wine and set the glass down. "Anyway, the goal was to see who could give the most elaborate ball or which woman would wear the most *outré* clothes. I remember one chap riding a fully caparisoned horse up the front steps, through the hall and into the ballroom of one of Paris's most grand and old hotels. The owner was not thrilled, but could say nothing when all his guests cheered on the brazen fellow and his mount.''

Felicia felt indignant for the poor host. ''I dare say he did not appreciate such treatment. I imagine you would not like anyone doing such a thing here.''

''I would have the churl horsewhipped.''

She blinked. He had gone from amiable to blood-thirsty so quickly. ''I beg your pardon?''

He smiled, thin and cruel. ''I would have him horse-whipped.''

Her appetite for turtle soup gone, she sipped the fine, dry French wine Oswald had poured. ''You have a magnificent estate. I can understand that it would upset you to have someone do such a thing.''

''Yes, it would.'' He set down his glass and sig-nalled Oswald to bring the next course. ''The Folly was started by my father, but he died before finishing it. I had it completed and the grounds landscaped. Capa-bility Brown started them, but fashion has changed.''

She nodded, following what he said. ''In what way has fashion changed?''

Oswald delivered the next course, which comprised several meats and removes. He poured a clear red wine this time.

Chillings warmed to his topic. ''We are more infor-mal than our fathers were. In the past years, I have had the course of the Rye River diverted by weir dams so that it runs closer to the house. There is even a lake within several minutes' walk, which you can see from the library. The plantings are wilder and less structured, more casual. Things like that.''

Felicia understood what he was saying, but was positive that she had no personal experience of these changes. ''That sounds very different. Something the Prince Regent might do.''

Chillings smiled. ''Something he has already done at Brighton.''

''Ah, the Pavilion.''

Chillings sipped his wine and watched her over the rim. ''You have no memory about yourself, but you are remarkably well versed with many other subjects. Strange how the human mind works.''

She cut into her roast beef with its fine French sauce. ''It is disconcerting, to say the least.''

''I can imagine so.''

He finished his wine and Oswald immediately poured more. Seeing the butler's attentiveness, Felicia told herself to remember not to drain her glass. Somehow she did not think she had a head for drink of any sort.

''Well,'' she said, wishing to take the talk away from her, ''you seem very interested in your estate.''

''It has occupied a great deal of my time in the past ten years or so. I have even considered building a seaside cottage, but have contented myself with building a small lakeside cottage for picnicking and such.''

''If it is anywhere even remotely as well done at this house, then it must be delightful.''

''Thank you. If time permits, I will take you there tomorrow. It is just outside the terrace.''

''I don't wish to cause you any more trouble, Lord Chillings, than I already am,'' Felicia said steadily, looking him in the eye.

"As you wish," he drawled.

Oswald removed the latest course and set out the dessert trays. There was a dizzying array of sweets. Felicia found herself tempted to try everything, so she did.

She laughed lightly. "I must have a prodigious sweet tooth."

"It would appear that way," Chillings said, helping himself to a syllabub.

Felicia rose after dessert. "Thank you so much for inviting me, Lord Chillings. I have greatly enjoyed talking to you about your estate and the building and improvements you have done."

He rose and bowed. "My pleasure, ma'am."

She turned to go and noticed the painting hanging above the door she had entered. It was a single portrait of a young man in a dashing Hussar's uniform. Chillings.

He was debonair and rakish all at once. Posed with one leg crossed in front of the other and his shoulder propped against his horse's shoulder, he was the classic military officer that any woman would be interested in. His dark blue uniform crusted with gold braid made his shoulders look broader than they already were. The scarlet sash around his waist drew attention to his lean hips and strong thighs.

Felicia found herself mesmerised. Her breath was suddenly shallow and her heart beating rapidly. He was magnificent.

"That was in my younger days," Chillings drawled.

His words were like cold water on a fever victim's forehead. She snapped out of her preoccupation.

"Very well done, my lord," she managed in a credible imitation of nonchalance.

Without looking back at him, she stepped through the doorway and managed to smile at the footman who held the door open for her. An image of Chillings in his uniform seemed printed on her eye. No wonder he was engaged. He must have avoided all eligible females to have remained a single widower this long.

She needed something to take her mind off of him or her sleep would be fitful and unrestful. She headed for the library. Something in Latin would be just the thing.

She had not been in the library yet, but knew the direction. She stopped in the entrance and gaped. The room was, if possible, more impressive than the rest of the manor. Like the other public rooms, it was in the rotunda, so the outside wall was circular. Windows marched around the exterior with floor to ceiling bookcases spaced between them. As with the rest of the house, sage-green velvet curtains shut out the cold night.

A roaring fire warmed the room, but failed to light the corners where shadows held sway. As with every other room she had been in, a picture hung over the fireplace. This time it was a grouping of two young men with a woman posed between them. All three laughed at something the picture did not show.

She recognized one as a younger Chillings. The woman was very like him, with silver-blonde hair and dark eyes. She had his height and slim elegance. The second man was darker. His hair was black as pitch and his complexion was swarthy as a tinker's instead of being pale as fashion dictated. Unlike the other two in looks, he did have their high-bridged nose and the same dark blue eyes. All were dressed in the fashion of the first part of the century. Beau Brummell would have been proud of them.

Her host had a brother as well as the sister who was coming to chaperon.

She looked around some more and was relieved not to find any portraits of Chillings's wife. She told herself that it was no concern of hers, but she pitied the woman who fell in love with him. There was no room in his heart for anyone but the wife who was gone.

The thought caused moisture to prick her eyes, which was silly. He was nothing to her, and the unknown woman who would some day love him meant even less to her.

With more determination than she had felt on entering the room, she scanned the many books until she found a copy of the *Odyssey* in the original Latin. She opened the cover and began reading. She knew Latin.

Stunned, she sank into the nearest chair. She knew so much that many people would not know, yet she could not even remember her name. It was disheartening. She even knew that most women could not read Latin.

This was more than she could take. On legs grown weary beyond belief, she rose and started walking the seemingly endless distance to her room.

She reached the entry to the game room and stopped. Chillings stood bent over the billiard table holding a long, thin stick. To get to the hall that led to her room, she had to pass him. There was nothing for it. She was tired.

He used the stick to hit a white ball with black marks that then hit a red ball. The red ball ricocheted off the edge of the table while the ball he had hit stopped. It looked like a very boring way to spend the evening.

"Good night, Lord Chillings," she murmured politely as she passed by him.

"Ah, Madam Felicia. Would you care to play?"

She shook her head. "Thank you, but I don't believe I know how."

"I will teach you," he said, standing straight and setting one end of the stick on the ground so that the pointed end rested against the table. "My pleasure."

She eyed him narrowly. He had made it abundantly clear that nothing about him was her pleasure.

"Thank you, but I am tired."

She kept moving, although her steps were smaller and slower. There was a magnetism about him that made her want to be close. The attraction had been there from the start, ridiculous as it was.

"Afraid?" He drawled, lounging with his hips against the table, his legs crossed at the ankle.

Yes, she thought. I am afraid of what you make me feel. Out loud, she said, "Merely tired."

A slow, lazy grin lit his blue eyes. "Of course."

He turned away as though she had ceased to exist for him. She bit her lip in chagrin. She should leave.

Instead, she said, "Well, it might be interesting."

He turned back. "It can be."

Felicia looked around the game room and wondered what she had let herself in for. Unlike most of the house, this room was done in shades of blue. For a place where competition would be rife, it was very peaceful. Placed between two windows was a card table with sconces on the nearby walls and a candelabrum on the table itself. Cards were serious business.

"I think," Chillings said, "a smaller cue would suit you."

He took a long stick down from a device on the wall that held many sticks, some longer and fatter around than others. Felicia had no memory of any game like this.

"Now," he said, "the object is to hit the red ball with this ball."

She nodded.

"To do so, you use this cue to strike the first ball in such a way that it hits the second one."

Felicia nodded again. She could tell already that this was a game of hand-and-eye skill. She did not know if she would be able to play it. Chillings held the cue out to her. She took the stick, wondering if he would become angry if she played badly. For some reason, the possibility made her hands clammy, as though someone in her past had been that way.

She looked at him and saw him watching her. She knew he had a temper, but she also knew he controlled it.

"If you don't wish to do this, just say so," he said quietly, his voice smooth and beguiling.

"No, no…that is, yes, I do wish to try."

Her pulse increased, and she knew she would be hard pressed to refuse him anything he asked for in that voice. She was so susceptible to him. It was an unnerving realisation.

"I think to start, you should just practise hitting your ball."

She nodded. Lifting the stick, she put the pointed end against the ball as she had seen him do. She pulled the stick back and pushed it forward. It hit the ball lopsided, sending the ball bouncing across the table and on to the floor.

She frowned. "It is not as easy as it looked."

"No, it is not."

She whipped her head around to look at him. "Are you laughing at me?"

"I am merely enjoying the situation."

Part of her felt she should be insulted. But he was right. She must have looked ridiculous, bent over with this stick and then sending the ball flying.

He stooped and retrieved her ball, which he put back on the table. He quirked one black brow. "Again?"

"Again," she said firmly.

The need to master this skill lent her determination. Positioning the stick, or cue, again, she wondered if she had always been this stubborn. Was this part of who she was? From her desire to show Chillings and show herself that she could learn billiards, she rather thought it was.

Ten times later and ten flying balls later, she admitted defeat. "I don't think this is my game."

He studied her with a curious glint in his eyes. "But you want to learn it." It was a statement, not a question.

"Yes. I find that I don't want to be someone who gives up easily." She shrugged. 'I don't know if that is a trait of mine or just something that has come on since the amnesia."

"You have probably always had it. I believe the general thought on conditions like yours is that the person does not change. He merely does not remember."

"You are very well versed in my condition," she said a trifle tartly.

"I saw a number of men suffer from it during the wars."

His tone said he did not want to discuss the wars. He had made a statement of fact as he knew it and that was that.

Felicia counted to ten and lifted the cue again. Her exhaustion of earlier was gone. She took aim, shot and hit the ball on the left.

"A little left slide," Chillings said.

"What?"

"The way you hit the ball, although you did not intend to do so, is called putting slide on the ball."

"I see." But she did not and she knew that he knew.

"How badly do you want to learn?" he asked, leaning lightly on his cue, which was planted on the floor.

"I don't really know." She felt helpless, a feeling she was experiencing too much lately. She did not like it. "I suppose I would like to at least be able to hit that silly white ball so that it hits the red one."

"Right."

He pushed off, coming towards her. "Let me help you, then."

"How?"

She was getting a sense of unease. There was something about the way he was looking at her that made shivers skip down her spine.

"Pick your cue up. Now, use your left hand as a guide. Like this." He showed her. "Then pull back slowly on the cue and shoot forward."

She tried.

"You are angling your elbow too far out," he said, touching her upper arm so that she pulled the offending elbow to her side.

She tried again.

He frowned. "If you will let me."

Instead of waiting for permission, he went behind her and brought his arms around so his body cupped hers. Her posterior pressed into his loins. His chest lay fully along her back. Slowly, he bent her forward as he moulded her into the position he wanted.

Felicia thought she would pass out from the blood rushing away from her head and to other parts of her body. She tingled in areas she had not noticed before.

His breath was warm on the nape of her neck. His scent engulfed her. She gulped hard and hoped she could concentrate enough to hit the red ball so that he would release her. Her senses could not take much more of this.

"Now," he said, his voice a husky rasp, "let me guide you."

She licked dry lips. "Yes."

She leaned forward more until her back end pressed tightly to him. She gasped as she felt him stir against her. He jerked.

Without thought for the possible consequences, she turned her head to see his expression. It was a mistake.

His pupils were dilated. The angles of his face were knife blades of hunger, sharp enough to cut to her core. He tensed around her so that she could not have escaped had she wanted to.

She stared up at him.

"Felicia?" he said, his murmur a request.

Her eyes widened as he lowered his head the few inches that separated them. His mouth touched hers. His lips moved against hers, demanding and giving all at once. His beard scratched her skin and then she forgot all about it as her senses exploded outwards. She responded with a fervour she had not known she possessed.

He deepened the kiss until she whimpered with rising desire. As he plundered her mouth with his, he turned her in his arms so that her breasts pressed against his chest. One of his hands burrowed into her hair. The other slid down her back to cup her hip and pull her tightly to him.

He moved against her, an action so natural that she responded without thought. He groaned deep in his throat.

His hands skimmed over her body, coming to rest on her waist. He lifted her on to the billiard table in one easy flexing of muscles and straddled her so that his inner thighs embraced her on the outside. Her head fell back and her hair tumbled from the pins to fall in a golden puddle on the table.

He trailed kisses down her arched neck.

She had never felt like this. Even with her memory gone, a deep part of her knew that no man had ever done this to her. It was as though the ardour he created in her rose up from her depths and burst outwards to consume all thought, leaving only a woman in the throes of an uncontrollable response to a man's lovemaking.

One of his hands skimmed up her ribs to fold around one of her breasts while his other hand held her steady. He kneaded the aching mound of her flesh until all she wanted to do was rip her clothing off and press herself into his embrace.

She slid her hands to where his shirt lay open at his throat and started undoing the buttons until she could slip her palms inside the cloth and feel his flesh hot against hers. She began to shiver in earnest as he gasped.

He broke away from their kiss to stare down at her. His eyes were wild and his mouth was moist from her lips.

"I want you, Felicia."

His voice was so deep and so hoarse that she could barely understand him, but she knew instinctively. Her body could feel the tension that held him against her, his loins straining against her stomach.

"Now," he said with more force.

"Now," she murmured. "Yes, please."

A shudder ran through him. Holding her eyes with his, he started unbuttoning her bodice. He licked his lips and his eyes suddenly closed as stark hunger moved over his features. By touch alone, he pulled her clothing from her shoulders and slid the sleeves down her arms until the only thing between her and his passion was her thin cotton chemise. Only then did he open his eyes again to look at her.

He drew his breath in sharply as he gazed at the pink pricks of her nipples visible through the gossamer material. Her breathing became rapid and shallow as she watched his arousal. Every part of her ached with suppressed need.

He lowered his head until his mouth closed over her nipple. He nipped her gently with his teeth and she thought she would die. Through the cotton material he pulled and sucked and bit her until she was ready to scream. Then he went to the other breast.

She was lost.

Her release was a spasm that ripped through her entire body. She gripped him with arms grown so tense they hurt. Tiny gasps of pleasure and surprise escaped her. Her head collapsed on to his shoulder, his mouth still pressed to her bosom.

When she had stopped shaking, he released her. She lifted her head and met his gaze. His lips were swollen from suckling her and his eyes were glazed with unreleased passion. He caught her face between his palms seconds before he caught her mouth with his.

He kissed her long and deep. Her head whirled.

Then she was free.

He stepped back abruptly. His chest rose and fell in rapid, deep gulps.

Dazed, she swayed but managed to get her hands pressed to the top of the billiard table where she still sat so that she was balanced. Lethargy held her.

"I believe," he said, his voice not quite steady, "that you had better go to bed." He closed his eyes and added, "Alone."

Felicia slid from the table to stand on wobbly legs. Without a word, feeling a hot blush of shame mount her skin from the top of her chemise up her exposed bosom to the top of her hair, she walked away.

She reached her room, thankful that no servant waited for her. She could not stand to face someone after what had just happened. She finished unbuttoning her dress, which was easy because Chillings had done most of the work for her. The black bombazine fell from her to crumple on the floor. She left it there. Next came the stays.

She crawled into bed with the chemise still on. The cotton was damp where her breasts poked upwards. She brought one hand slowly to her bosom. Chillings's— Guy's—mouth had been pressed here. Her nipples ached.

"Lord, what have I done?" she whispered into the silent night.

She had behaved as a wanton. Not only had she let him ravish her, she had encouraged him. The breath caught in her throat. She had…she had… She had no word for what had happened to her.

She twisted to her side and curled tightly around her stomach. She was a widow so she must have known a man before. Somehow she did not think she had ever had that overwhelming experience that was a pleasure unlike anything she could have possibly imagined.

No wonder men wanted to make love. But tomorrow she would have to face him in the bright light of day.

She groaned in embarrassment and buried her head in the pillow, as though by doing so she could as easily bury the desire that ran unabated through her blood. Somehow, she had to find the strength to look at him and not throw herself into his arms, begging for more.

Somehow, she had to leave here before more happened between them. Not only was her virtue in jeopardy, but so was her heart. Neither was a possession she could give into another's keeping.

Chapter Five

Guy woke, his entire body tense and feeling as though he might explode at the slightest provocation. Then he remembered.

He had made love to Felicia, or very nearly done so. They had come so close that not finishing what they had started was the reason he felt so irritable this morning. Although, he thought wryly, she had got more pleasure than he had. A heavy fullness settled in his loins at the knowledge. He had enjoyed many women, but never had he had one who responded as completely as she had.

He flung his arm across his eyes, only to have the scent of lavender—of her—fill his senses. She had been eager and responsive, as anxious to go where they were headed as he had been. He still did not know how he had managed to stop. Probably when she had experienced her release. Her total involvement had aroused him at the same time as it had sobered him.

He groaned.

If he hoped to accomplish anything today other than going to her room and taking her without regard for the consequences, then he had better get up and find a way to release the pent-up energy that held him tight as a bowstring.

"Jeffries," he bellowed. "I am going riding."

The valet appeared. "Yes, my lord. Your clothes are laid out."

Guy eyed the valet. "You seem to know what I intend to do before I know myself. It is not always a comfortable habit."

Jeffries shrugged. "I try to always be one step ahead of your needs, my lord. If I fail to please, I beg your pardon."

Guy got out of bed, thankful that his nightshirt covered his reaction to the memory of last night. Jeffries was too aware by half as it was.

"You know you are indispensable. Now, just help me get dressed."

After what seemed far too long a period, Guy found himself dressed and on his way to the stables. Dante stood ready, pawing the ground in impatience.

"Easy, my friend," Guy said, stroking the gelding's strong neck. "We will be gone shortly."

And they were.

Hours later, the sun fully risen, Guy decided to visit his mistress. Jane could easily help him get rid of the physical discomfort that rode his loins like a harpy. He was surprised that he had not thought of her first.

He arrived at Jane's modest dwelling on the village outskirts cold and more than willing to be made warm. She answered his knock quickly.

"My lord," she said, delighted surprise making her prettier than she actually was.

He smiled at her. "May I come in?"

She smiled back and opened the door wide. "Please."

He stepped past her, catching her earthy scent that had always made him more than ready to enjoy their joining. Today he felt nothing. He was still tense with unreleased passion, but he was experienced enough to know that his condition was not caused by this woman. But he was here.

She wiped her flour-covered hands on the apron that was tied around her small waist. He appreciated the sight of her. Petite in height, but buxom and wide-hipped, she was a woman made for lovemaking. He had always been able to lose himself in her ample charms and skilled hands.

As usual, she waited for him to take the initiative. He closed the distance between them and wrapped his arms around her so that her breasts pressed into the hard muscles just below his nipples. His mouth took hers and her fingers found their way to the buttons of his shirt.

He was naked from the waist up when he gave up.

"I am sorry, my dear," he said, feeling true regret. "But it seems I have started something I cannot finish."

She gave him a bewildered smile. "That is perfectly fine, my lord. We have never fully completed our lovemaking. That is, you have never—"

He put one finger on her lips. "I know that, but this is different. It has nothing to do with you, Jane." He gently took her hands from the tabs of his breeches. "I wish there were an easier way to say this."

She stepped away from him. "I understand, my lord. It is over between us."

He nodded.

She took a deep breath, her ample bosom rising and

falling under the brown wool of her dress. Always before the sight had aroused him. Now he watched with regret only.

"It is just as well, my lord. Farmer John has asked me to marry him." She flushed. "I was not sure what to tell him because of what was between us. Now I will accept."

"Is that what you want, Jane? I will provide for you so that you need never marry if you don't wish to."

She nodded. "I want children and a home. I am ready."

It was just as well. He had never had anything to offer her other than money and the physical pleasure he could give her. Now he had nothing.

"I understand. I am engaged to marry because I need a son."

"I wish you very happy," she said, formally.

"And I you," he replied.

He turned away and pulled on his shirt, his coat and greatcoat. When he was fully dressed, he went back to her.

"I will see that you have a tidy nest egg for you and your farmer, if you wish to share." True regret darkened his eyes. "I have always enjoyed my visits."

She smiled wistfully. "And I, my lord. But I always knew it would end."

He took her hand and raised it to his lips. "I wish you the best of everything, Jane. Let me know when the first child arrives."

He released her and left. There was no sense in lingering. They had each made their decisions. He did not even regret that they had not slept together. Somehow it had not felt right to do so.

Damn Felicia. What would she change in his life next?

* * *

A good hour later, Guy cantered Dante on to the circular driveway in front of The Folly and noticed a travelling carriage. The Fenwick-Clyde coat of arms stood starkly against the black door. Annabell was here at last, and not a day too soon and almost a night too late.

He handed Dante to a groom and strode towards the travelling chaise.

He was in time to help her out of the coach.

"Guy," she said, pleasure lighting her face. "I came as quickly as I could. I hope I am not too late." She smiled at him as though her words were to tease him, but her eyes held concern.

He chose to respond to her humour. "Minx." Then glanced at her luggage. "You seem to have brought everything you own. I swear, I will never fathom how you have travelled the globe when you seem to take half of the British nation with you."

She laughed. "I travel in luxury while here. Otherwise, I travel like a Bedouin, with the clothes on my back and my tent and tea kettle, only they drink coffee. Nasty drink," she finished, wrinkling her nose.

He shook his head. "However you travel and however much paraphernalia you bring with you, there is room in your old suite." He put his arms around her and hugged her tightly. "Thank you for coming, Bell, and for being so prompt."

She hugged him back. "I gathered from your uninformative note that it was rather urgent."

He grimaced as he led her to the front door. "I am in a potentially compromising situation and through no fault of my own." He grinned. "For once."

She raised one black brow, so much like his. "Not of your making?"

"No, dammit." He rubbed his jaw, feeling the short growth of his beard. "I have only done what any decent person would do. Taken her in and given her shelter."

Annabell's brow rose higher. "Her?"

"Yes, Bell, her."

"The plot thickens," she said, her voice lowering into an exaggeratedly conspiratorial tone.

He grinned in spite of his worry. "Melodramatic as always."

She shrugged out of his embrace. "You are the one who is carrying on as though this situation will be the ruin of you, not me."

He allowed her to put some distance between them as she mounted the steps to the entrance. Her making light of the situation irritated Guy. What had happened between him and Felicia just the night before over billiards had not been nearly enough for him. And he thought she felt the same. No matter how Bell might tease about the situation, it was serious.

"Good morning, Miss Annabell," Oswald said, bowing.

She grinned at him as she stepped into the foyer. "Good morning to you, Oswald. And it is Lady Fenwick-Clyde."

"Yes, Miss Annabell," the always-perfect butler replied.

The exchange lightened Guy's mood. "He always thinks of you as the small girl you used to be, running wild around here. I doubt he will ever call you by your new title."

Annabell shrugged. "That is fine with me. I often

wish that I were still that small girl." She shrugged off her heavy wool-and-beaver cape, giving it to a footman who had appeared. "My trunks are still in the carriage."

"I will have them taken to your rooms, Miss Annabell," Oswald said.

She thanked him and turned to her brother. "So, where is this beastie who has you scared for your honour?"

Guy glared at her. "This is not a laughing matter, Bell. The woman has lost her memory, and I am stuck with her until I learn who she is."

"An onerous burden indeed," Annabell said. "But that does not answer my question."

Guy gave a long, put-upon sigh. "She is likely in the library. The room seems to have ensnared her."

"She has good taste." Annabell moved in that direction.

Guy kept pace with her. "What are you doing?"

"I am going to meet her."

"You can do that later."

She stopped and looked pointedly at him. "No, I cannot. If she has got you in such an uproar, then I need to find out what she is like."

He knew there was no keeping her from something she had decided to do. He moved aside. "You always were the most stubborn of us."

"I was also the most practical."

Guy watched his sister sail away, the skirts of her silver-grey travelling dress swishing behind her. He might as well have tea and refreshments served in the library. It would be some time before Annabell went to her rooms.

* * *

Felicia looked up from her book to see a woman framed in the library door. She was tall with silver-blonde hair and black slashing brows. High cheekbones and a strong chin gave her face character. Her clothing was the height of fashion with a high waist and grey piping. A grey spencer made her elegant figure look trim.

Felicia stared. She was a female version of the Viscount, even to her well-defined, sensual mouth. She was the young woman in the portrait.

"Good morning," the woman said in a husky contralto. "I am Annabell Fenwick-Clyde. I dare say my brother has not told you he has a twin sister—or a younger brother, for that matter."

Felicia set the book aside and stood. She returned the woman's smile. "No, he has not, but the portrait over the mantel told me such."

Annabell's gaze went to the picture. "Ah. It is a reasonable likeness. Especially considering that it was nearly thirteen years ago."

Annabell took off her gloves and spencer and tossed them on one of the many blue-and-green velvet upholstered settees. "So, you have lost your memory."

Felicia nodded and sat back down, resigning herself to another interrogation. She cast one wistful glance at the book she had been reading before focusing her attention on the other woman.

"But you know your first name," Annabell continued.

She sank into a leather chair with a natural gracefulness that reminded Felicia of Chillings—Guy. After what they had done last night, using his title seemed too impersonal. She felt herself flush from the remembered passion, his lips, his hands, everything.

"Ahem," Annabell said. "You seem to know your first name."

Felicia felt like a child caught where she should not be. With an effort of will, she put last night's sensations aside.

"It seems that my toiletry case has my initials and a wedding band..." She paused, wondering why every mention of that ring caused her stomach to tighten uncomfortably. She raised her right hand. "There was a wedding band with mine and my husband's names engraved on the inside. Or so we think." She shrugged, uncomfortable with the situation. "It seems that I am likely a widow because of my black clothing."

She hoped she was a widow. What she had done last night would nearly be adultery if she were still married. The fact that Guy was engaged paled beside the knowledge that she might have been unfaithful to a man she could not remember. But she had wanted what they had shared. Even now, in the cold, sparse light of day, she knew she would do it all over again. Her body was in control, not her reason.

Annabell pinned her with a piercing look. "Is that what you really think?"

More uncomfortable than ever, Felicia shrugged. "I don't know."

"Don't know or don't want to know?"

Exasperation at the other woman's pointed questions made Felicia's voice sharp. "I don't know. Plain and simple. If it is because I don't want to know, then so be it. If it is simply because of the hit to the head I took, then so be it. I do not know."

Annabell grinned, so spontaneously and genuinely, that Felicia returned it without thinking.

"You are feisty," Annabell said. "That will stand you in good stead here."

A knock on the door preceded the entrance of Oswald with the tea tray. "His lordship thought you might like some refreshments."

"My brother, the perfect host," Annabell said.

"I try to be," Chillings said smoothly, following the butler and tray in. He glanced from one flushed face to the other. "I hope we don't intrude."

Annabell waved a long-fingered hand. "Of course not. I was merely quizzing your guest, much to her irritation. I would wager that Felicia is grateful for your arrival."

Felicia, already warm, turned warmer. Just looking at him, she felt his lips on hers and his hands doing things to her that had nearly made her crazy with longing for more. She wanted things that would be improper under any circumstances, but because of her situation were doubly so. Yet, she could not help herself.

He cast her an inscrutable look before crossing to the desk where a decanter and several glasses sat on a silver tray. He unstoppered the container and poured himself a drink.

"Whisky, as usual?" Annabell said.

Felicia glanced sharply at Annabell. Did she disapprove of her brother's drinking? Most men drank liberally.

Guy raised his glass. "To my sister and our guest." He downed the contents in one long swallow.

"You don't even cough or gasp," Annabell said. She turned to Felicia. "That stuff burns all the way down your throat and it explodes in your stomach. Normally. But when you drink it constantly, it seems the effects are not so strong."

Felicia said nothing. There were undercurrents here that she did not understand and was better out of. Just as she was better out of this room and away from the Viscount. The last thing any of them needed was for her to make a fool of herself over him in front of his sister. The other woman was here to preserve their reputations, to keep them from doing what they had done last night. Definitely to prevent them from consummating what they had started.

She rose abruptly. "If you will excuse me." She looked at Annabell, unwilling to see what the Viscount's face might reveal. "But I am tired and my head is beginning to ache."

Not waiting for a reply, she grabbed her book and skirted the table where the tea tray sat. She caught a glimpse of movement from the corner of her eye.

Guy stood at the door, his hand on the handle so she could not open it herself. She hardened herself to meet his gaze. His eyes were dark as the sea during a storm and his mouth was a sensual slash bared in a predatory smile. Her knees weakened and it was all she could do to remain standing.

"Yes, my lord?" she said, her voice barely a whisper.

"I will send Mrs Drummond to you."

His melodic baritone made her nerves sing. She remembered all too clearly how he had spoken to her last night, telling her how desirable she was, how beautiful she was. Need, hot, heavy and sudden, engulfed her.

"That is a very good idea, Guy," Annabell said loudly, breaking Felicia's concentration just in time.

Felicia pulled herself up short and ground her nails into her palms in an effort to take her mind off of the Viscount. "Thank you," she murmured, slipping through the door he now held open and not looking back.

Heaven only knew what she would do if he continued to watch her with eyes that spoke of shared passion, because *she* did not know what she would do.

Guy waited until Felicia was no longer visible before closing the door and turning back to his sister. Condemnation met him.

"What have you two been doing?" Annabell demanded.

He shrugged. "What does it matter? You are here now."

Annabell shook her head. "It matters to her, Guy. And unless I miss my guess, it matters to you. You looked ready to devour her."

He crossed to his empty glass and refilled it. "That is why you are here."

She sighed in resignation. "I doubt that my presence is going to do much after what I just saw. There is an electricity between the two of you that is palpable." She rose and went to him. "And you are engaged."

"And she is a widow," he said, downing his whisky.

"That is not the point. If Miss Duckworth hears of this, your engagement will be over. If the *ton* gets even a hint of this, it will be all over town." She put a cautionary hand on his arm. "Are you prepared to marry this woman whom you know nothing about?"

He scowled at her. "You always were adept at calling a spade a spade, Bell. I am marrying Miss Duckworth. That is settled and the notice in *The Times*. Nothing can change that. A gentleman does not jilt a lady, no matter what the provocation."

"Then you had best find out who this Felicia is as quickly as possible and get her out of your house," Annabell stated flatly. "Or else, you will find yourself where you do not want to be."

Chapter Six

"Faugh!" Annabell threw her cards onto the table. "You are unbeatable, Guy."

Felicia laid her cards down more sedately. "He certainly has the Devil's own luck tonight."

He smiled faintly. "If I were at Brook's tonight, I probably would not lose my inheritance."

"Definitely not," Annabell said, rising. She sobered. "Have you heard about Dominic's latest?"

Guy raised one brow and cast a quick glance at Felicia. "Is it polite conversation?"

Annabell looked at Felicia, who still sat at the table with her hands folded calmly in her lap. "No. Nothing Dominic does is ever acceptable conversation for a drawing room."

Felicia, realizing they were discussing their younger and feckless brother, rose. "If you will excuse me, I will retire."

"No, no," Annabell said quickly. "I should not have brought the subject up. I am just restless."

She paced to the fireplace, picked up the poker and jabbed at the embers. Having excited the fire so that sparks shot out and landed on the tile surround, she moved to the window. She threw wide the window and stepped on to the terrace that ran the length of the house. Cold wind whipped into the room.

From outside, Annabell said, "The moon is full, Guy, and your lake is frozen. What do you say to ice-skating? We can see well enough."

Guy rose and joined her. "Sometimes you are as volatile as Dominic."

She slanted him a look full of meaning. "And you, brother."

Felicia stayed inside, bundled tightly in her shawl, and moved to the fireplace. She should go to her room, but she was not sleepy and the idea of ice-skating under a full moon was appealing. It smacked of something slightly dangerous and exciting. She even thought she knew how to do it.

"What do you think, Felicia?" Annabell said, coming back inside. "If you want to skate, then I know Guy will agree."

Felicia blinked at Annabell's words. "You jest, I am sure. But, skating does sound exciting. Only I have no skates and not enough clothing to stay warm."

Annabell let loose her infectious laugh. "I have everything you will need." She turned on Guy, who was closing the French doors behind him. "What say you now?"

Guy looked from one woman to the other. Annabell had colour in her cheeks from the cold. Felicia had colour in her cheeks from the fire, and her eyes danced with interest. His inclination was to decline. But he said nothing.

"No answer is a yes," Annabell said. "Come along," she said to Felicia. "Some of my old clothes that are stored here should fit you."

Felicia looked at Guy, who shrugged his shoulders. His eyes watched her with an intensity that put the lie to his casual gesture. She shivered, but not from the cold.

''It seems I have no say in this,'' he said. ''Shall we meet back here in thirty minutes? I will have Oswald dig up our old skates.''

Both women burst into smiles. He watched them hurry down the hall and knew why he had agreed to something so ridiculous. Felicia's face had told him that she wanted to skate. Nothing else would have swayed him, certainly not Bell's restlessness. He would have talked with his sister instead. Very likely Dominic's latest escapade was bothering her. But he had said nothing, and now the three of them would freeze on the ice and might or might not have fun doing it.

Annoyed at himself, he stalked from the room. There was no telling what he would do next. He had already done things that if someone had told him a fortnight ago he would do, he would have laughed until they slunk away in embarrassment. He did not like to think what he would do next.

They met back at the game room's French doors in exactly thirty minutes. Annabell grinned in anticipation. Guy looked bored and Felicia wondered if she was doing the right thing.

Oswald joined them with three pairs of skates hanging from his gloved hands. ''I hope these fit, my lord,'' he said, handing them to Guy.

''If they don't,'' Felicia said, ''we will make do.''

As she had made do with Annabell's old clothing. The other woman had lively tastes and there had been no black for Felicia to wear. She had settled on a navy spencer and matching pelisse and a cape lined with rabbit fur. The second pair of stockings she wore were pink and the two extra petticoats were cream and white. At first she had been uncomfortable in the colours. Now, she accepted them. At least her outer clothing was dark.

Guy gave her a quick perusal. "It appears that you found something in Bell's castoffs."

Felicia smiled. "She has lovely things."

"Mostly out of fashion," Annabell said.

"But they will keep me warm," Felicia said calmly. Somehow she knew that she had made do most of her life. This was nothing new and it did not bother her.

Guy opened the doors and they all walked outside. Felicia caught her breath at the cold and the beauty. Moonlight limned the terrace in silver and sent moon shadows to dance along the frost-tipped grounds. It was like a fairy-tale world, and Felicia was suddenly glad they were doing this.

"It is as though we have left the world behind," she murmured.

No one responded, but that was all right. She was happy.

They reached the artificial lake quickly. Willows towered above the shore with their limbs dipping like maiden's hands to skim the ice. Ornamental bushes in casual clusters provided texture.

"This is truly beautiful," Felicia said, knowing she sounded redundant, but unable not to comment on the magnificent simplicity Guy had created. "You have made this into a magical place."

"Thank you," Guy said. "It was done over the past few years. I wanted the grounds to reflect the more casual aspect of country life. Not like the stately and staid vistas from my father's time."

"Come along, you two," Annabell said. "You can talk about Guy's passion for landscaping and building another time."

Nestled next to an elegant little pier was a bathhouse done in Grecian lines with a more casual green-and-white striped awning that seemed to float over the lake's edge. At the moment, frost and snow made the awning sparkle as though diamonds were strewn across it.

"Do you swim in the summer?" Felicia asked.

"As children we did all the time," Annabell answered without looking back at them.

In a lower tone, like rich thick chocolate, Guy said, "I still do. When it is hot, the cold water against my skin is like a refreshing tonic."

Felicia glanced at him, only to be caught by the dark hunger in his eyes. She knew they reflected the emotion in her own. For some reason, when she pictured him swimming, he was without clothes. His wide shoulders and lean hips would slice through the water, and then he would stand up.... She licked suddenly dry lips.

"Really?" She forced herself to look away, but could do nothing about her breathlessness.

"Yes, really," he said, a hint of laughter in his voice now.

Disconcerted by his abrupt change of mood, she turned back to him. "You are the most contrary man."

"The same might be said of you," he murmured, holding out his hand to help her over an icy patch.

Without thought she placed her hand in his. When he was near, she felt safe. Then the heat from his body penetrated his glove and hers. She sucked in cold air that did nothing to cool the curl of smoke in her stomach. Her sense of safety fled.

She made it across the slippery area, but he did not release her. Instead he pulled her closer until she could smell the clean fresh scent of lime. It was a scent she would always associate with him, no matter what happened.

They reached the stone bench where Annabell sat donning her skates without Felicia realizing it. She smiled at the other woman and saw that the Viscount's sister was studying her through narrowed eyes. But Annabell smiled back.

"Are you sure you know how to skate?" Annabell asked, as she stood.

"No," Felicia said, laughing lightly, "but I think I do. Surely I do. I can picture people skating."

And she could. She really could. She stared at nothing as her mind played back a scene. It was daytime, but the sun was in her eyes and she could not make out any of the figures she saw skating. They were all blurred, although some seemed smaller than the others. Children, perhaps?

"What do you see, Felicia?" Guy asked.

"People. Some are small. Children?" Then the image was gone. She shook her head. "I must have been seeing people I know." She sighed. "But I could not see them clearly."

"That makes sense," he said, releasing her hand.

She felt bereft. But she should not. To take her mind off the unexpected sense of aloneness, she sank to the bench Annabell had just vacated. Guy handed her the skates to be strapped to her boots. She took them and started to attach them only to realize that she did not know how, and there was not enough light from the full moon for her to figure out how to do so. She frowned.

"Having problems?" Guy said, squatting down in front of her.

"Yes," she said, impatient with herself. Her hands fisted. "I don't know how to attach these. I thought I did or would or something. And now, it is as though I know nothing."

"Easy," he said soothingly. "I will do them for you." He looked up at her and a frown marred his patrician forehead. "You may never have had to fasten them. A man might have done it for you."

She returned his frown. "If I am a widow?"

"That seems likely, as we have discussed."

"Then that makes me a very silly woman if I did not learn how to fend for myself but always depended on a man."

His brow smoothed. "Many women would disagree with you."

"I suppose."

He finished fastening the skates and sat beside her. His thigh met hers and, even through the multiple layers of clothing, she could feel his hard muscles. She inched away until she was barely on the bench. Better to fall on to the ground than touch this man in a manner that felt intimate enough to spark a desire in her that would burn with the intensity of an inferno.

He paused a moment in fastening his skates, his face shifting so that his dark eyes met hers. She looked away and jumped to her feet, determined to put some distance between them before she lost all sense of propriety and threw herself into his arms.

She wobbled and her left ankle buckled. She fell sideways, right into Guy's arms as he stood to catch her. She leaned into him, telling herself it was only for support. Still, her side felt scorched as awareness of him radiated out to every fibre of her body.

Memories of what they had done just several nights before, and of what they had not done, played through her mind. He had lifted her on to the billiard table, scattering the balls to the floor, then he had touched her. His fingers had caressed her in places so intimate that she had not realized what it would feel like to have someone stroke them. And she had done the same to him. Tremors of desire took her and she wondered if she was the only one remembering. She looked up at him and knew she was not alone.

There was a wild look about him. His eyes were a little more narrow than usual, his jaw a little firmer, his body tighter.

His head angled down until his breath brushed across her cheek. "I would do it all over," he murmured.

She gazed up at him. Part of her wanted to tell him she would not. The part that did not know who she was or if she might be married. The part of her that was her heart told him, "So would I."

His grip on her tightened and she thought he would kiss her. His lips were nearly on hers.

"Guy," Annabell said loudly, "we came here to skate."

Guy moved back, but did not release Felicia. "So we did, Bell."

As though he had not just nearly seduced her with nothing more than the promise of a kiss, he helped Felicia with all propriety until they stood side by side on the ice. Frustration took Felicia as her ankles gave out and she slid down, saved only by Guy's arm around her waist.

"Easy," he said.

"It seems that I don't know how to skate after all."
Her fingers tightened on his forearm.

"Come along, you two," Annabell called from farther out on the lake. "Come skate in the moonlight."

Felicia looked at Annabell and forgot her irritation for the moment. Guy's sister did figures of eight and glided by on one foot with the other held gracefully in the air, and all on a lake of ice that sparkled like molten silver in the moon's glow. Annabell's elongated shadow swept behind her like a swan gliding across water.

"Oh," Felicia breathed, "how beautiful. She is so graceful."

Guy did not glance at his twin. "Yes."

Felicia's gaze snapped back to him. "Again?" she asked softly. "Annabell will see us, you know."

"To hell with Annabell. She is a grown woman."

Felicia shook her head. "No, it is not comfortable."

"Nothing about this is comfortable." He bit off each word.

"No," she murmured, "it is not."

"Shall we return to the house?" Annabell asked from not more than four feet away.

Felicia had been so involved with Guy that she had not noticed Annabell approach. The realization of how mesmerized she was by him was sobering. She stepped away, forgetting she was on ice skates.

Her feet slid and slipped. Her arms windmilled as she tried to keep her balance. She squeaked.

Guy caught her to his chest and held her tight until her breathing returned to normal. A thick strand of hair had come loose and hung like spun copper down the back of her coat. She brushed futilely at it before giving up.

"Leave it," Guy said, his voice deep.

She nodded. "You can let me go now. Or just hold my hand."

He released her and skated back only far enough to put some distance between them, but he continued to hold her hand. "Move slowly," he said. "And don't look down."

She scooted her feet along in tiny slides. Her fingers gripped Guy's hand like pincers.

"That's the way," he crooned. "Slow and easy."

She darted a glance at him, wondering if he knew how seductively suggestive his words and tone were. The knowing glint in his eyes told her that he did. She tried to ignore him. Next to impossible, but she tried.

Then, as though by magic, she got her balance. "You can let go," she said, her voice barely above a whisper. "I think I have it now."

His fingers loosened on hers, but he did not withdraw his hand. Slowly, so as not to lose her newfound balance, Felicia let his hand go. She found it felt safer if she held her arms slightly out at her sides. Elation filled her as she moved on her own.

"Bravo, bravo," Annabell said, skating up to Felicia. "I believe you have got the idea now."

Felicia did not dare nod. She was not even comfortable speaking in case her concentration broke. Instead, she skated towards the centre of the lake where Annabell had been. She reached the spot where the moon shone down like a spotlight. Giddy with delight, she did circles, her arms held wide. Her skirts belled around her. Her coat flared out. Her hair escaped from the pins that had only managed to barely hold it in proper confinement.

Guy smiled at her exuberance. This was a side of

her he had not seen yet. But then, he had only known her for a matter of weeks. It seemed longer.

"She is lovely," Annabell said, coming up to Guy's side. "It is a pity you are already promised to Miss Duckworth."

Guy tensed. "A pity for whom?" he drawled. "Not for me."

"Hah. I have seen the way you look at her. You would devour her if you could." She paused to let her words sink in before adding, "And she feels the same."

"Rubbish."

Even as he said the word, Guy knew in his stomach that he did not mean it. Nor could he lie to his sister. Not that she would not see through the lie, for she would, but simply because he and Bell had always been honest with each other. He thought it might come of being twins.

"It is better this way," he finally said. "She does not know who she is or what her life is. I am looking for a marriage of convenience, not passion."

"Or love?" Annabell queried softly.

"Or that."

Felicia, gaining confidence with every second she remained on her feet, did a twirl. Guy watched her, noting the way the moonlight emphasized her elegant cheekbones and the fine way she tilted her head back so her long neck showed graceful as a swan's.

The next instant she fell.

Felicia shrieked in surprise and consternation. She hit the ice with an impact that knocked her breath out.

Guy watched her slam into the ice and bounce up from the force of the fall. Then, to his horror, dark lines started forming.

"Felicia," he shouted, "get up. Now. Come back."

She rolled to her knees and looked around. "Oh, no," she moaned. She tried to stand and fell back. More cracks appeared.

Guy's heart sped like a galloping horse as he rushed to her, stopping just short of the cracks. He did not trust the ice with his added weight.

"Don't try to stand again. Crawl toward me. Quickly, now," he finished, keeping the panic he felt from showing in his voice. The last thing she needed was his fear added to her own.

Felicia looked up at him. She knew that when she reached him she would be safe. On hands and knees, she scrambled towards him.

The ice cracked again, the sound reverberating in Felicia's ears. Distantly, logically, she knew the noise had not been great, but she also sensed that this crack was crucial. Seconds later, she sank. Cold water closed around her. She gasped and freezing liquid rushed down her throat and filled her lungs. She thrashed until her head broke the surface. She coughed and gasped and went under again.

"Oh, my God, no," Guy said.

He inched forward, afraid to go too far and fall in with her. He would not be able to help her if he was submersed.

He looked back at Annabell. "I am going to lie on my stomach and move slowly toward her. The less weight on the ice near her, the less chance that it will break too."

Annabell nodded, too stunned to speak.

Guy sprawled on his belly. He was distantly aware of the cold seeping through his clothes and into his muscles. He inched forward. He had to reach her. He was almost to her when the ice beneath him started to creak. He did not have much time. He pushed himself to the edge and looked into the dark water. He could see Felicia just below the surface.

The ice creaked again. A fresh crack started.

Time was against him. He shoved his arms into the freezing black water as deep as they would go. He felt her fingers but could not get a grip on her. He inched forward and took a deep breath then plunged his head in along with his arms so that he was in the water to his chest. He caught her.

His heart pounded until he thought it would burst. His muscles clenched until they ached, but he held on to her. Slowly, ever so slowly, he used the strength in his legs to move him backwards. Too slowly.

He felt hands on his ankles and realized that Annabell had come out behind him and grabbed him. She pulled and he slid backward more than he could do on his own.

His head broke the water and he gasped for air. ''More, Bell. More. She is like a dead weight with all her clothing.''

Annabell grunted.

Felicia's head popped above the surface. She gasped and coughed and choked.

Relief was a sharp pain in Guy's chest. ''Come on, Felicia. Help me if you can.''

Her eyes opened wide. ''I...I..''

Her teeth chattered and her fingers were stiff in his. He could see her fear. ''I have you.'' Without looking back, he said, ''I need more help, Bell. I don't think it is safe for me to stand yet.''

''Yes,'' Annabell said breathlessly. ''I am trying.''

''I know, Bell.''

He kept his gaze on Felicia. Her eyes had closed and she looked lifeless. Fresh fear speared his stomach. They had to get her out. Now.

"To hell with it," he muttered. "Let go, Bell. This is taking too long."

Annabell barely released him when he worked his way to his knees, keeping a firm grip on Felicia's hands. He changed his hold to her wrists and stood, pulling her up with him. The weight of her clothing was enough to bend him over, but he persevered. Then she was out and in his arms. He gripped her tightly. The ice under his feet cracked.

"Move," he shouted at Bell. "Now."

He leaped away from the breaking ice, landed precariously because of his skates, and sped toward shore. He saw Bell safely ahead of him. At least he did not have to worry about her.

He knew it had only taken seconds to reach the shore, but it had felt like an eternity. Bell was beside him instantly.

"How is she?" his sister asked.

"Cold and still," he said quietly, keeping his voice calm. The last thing any of them needed was for him to give in to the fear he felt. "We need to get her to the house."

Bell knelt down and undid his skates without being told. He smiled. She had always been one to take action. Sometimes it was the wrong action, but she never stood by and did nothing.

He started up the path as quickly as he could. Felicia lay in his arms like a leaden weight. She did not move or open her eyes. Her glorious hair, sodden and heavy, fell nearly to the ground in lank strands. Her breath came in shallow little puffs that looked like smoke in the cold air. He sped up. His feet slipped on the frosted gravel but he did not slow down. He did not dare.

He heard Bell behind him. "Go ahead and notify Mrs Drummond."

"Right." She passed him running.

Guy's arms ached and the cold from Felicia's body and wet clothes penetrated his own clothing. The closeness of their bodies and the warmth he exuded from exertion did not make a difference to the chill he felt in her.

He was at the door just as Oswald opened it. "Mrs Drummond is in Madam Felicia's room, my lord."

"Thank you," Guy said, hurrying past. "See that a hot bath is prepared."

"Mrs Drummond has already ordered one, my lord."

Guy heard Oswald's words as though from a distance. He was already rushing down the corridor. He passed through the games room. One more set of stairs to climb up to the first floor where the guest chambers were. He was nearly out of energy. The door to Felicia's room stood open. He burst through and made straight for the bed where he gently laid her. She did not stir.

"Dear me, dear me," Mrs Drummond said, coming up behind him. "She is drenched to the skin." She spared a glance for the Viscount. "And so are you. Go change. You cannot do anything for her that I cannot do better, my lord."

A wry smile twisted Guy's lips. Mrs Drummond was nothing if not confident of her skills.

"I will stay here and help." He took off his coat and tossed it on to a chair. The housekeeper opened her mouth to speak, but he cut her off. "Two pairs of hands are better than one. Someone used to tell me that.''

''Using my own words against me, my lord. It is not playing fair.''

He shrugged. ''I don't intend to play fair where this woman is concerned.''

Mrs Drummond gave him a startled look before focusing her attention on the frighteningly still woman. ''Her lips are blue and her breathing is shallow and irregular. Best get her out of those wet things.'' She all but elbowed her way past the Viscount. ''You had best turn away, my lord.''

He gave her a fleeting grin. ''I don't believe I will do that. I have seen and undressed enough women to know what to do here.''

Mrs Drummond's sharp intake of air was loud in the quiet room. ''As you say, *my lord*.''

He did not even look at her. ''We have more important things to do than waste words.''

''True.''

Mrs Drummond started unbuttoning Felicia's coat even as Guy put an arm around Felicia's back and raised her enough that they could pull the clothing off. It hit the floor. Next was the pelisse. After that a spencer. Now her dress.

The buttons and ties were at the back so Guy held her propped forward, resting on his chest. He continued to hold her thus while Mrs Drummond stripped the chilling material from Felicia's skin.

''She is clammy and cold as an eel.''

Guy grimaced. ''Not a very flattering description.''

''But accurate. Hold up her hips, my lord, so I can slide this off.''

He did as ordered. Under it all was a simple set of

stays over a thin chemise, which was transparent from the water. The pink aureoles of her breasts thrust upward, the nipples taut as though she were caught in the throes of passion. As they had been several nights before. The breath caught in Guy's throat.

He had to look elsewhere while Mrs Drummond unlaced the stays and the ripe fullness of Felicia's bosom tumbled loose. The urge to touch her, even now, was nearly undeniable. He berated himself for his lack of control.

"My lord," Mrs Drummond said sharply. "I need you to help me undress her, not hinder me by holding her so that I cannot get her chemise off."

He jerked. But her scold had broken the spell. For the moment. He knew it would not last. He desired Felicia too greatly.

He clenched his jaw and did as directed until Felicia lay naked on the coverlet that was now wet and needing to be replaced. Her skin was pale as alabaster. It had been that way the last time he had seen her naked, although he had not seen more than her bosom. Without forethought, his gaze travelled down the length of her.

Full, tip-tilted breasts led to a slim ribcage and tiny waist. Her hips flared in lush welcome. Her legs were long and her ankles neat. She was lovely.

She was also a mother. There were nearly transparent stretch marks across her abdomen. They were not easy to see. The light had to hit them just right as it did now. His gut clenched. A fleeting memory of Suzanne crying out in pain from birthing sped through his mind and disappeared. The sight of Felicia was too immediate for anything else to matter.

He traced one of the spidery stretch marks that told

him she had birthed at least one child. Other men might think it an imperfection, but to Guy it added to her beauty. His finger skimmed the line from her right hip to her belly button where another barely visible mark started. This one went to silken hairs—

"Stop that." Mrs Drummond swatted his hand.

Guy jerked back and took a deep breath. Closing his eyes to Felicia's beauty, he carefully covered her with the sheet. "Thank you, Mrs Drummond," he murmured, not sure he truly meant it.

This was the second time tonight that his passions had got the better of him, and he had acted indiscreetly with other people around. What was this woman doing to him?

Then the realization hit him. This was proof that she was a widow. But where was her child?

Mrs Drummond sniffed. Once more she disrupted his thoughts. "I will go get clean bedding myself. Calling a maid will take too long." She eyed the Viscount. "See that you do not do anything. It is improper enough that you are seeing her like this. Not that I can do anything to stop you."

Knowing her reprimand was deserved, Guy said, "At least credit me with the decency to realize that she is too sick for me to seduce her."

"Miss Annabell should be here," Mrs Drummond said pointedly.

"And she will be," Guy said. "She is changing before she catches an inflammation."

Mrs Drummond turned reluctantly away. Felicia's eyes flickered open. Guy leaned forward, gripping her hand hard.

"Felicia?" he said. "Do you hear me?"

Her head moved in a nearly imperceptible nod.

"You are safe," he said.

"Don't leave me," she whispered.

"Never," he said.

Chapter Seven

Her eyes drifted shut again. Her body relaxed.

Mrs Drummond, who had stopped when she heard Felicia's voice, started out again. She reached the door just as two footmen, supervised by Oswald, arrived with the hip bath and cans of steaming water. She waved them in and turned back to stare at the Viscount.

"I will be back before they have the water poured, my lord."

Guy understood what she was not saying. He was to wait for her before putting Felicia into the bath. He did not deign to answer. Favored and loved servant she was, but he would do as he determined best.

Painfully aware of Felicia's nakedness under the sheet, Guy hastily grabbed the corner of the coverlet from the opposite side of the bed and pulled it over her still form. Only then did he direct them to place the bath by the fire, something they were already doing. This woman had addled his brain along with his body.

They poured the water into the bath and left. The door closed behind them before Guy uncovered Felicia again. The hot water would take some of the cold from her flesh. Something needed to. If she remained like this, she would catch an inflammation of the lungs or worse.

He would bathe her while Mrs Drummond was gone. He flipped back the coverlet and picked her up as gently as possible and carried her to the tub. Careful not to get her hair into the hot water, he lowered her. Her skin flushed like a pink rose as the water enveloped her.

He folded a towel and placed it beneath her head so she was not resting on hard metal. Next he fanned her hair out so that it hung down the back of the tub where the heat from the fire would dry it. Unable to resist, he combed his fingers through the thick mass. It was like stroking the finest silk. His loins tightened instantly.

He groaned. Heaven help him. His response to her was beyond reason.

When he was sure she would not slide under the water if left unattended, he positioned a screen around the tub so she would not be seen by someone entering the room. He wanted to protect her privacy from other people. His mouth twisted. He could appreciate the irony. He had dug through her belongings without a thought for her feelings. Now he intended to bathe her, an act almost more intimate than making love. He was not her maid and he was not her husband. He wanted to be her lover, and he wanted to keep others from seeing her this vulnerable.

Guy turned back to her.

She watched him, her eyes half-closed. Her lips drooped. But she was awake.

He knelt by the bath. ''Felicia.''

Her mouth twitched in a weak attempt at a smile, but she did not speak. Her eyes drifted shut.

''Felicia,'' he said, projecting confidence into his

voice. "I am going to bathe you. The warm water will help bring heat back into your body. Next we are going to get you into dry clothes and into bed with a posset."

He did not often feel helpless, but he was close to that emotion now. To occupy himself, since the purpose of the hot water was not to clean her but to warm her, he fetched her brush.

Sitting to the side of the tub so that his body did not block the heat from the fire, he began brushing her hair. The damp tendrils did not take well to the bristles, but he slowly worked out the knots.

"Ahem," Annabell said, looking around the screen. "I thought Mrs Drummond was here."

"She was. She is fetching dry linens."

"And left you alone with Felicia?"

He shrugged and stood up. "I am the master here. She did as I told her, which is more than you have ever done."

He was irritated at himself for not having heard Bell come in. He had been so enthralled by Felicia's hair that nothing else had registered. This had to stop.

"Here," he said, handing her the brush, "you finish."

She raised one quizzical brow. "Is that an order? A maid could do it."

"No." He gave his twin a hard look. "She is ill and floating in and out of awareness. I won't have someone tending her whom she does not know."

Annabell said nothing, but took the brush from him and sat in the chair he had vacated. Guy nodded before going around the screen. He stopped, his jaw clenched tight and his hands fisted until the knuckles hurt. He had to get control of his reactions.

Felicia was only a woman. A desirable woman, but

only a woman. He had had his share of women, many more lovely than her. Suzanne had been a beauty. If his wife were alive today, she would eclipse Felicia without even trying.

But he knew, in some part of him, that it would not matter. Suzanne had never held him captive as Felicia did. He had cared for Suzanne, even loved her, but he had never been consumed by passion for her.

Mrs Drummond entered, stopping his thoughts and making him glad to see her. "About time," he grumbled unfairly.

She cocked her head to one side. "Where is madam?"

He waved a hand at the screen. "In the hot water with Annabell brushing out her hair."

The housekeeper gave him a sharp look, but said nothing. She quickly changed the linen. That done, she went to join Annabell. Guy knew his help would no longer be needed. If he stayed, the two of them would hound him and let him do nothing. Mrs Drummond he could have overrode, but not Bell.

It was better this way. No telling what he would do next. He left without a word.

Guy sprawled in the same slipper chair he had sat in several weeks earlier while questioning Felicia. His unwelcome guest. He laughed, but it was more sardonic than humourous.

The fire crackled and leapt up the chimney, but its heat was faint by the time it reached the bed. The bath had warmed Felicia, but that had been temporary. Since the small hours of the night, he had watched her get worse. Her teeth chattered and she tossed and turned.

The next thing, she was hot with perspiration on her brow.

She turned towards him and he thought her eyes were open. There was no candle, only firelight, so he stood up and moved to the bed.

"Guy?" she said, her voice a hoarse whisper.

"I'm here," he murmured.

She smiled at him, but it was weak. Dark circles made her eyes appear huge. He smoothed the hair back from her face, delighting in the feel of the silken strands. He did not think he would ever tire of running his fingers through her hair.

"I am so cold," she said, her jaw clenched to keep her teeth from chattering.

Consternation gripped him. They had done everything they could. There were extra covers on the bed. An earthenware hot water-bottle nestled near her feet. Warm stones had been put in with her.

"So cold," she said, her voice cracking with exhaustion.

He studied her carefully. She looked so frail, as though she was too weak to fight off the chills that wracked her body. Mrs Drummond had been afraid this would happen. If they were not careful or were unlucky, Felicia would have a severe inflammation of the lungs.

There was only one other thing to do.

He stood and slipped out of his robe and shirt. He went to the other side of the bed and slid under the covers. Then he moved to her side and pulled her into the curve of his body. She felt like ice, as she had when he'd pulled her from the lake. This had to work.

A soft sigh came from her as she snuggled into him. Lying on his side, he wrapped his arms around her.

The flare of her bottom flush with his loins, the smooth flow of her flank running the length of his thighs and the heavy fullness of her breasts resting against his forearm all combined to make him groan.

He chastised himself. He was here to take the cold from her body and hopefully help her recover. He was not here to make love to her. The last thing he wanted to do—or needed to do—was make love to her. That basic act would complicate too many things. And he could not, would not take a chance on getting her pregnant.

No, he had to control himself better than he had in the past. But this was temptation so great that it was torture to resist.

She wriggled in closer. He thought he would explode. And her breasts. Even through the nightdress she wore, he could feel their fullness. In his mind, he could taste their sweetness and delight in their response to his touch.

Madness.

''Guy? Guy?'' She twisted in his arms until she faced him. Her eyes were wide, her mouth a soft blur. ''Hold me. Make the cold go away. Please.''

He knew she had to be delirious. ''I'm trying, Felicia. I'm trying.'' His voice was hoarse with desire, his loins tight with the need to love her.

She burrowed into him until her lips pressed against the bare skin of his chest. Her arms slid up and around his neck. Her breasts pushed against him. Her nipples were hard pebbles that abraded his sensitized flesh. She might as well be naked for all the barrier her nightdress provided. They touched in every area that mattered. Guy ached and still she clung to him as though she were trying to absorb him or be absorbed by him.

"So cold," she murmured, her breath hot and moist against his flesh.

He groaned, all his good intentions beginning to evaporate in the heat she created in his body. "Felicia," he said, his voice cracking on her name. "Stop. Perhaps this was not such a good idea."

She held him tighter. She tipped back her head to look at him and her eyes glittered feverishly. "This is a very good idea. Very, very good."

Her lips parted and her eyelids drooped, but her body clung to his. Guy knew he was lost.

No longer able to resist the temptation of her, no longer caring about why he had first entered her bed, Guy lowered his face. His mouth met hers and the shock of it rocked through his body, more intense than the first time. Her lips moved beneath his, opening and welcoming him. The pulse pounded in his loins as he accepted her invitation.

Little soft sucking sounds punctuated each kiss. He nipped her lips, then gently suckled them. She sighed in pleasure. Her fingers tangled in his hair, holding him close.

"More," she demanded, straining against him.

Guy did not know if she meant more kisses or just to hold her tighter. He was beyond himself with desire. All reason fled as his body rose to meet her need.

He undid the ribbon at her neck and then slid his hands down her side, revelling in the sleek feel of her under his fingers. He caught the hem of her gown and started working it up her body. She moved to help him until the clothing was over her head and on to the floor with his robe.

He shuddered as the silken flesh of her bosom rubbed the raw nerves of his chest. It took all his control not to push her to her back and enter her then and there. Her mouth sought out his neck where she suckled until he thought he would go crazy.

It became harder to breath. "Damn these trousers," he cursed.

He fumbled with the buttons, his fingers all thumbs. She continued to kiss him and nuzzle him until he thought he would go crazy if he did not take this to the next level. Finally his trousers were undone and he pulled them down his legs, taking his stockings and underclothing with them.

He sprang free and lodged in the soft warmth between her legs. He jerked and nearly ended everything then.

"Guy." She stopped kissing him long enough to look at him. "I want everything."

Her eyes held a glittering intensity. He stared back at her, wondering if she knew what she was saying. She was sick and had been freezing. Dimly he remembered that her coldness had started all of this. Right now, she felt like a flaming brand in his arms. Her face was flushed and her skin was hot against his.

She moved, trapping his hardness between her thighs and it no longer mattered. Nothing mattered but being inside her.

"I will give you everything I have," he promised.

Determined to pleasure her until she cried out for him, he slid down the length of her, kissing and nipping her as he went. In each hand, he held a breast and gently kneaded them, revelling in the firmness and the way they responded to his touch. Her entire body seemed to hum.

He reached the juncture of her thighs and regretfully released her breasts. She made a soft sound of protest.

"It is all right, Felicia," he said, his voice deeper than he had ever heard it. "You will like this."

He spread her legs and positioned them so he could reach her soft core. Then he began to kiss and lave her with his tongue.

"Guy," she gasped, her body bucking.

"Easy," he said, holding her hips firmly.

He used his fingers to massage her belly, never stopping his mouth and tongue. When her gasps became soft and quick and her stomach knotted, he knew she was ready. He rose to his knees, ignoring her protest, and slid into her. Her back arched and her nails bit into his thighs. He pulled out and thrust deeper, setting up a rhythm that she followed as though they had been lovers for all eternity. It was bliss.

Sensation overwhelmed him. He lost control. He tightened to the point of near pain, the pleasure was so intense. Shudders racked his body and he knew he was near his end.

"Guy…" Her voice rose, her nails raked his skin.

A glimmer of sanity entered his brain. He could not—he panted, trying desperately to gain control of himself—would not lose himself in her. She would not bear his child and all the danger that entailed.

Somehow, some way, he pulled out of her. His body protested, his muscles spasmed. He released his seed on the soft whiteness of her belly.

"My…" He trailed off, spent, with no breath to speak.

"Guy," she moaned. "Please, please, help me."

He realized with a start that he had ended it too soon for her. "Easy, Felicia," he said, rolling to her side and gathering her close. "I will make it right. I promise."

He caught her hungry mouth with his and slid his hand down. He stroked her with a passion that reignited his own. This time, he controlled himself. He might have spent himself once already, but he would not take another chance of being able to pull from her in time. Instead, he increased his motion to match the movement of her hips.

He felt her muscles clench and knew she was almost there. She thrust hard against his hand. Her mouth left his as a high moan escaped her. She exploded around him. Only after he was sure she was satisfied did he ease his stroking and bend to kiss her gently. Her sigh of relief filled his lungs.

He turned her so that her back fitted against his chest and pulled the covers around them, careful to see that she was tucked in. Instead of cold coming from her now, she radiated the hot heat of satisfaction. He shifted her hair aside and kissed the nape of her neck. She murmured something he could not hear and then her body relaxed. She had fallen asleep.

He lay awake into the early hours of morning.

Guy started awake. Where was he? What had woken him? Felicia. He was in her bed.

Memory flooded back. Felicia falling into the lake. Making love to her. Her calling out. Words he could not make out. That was what had woken him.

She tossed. "Nooo... Please, Lord, no." Her breath caught on a sob. "Not Colleen, please. Ced..."

She was calling out to someone. He rose on one elbow to see her, but the fire had died and she was only a darker shadow in a dark room. The covers fell from his shoulder. A cold dark room. Her body was in complete contrast. She was like a smouldering cinder. Something was wrong.

He had to see her better. He crawled from the bed. Naked as the day he was born and covered in goose-flesh, he went to her side and fumbled at the nearby table. He found a tinder box and the candle. Soon there was enough light to find his clothes where they lay strewn on the floor. Her nightdress tangled with his trousers as intimately as her body had tangled with his.

Instantly, uncontrollably, he hardened. It was as though he had not quenched his ardour no more than a couple hours before. He groaned as he pulled his trousers up and fastened them.

He went to Felicia. She was drenched in perspiration. Her beautiful hair lay in tangles on the pillow, its shine dulled.

"Dammit," he muttered. "This is not good."

"Please," she begged, eyes closed, body twisting. "Don't take them."

Tears streamed down her face. Her lips moved as she continued to plead. She was delirious. He had to get her temperature down.

He pulled back the covers and tucked an extra sheet that Mrs Drummond had left around Felicia, then went to the washbasin and soaked a cloth with the icy water. Mrs Drummond had left instructions to bathe her like this if her temperature rose, which it had.

He pulled the covers from her again and the musty odor of their lovemaking met him. His body responded instantly. He grimaced. He had to stop this. She needed his help, not his passion.

Gently, and more aroused than he wanted, he washed her heated skin. Already the cloth was warm and needed to be dipped in the cold water. He brought the washbasin and its stand by the bed.

Next he rinsed her face. The flush left her skin as the coolness touched it, only to return as soon as he stopped. He dipped the cloth again and moved down her body.

He bathed her without stop, starting at her forehead and going to her toes and then repeated it, again and again. The repetition eased some of his aching desire for her. She was so sick, he felt like a heartless rogue to want her so badly. But he did.

The water in the basin was lukewarm when someone knocked. "Come in," he said.

"Guy?" Annabell said.

He glanced over his shoulder as she stepped into the room. Before she could speak again, he said, "Bell, please go for more cold water and have a maid come in and start the fire. I am freezing."

Instead of immediately doing what he said, which was usual, she came to the bed and stood beside him. "She looks bad."

"I know," he said.

"But even so, she is lovely."

"I know," he said, wondering why his normal sardonic answers would not come.

Annabell glanced at him. "Are you in love with her?"

Guy tensed and with an effort of will looked his sister in the eye. "Don't be a silly romantic, Bell. I am not in love with her."

"A good thing," Annabell said drily, "since you are engaged to Miss Duckworth."

Her words were a blow to his solar plexus. He had forgotten. He had not thought about Emily Duckworth since he left her in London wearing the engagement ring he had just bought. He had not given her his mother's, the ring that passed from bride to bride. Suzanne had worn it and now it stayed in a safe here at The Folly.

"Go get the water and maid, Bell," he said, his voice sounding more tired than he wanted.

She gave him one searching glance before leaving, but said nothing further. Guy was thankful for that.

He looked down at Felicia. Her lashes were a sweep of chocolate above her cheeks. Her lips were swollen and scarlet. The dark circles under her eyes were deeper and blacker than they had been just hours before.

He had told her about Emily Duckworth, intending to put distance between them. It had for all of a day. And now they were to this point. It was no good. Emily Duckworth was the woman he intended to marry and have an heir by. Felicia had been an unwelcome houseguest.

Now she was his mistress.

This was not what he had planned. Widows frequently became men's mistresses—Jane in the village had been his for some time. But somehow he did not think Felicia was the type of woman to be a man's lightskirt.

That did not answer what he was to do about Felicia. Ideally, he would apologize to her and walk away. He knew he could not do that. Not yet. Not while she was in his house. Not while his need for her was greater than his reason. He groaned and rubbed his jaw where his beard itched.

The arrival of Bell, a maid and more water turned

his concentration. He yanked the covers over Felicia's nakedness and turned to his sister.

"Thank you for hurrying, Bell."

"A better greeting than before," she said, a smile in her eyes. "But you still look like something Dominic dragged home with him."

Guy laughed. He could not help it. He had seen some of the strays—four-legged and two—Dominic had brought home with him.

"Then I must look like something to scare children."

Now she smiled with her lips. "Or worse. Get some sleep." When his jaw tightened, she added, "I will stay with her until you are able to return."

He looked at Felicia. She seemed to be resting more comfortably. "Good advice, Bell, but call me immediately if her condition changes."

"I will," she promised with an indulgent look on her face. "Although I should not."

Chapter Eight

Guy woke feeling like he had drunk too much whisky the night before. His head felt like it was stuffed with wool and his limbs had no strength. He forced one eye open and then the other. From the faint light peeking through the drapes, he knew it was late afternoon.

He staggered out of bed and instantly regretted it. He wore no clothes and did not even remember removing them. His room was as cold as the lake Felicia had fallen in or so it seemed.

"Jeffries," he said, his voice louder than normal but not a shout.

His valet responded immediately. "Yes, my lord?" a very proper gentleman's gentleman answered from one of the many shadows.

Guy twisted around to see Jeffries crossing the room towards him. The valet was a short, trim man with a pointed chin and a decided dapperness about him. At the moment, he was impeccable in a plain black coat and pantaloons with a white shirt. Even his shirt points stood tall. A gentleman's gentleman of the first water.

Guy grinned.

He and Jeffries had been together a long time. Prior

to his elevation, the valet had been a footman at the Chillings's mansion in London. When Guy had chosen him, the man had contacted Beau Brummell's valet on his own initiative in order to learn his new job from the best. There were many men of fashion who would do anything to lure Jeffries from Guy, but the valet was loyal. However, he never failed to mention his desirability when Guy would not follow some dictate of Brummell's.

"Jeffries, I need to bathe and dress immediately."

The valet nodded. "As you wish, my lord, but she is no worse than when you left her."

Guy stopped in mid-step. "What did you say?"

Jeffries coughed. "I merely thought you wished to know that Madam Felicia is still sleeping and seems in no immediate danger. Her fever is down. I believe Mrs Drummond has a mustard poultice on the lady's, ahem…chest to ward off any inflammation."

Guy nodded. That was exactly what he wanted to know, but he did not like it that his valet knew the answer before he asked the question.

"Thank you."

"I am always glad to be of service."

Guy eyed the other man. Jeffries could be tongue in cheek when he chose. It was his only failing.

"Then you will be glad to arrange for my hot water to come immediately." Guy turned away with a grin. That would put Jeffries on his mettle.

"Absolutely, my lord," the valet said, his tone only the slightest bit huffy.

Twenty minutes later, Guy sank into the welcome heat of the bath. "Ah," he sighed. "This is perfect, Jeffries."

"I know, my lord."

Guy shook his head slightly. "As will be my clothes."

"You arrange a beautiful cravat, my lord."

Guy laughed outright, some of the night's worry leaving him. "Generous of you."

A knock interrupted them. Guy heard the door open.

"Lady Fenwick-Clyde," the valet said in his most disapproving tone. "His lordship is indisposed."

From behind the privacy of the screen, Guy said, "I am bathing, Bell. Can't this wait?"

"I don't think so," she said.

Guy caught the anxiety in her voice. He sat straight up and grabbed for the bath sheet laid across the hearth. He stood and wrapped the length around him.

"Has Felicia got worse?"

He heard Bell sigh and could picture her selecting a strand of hair and starting to twirl it around her fingers. "This is not about her. We—you—are in a pickle. Miss Emily Duckworth is here."

"What?"

Guy nearly dropped the bath sheet into the water. He managed to catch it with only one corner sopping. Securing it so that it covered his hips and legs, he stepped out of the tub and around the screen.

"What the devil is she doing here?"

Bell shrugged, but she twirled the strand of hair. "I have no idea. She won't speak to me, other than civilities."

"Fine pickle indeed," Guy muttered. "Jeffries, fetch my things. Bell, go back and keep her company." Bell raised one black brow. Guy caught her action just before turning away. "Please go back and stay with her."

"That is much better. I am not one of your servants

or horses,'' Annabell said. ''I don't like her showing up like this either. It makes me think that she knows about Felicia, but I don't see how she could.''

''Neither do I,'' Guy said, nodding to Jeffries his acceptance of the clothing the valet had selected. ''But I did not invite her.''

Annabell groaned. ''Oh, dear. Well, I had better get back. No telling what is happening while I am here. Perhaps I can get something out of her before you come down.''

''Let us hope so,'' Guy said.

''This is a very uncomfortable situation,'' she said tartly, retreating to the door.

''Yes, it is, Bell, and not one of my making. I did not bring Felicia here to flaunt the proprieties. I brought her here because she was hurt. Nor did I invite Miss Duckworth,'' Guy said, his mouth twisted.

Fifteen minutes later, Guy stood outside the door that led to the north drawing room. He was dressed in the height of fashion and knew that no matter what kind of physical and emotional mayhem had been going on between him and Felicia, he looked the part of the consummate aristocrat without a concern in the world other than the perfection of his cravat, which was done in a perfect Chillings Crease.

When the footman moved to open the door and announce him, Guy shook his head. Miss Duckworth should not be here. He wanted to see her face before she saw him. Perhaps he could learn something from observing her.

Guy entered the room quietly. Annabell sat at her ease, feet on a stool and posture anything but elegant. Miss Duckworth, on the other hand, sat with back straight, hands folded in her lap, and head held high. She was the perfect picture of a highborn lady. She also looked uncomfortable, as well she might. Ladies of Quality, which she was, did not call on unmarried gentlemen who were not their relations.

He scowled. "Miss Duckworth," he said in a voice that carried the distance of the room to where the two women sat in chairs grouped around a roaring fire. "So pleased to see you."

Miss Duckworth started, her head and upper body jerking around so that she could see him. He studied her dispassionately. She was not a Beauty, but she was striking. Her hair, red as a rowan berry, was pulled back from her strongly angled face and into a chignon at the nape of her long neck. He knew her eyes to be grey. Her figure was tall and slim. She would make him a more than acceptable wife.

She would also be biddable, or so he had thought. This visit, however, made him think he needed to re-evaluate her. Not that it mattered now. He had offered for Miss Duckworth and she had accepted. It was a bargain only a man of no honour would break and he was many things, but not honourless.

Annabell rose and came toward him. "I was just telling Miss Duckworth that you would be with us shortly."

Miss Duckworth also stood, and her brown sarcenet pelisse trimmed with ermine moved gracefully with her. Beneath she wore a plum kerseymere carriage dress. Brown was not a popular colour, but it became her. Her ermine muff lay on a nearby chair. She wore Wellington boots. Her style was what had first attracted Guy. He still admired it.

"Lovely, as always," he said.

Annabell linked her arm in his and pulled him to the other woman. Guy felt his sister's tension. He shrugged slightly so that his coat settled better on his shoulders and some of the tightness in his muscles eased. When they were within feet of Miss Duckworth, Bell released him. He stepped forward and took his fiancée's outstretched hand and brought it to his lips. The fine leather of her gloves was soft.

She smiled at him, but it did not reach her eyes. "Courteous, as always."

If he did not know better, he would say she was irritated, not nervous. He realized that, much as he hoped differently, she very likely knew about Felicia. News travelled quickly in their world, even here in the country in the dead of winter.

"Is tea on the way?" he asked Annabell, deciding to ease some of the discomfort that was so palpable.

"Of course," his sister said in tones that implied he had insulted her by asking.

"I never doubted you would organise this, Bell. The issue was timing." He ignored his twin's scowl and turned to Miss Duckworth. "You must be frozen after your trip."

"December is not the best month to travel in," she conceded and cast a quick look at Annabell. "But we cannot always choose when we must visit."

He raised one eyebrow, a trick that normally quelled most people. However, it had never worked with Felicia, and he realized, as Miss Duckworth returned his look without flinching, that it did not work with his fiancée either.

Tea came and Annabell poured. After handing Miss Duckworth hers, she turned to Guy. "Would you care for some?"

She was being provoking. "Thank you, Bell, but you know it is not a favourite of mine. Did Oswald bring coffee?" He knew the butler had done so. Oswald was meticulous.

Bell poured the coffee black and handed the cup to him. She shuddered dramatically. "I don't see how you can stand to drink this without cream or sugar. It is a bitter drink. Even in my travels I never developed a taste for it."

He drank the beverage down. "It cuts the sweetness of the cakes and gives me a jolt of energy. Something I may need." He looked at Miss Duckworth as he said the last. His gut said he was not going to like the reason for her visit. Deciding to bring this meeting to a head, he asked, "What brings you here, Miss Duckworth?"

He caught her unawares, and she choked on the tea she had just sipped. She set her cup and saucer down just in time to keep the liquid that spilled over the edge from landing on her clothing. Annabell glared at him at the same time as she handed Miss Duckworth a white napkin embroidered with the Chillings arms. His fiancée dabbed at her mouth and then her spotless clothing.

Nerves, Guy decided.

"I think," Miss Duckworth said, her cultured tones back, "that my reason for being here is best discussed in private, Chillings."

"That bad?" he drawled.

Miss Duckworth's ivory skin reddened.

Annabell sighed and shot Guy a reproachful look. "I shall be in the Sylph Room." What she did not say was, with Felicia.

He cast his twin a minatory look. Bell grinned roguishly, her expression telling him that tit for tat was fun.

He could be pushy and rude to Miss Duckworth, but Bell would put him in his place.

As soon as the door closed behind Annabell, Miss Duckworth rose and started pacing. She reminded Guy of Dominic, and he nearly told her to sit back down just as he would have ordered his brother. She stopped on her own and looked squarely at him.

"I can hedge and simper and beg you to tell me this is nothing but a Banbury tale," she sighed. "But I do not think it is."

The reproach in her grey eyes told Guy she knew about Felicia. How much more she knew remained to be revealed. But she could not know about last night. No one but Felicia and he knew about that.

Memory rushed through his mind and body without his volition. The feel of her hair against his bare skin, the touch of her lips on his and the ecstasy of their joining. A shudder of desire racked his body.

"Are you quite all right?" Miss Duckworth asked, her brows drawn in worry.

"Of course," Guy said, his voice deeper than he liked, and wondered if he truly were fine. "A draught. Nothing more."

Her expression remained skeptical but she said nothing else on the matter.

"You were saying…" he prompted, his tone normal, his mind once more in control of his treacherous body.

"It has come to my attention, and goodness only knows who else's, that you have a female guest here." The words were a spurt that ended as abruptly as they had begun.

Guy lifted one black brow. "Yes?" He invited her with his tone to confide in him.

Her eyes narrowed slightly. It seemed she had more spirit than he had thought.

"I know you very likely think it none of my business, Chillings, but I must disagree with you. We are betrothed."

His jaw tightened. "But we are not married."

She took a step back. "True. Is this how I can expect you to go on after we are wed?"

Guy rubbed his bearded jaw with long fingers as he considered his answer. The tone of this conversation would tell how they would deal together. He had thought she knew his terms better than this. And he had not decided what to do about Felicia.

"Annabell is here to chaperon."

She nodded. "My information did not have her here."

"Ah." So the tale had reached her early in the unfolding. "Might I ask how you found out?"

Her sigh was deeper, and she turned on her heel and walked to the window where she stared outside. "One of your footmen is stepping out with a maid in another house. The maid is a distant cousin of one of the dairymaids on my father's estate. And so the thread of connection goes."

He understood perfectly. The aristocracy and their servants lived in a small world, intertwined in so many ways. The links of relationship were not surprising. This was also another reason why he had been fairly sure from the beginning that, while Felicia was a lady of Quality, she was not from his circle. He would have known her otherwise.

"She was in a carriage accident." He told his fiancée what had transpired over the past weeks, leaving out only his growing involvement with Felicia. "And there you have it, Miss Duckworth. The lady is upstairs now with a fever and delirium.'' He paused to let the information sink in. ''Would you like to see her?''

Emily Duckworth shook her head emphatically. ''No, thank you, Chillings. I did not come to quiz the woman.''

''Only me,'' he said with a cynical twist of his lips.

She shrugged. ''You have a reputation.''

''Which you knew when you accepted my offer.''

''Yes, I did. I did not think it would matter.'' She gave him a candid look. ''We are not in love. We don't even know each other beyond a passing acquaintance.''

''Enough for you to know of my proclivities.''

''True. But then, most gentlemen of the *beau monde* share your *proclivities*. It is a trait a married woman must endure.''

He did not like the direction of this discussion. ''A marriage of convenience is like that, Miss Duckworth.''

''Yes, I know.'' She took a deep breath. ''Does she mean anything to you?''

He stared at her. ''You are impertinent.''

''Yes, I suppose I am,'' she said softly, turning away. ''I had not intended to be. As I said before, ours is not a love match. Yet, I find my pride pricked.''

''Then accept the situation as everyone else of our acquaintance does, even the gentlemen.''

His cynical words dropped between them like stones. He knew he should tell her that Felicia was a houseguest, nothing more. He should reiterate that Bell was here, had been here before anything happened. He said nothing. Instead he stood so she would know this interrogation was over.

She turned back to him. ''I wish that I could, Chillings. But pride is my besetting sin. Even Lucy says so, and she is barely old enough to come out this next Season.''

His shoulders hunched. This was the moment for him to tell her that nothing had happened, that gossip—if it reached the *ton*—would die soon. The Quality lived life to the fullest and then moved on with very little thought for the past. Again, he said nothing. He had many faults, but he did not lie.

Her hands, buried in the folds of her pelisse, moved as though she could not control them. He wondered why he had not noticed before that she was not truly the calm and reasonable spinster he had first thought her. She hid herself well.

''Pride can be difficult,'' he agreed. ''But I repeat, ours is to be a marriage of convenience. All I ask of you is an heir. After that, you may go on as you please. Just as I will.''

He watched her straight back stiffen. Remorse and a hint of sorrow that their marriage would be so sterile took him. ''I am sorry if you wished for more, Miss Duckworth. It is not too late for you to call off.''

Even as the words left his mouth, he found himself hoping she would do so. Suddenly, a marriage of convenience was the last thing he wanted.

She turned back to look at him. Her face told him nothing of her feelings. ''I understand what you want from me, Chillings. I knew it from the start and am willing to comply. I just did not think you would throw your infidelities in my face, and I hope that once we are married you will not bring your mistresses home with you.''

His eyes narrowed and the urge to lambast her was strong, but she had not said anything that was not the truth. And she had a right to be angry, no matter what he had said earlier. But he was not willing to stay and receive more of her sharp tongue.

He gave her a curt bow. ''If you will excuse me, Miss Duckworth. I will send Oswald to escort you to your rooms.''

She still said nothing, so he pivoted on the heel of his Hessian and left. The jangle of the boot's gold tassel was loud in the silent room.

Felicia lay still with her eyes closed. She was kept warm and cocooned by the covers. The scents of lavender, lime and musk mixed in the air along with the smell of burning coal.

She opened her eyes and looked around for Guy. When she did not see him, her spirits fell. She told herself not to be a goose. There was no reason for him to here. The lime and musk had misled her and meant nothing.

She sighed and closed her eyes, thinking she would nap. She was so tired. But her mind insisted on racing so that she could not mentally relax no matter how badly her body needed rest.

The last thing she remembered clearly was skating on the frozen lake. Everything after that was a blur. Cold, freezing cold and then hotter, hot as flames. Guy, Chillings, Viscount Chillings was mixed in with everything.

And before that. An accident in a carriage on her way to London where she was to meet with…

She sucked in air.

She remembered everything, who she was, why she was in mourning, why she was going to London in such a hurry. Everything.

She heard movement, sensed someone by the bed. She had been so lost in her returning memories, that she had not heard the door open.

"Felicia?"

A man's deep voice folded around her like the thickest, most desirable of honey. Her chest ached with longing. She opened her eyes.

"Chillings?" she whispered. "Guy."

"Felicia." She heard gladness in his voice and relief.

He leaned over her so close that she could see the fine lines that bracketed his mouth. There were dark circles under his eyes, accentuating their deep blue colour. His hair was dishevelled and his shirt open, the cravat untied and hanging down on each side of the collar. His pulse throbbed strongly just below his Adam's apple. Felicia's senses quickened with desire for him.

He was her safety, her warmth—her passion.

She forced a smile but knew it was weak. She was so tired. She said the first thing that came to her mind. "I love you."

"What?"

His voice held surprise and…and withdrawal. Her head hurt, whether from his rejection or her illness she could not tell, nor would she make herself decide. Some things were better left alone.

Her smile faded and she turned her head just enough so she would not have to look at him, see the rejection spread across his face. She remembered too many losses and too many rejections already to be able to watch him push her away too.

"Felicia," he said softly, his tone commanding her to listen to him. "You have been ill. We were worried about you."

She nodded, a barely perceptible movement, but still could not bring herself to look at him. She had to come to terms with the memories that poured into her before she could face him with equanimity and acceptance of the fact that she loved him and he did not feel the same. Her mouth twisted. Not that any of this mattered. She was married to a man very much alive.

Her stomach cramped sharply and painfully. Now she remembered that this spasming occurred when she was upset.

''Mrs Drummond has left some laudanum for the pain she says you will feel in your chest. You have been coughing so much when you were not drenched with a fever.'' She heard glass clinking and the slosh of water. ''Drink this. It will help.''

''Yes, it will lessen the physical pain,'' she murmured. ''But I don't wish to take it.'' She had never liked blunting her senses with drugs. ''I remember who I am.''

She could not see his face. She sensed rather than saw his shock. Finally, knowing she could not continue to hide behind her sickness, she turned back to him.

He stared at her, his expression unreadable. The stark lines of his cheeks and jaw showed his strength and his determination. She might be stupid and have told him she loved him, but she knew in this moment that he would never feel the same for her. He desired her. He had proven that when he taught her billiards. Instantly, she was hot, something she realized that came from her memory of what they had done.

Fortunately for her and her vows of marriage, Chillings was not as susceptible as she. His body was involved. Her heart was involved. Two very different organs.

Quietly, he asked, "Who are you?"

In a barely audible voice, she told him. "I am Felicia Anne Marbury, married to Edmund Douglas Marbury, mother of Cedric and Colleen Marbury." Tears blurred her vision, as unexpected as they were painful. "Or I was their mother. They…" Her voice trailed off and no matter how she tried, the words would not come out. "I…mourning."

Sobs welled up inside her to spill over as a torrent. Her shoulders shook and her stomach bunched. Breathing seemed impossible. She curled into a ball. The remembered loss was as sharp and torturous as though it had happened yesterday instead of nearly a year ago.

"Felicia," Guy said.

She could not answer him.

A part of her felt him wrap his arms around her and bundle her and her covers up. He carried her to a chair and sat down with her in his lap, held securely against his chest. She turned her face into his warmth.

One hand held her shoulder while the other burrowed into the depths of her loose hair. His fingers began to massage the tight muscles at the base of her skull, bringing comfort and the healing power of touch.

Guy held her tightly, wishing there was something he could do to ease her pain, wanting to protect her from this agony. He knew only too well how heart-wrenching it was to lose a child. But to lose two children she had borne and raised must have been horrendous.

He also worried. This bout with grief could not be good for her in her frail condition. She needed all her strength to heal.

But she remembered.

They could go forward from here. He stopped himself from going down that road. She could go forward from here. There was no future for them, even if she did think she loved him. She was married. He was betrothed.

He continued to stroke and massage her scalp even as he held her close. The fire crackled, providing more warmth than he needed with her on his lap and the covers, coverlet and all, from the bed draped over them both. But the last thing he wanted was for her to get sick again. As it was, they would be lucky if she did not suffer a relapse.

He heard her hiccup at the same time as her head rose from his chest. He looked down into her tear-drenched eyes and it was nearly more than he could resist not to kiss her. But she did not need his passion right now. She needed his strength and protection. Instead of taking her lips with his, he stroked the tangled, damp hair from her forehead. She burned.

Then she smiled at him, a wavering one, but still a smile. He smiled back.

"I am so sorry," he murmured, continuing to stroke her hair back. "So very sorry."

She closed her eyes as though to shut out the memory, but soon reopened them. "Thank you, Guy. For holding me." She hiccupped again. "I've ruined your shirt. And it is—was—spotless."

"It doesn't matter," he said. "You needed to release your grief."

She sighed and leaned her head against him. "It was as though I had just lost them. As though nearly a year has not gone by."

"Your amnesia. I would be surprised if it has not

played strange tricks with your mind and your memories.''

She nodded, her hair tangling in his shirt buttons. "Ouch," she muttered.

"Careful," he murmured. "I will free you."

She gazed at him with trusting eyes as he carefully worked the strands loose. "I wish all my pain could be so easily dealt with."

"So do I," he said, finding that he truly meant it.

The realization made his fingers still. But it was too late for them. He hardened his resolve.

"It is best if you get back in bed. You need sleep and rest to get well." He stood and carried her to the four-poster where he laid her gently down.

Her hands fell away from his neck as she sank into the mound of mattress and pillows. Her mouth tightened. "I owe you an explanation of who I am and what I was doing when you found me," she finally said.

He stayed by the bed. "Later. You need rest right now."

Her mouth twisted. "Rest. I feel like I have not rested for a year. Even here, with no memory, I knew something awful had happened to me. No, I need to talk more than I need to sleep. Perhaps telling you will free me."

He saw her slender body shift as though her mind moved her to physical action. Perhaps this was better. Talking might release some of the pain, like lancing a festering wound let the poison flow out so the wound could heal.

"Go ahead," he said softly, taking her hand and squeezing carefully.

"My full name is Felicia Anne Marbury. I was born Felicia Anne Dunston."

The Reader Service™ — Here's how it works:

THE READER SERVICE™
FREE BOOK OFFER
FREEPOST CN81
CROYDON
CR9 3WZ

NO STAMP
NECESSARY
IF POSTED IN
THE U.K. OR N.I.

He sucked in his breath. "Dunston?"

"Yes. My father is Nathan Dunston."

"The coal baron." Guy whistled softly. "He is one of the richest men in Newcastle."

"Yes, again," she muttered. "And one of the most single-minded. My mother died giving birth to a still-born boy—" Guy jerked, releasing her hand, his re-action beyond his control. "Oh," she murmured, looking stricken, "I did not think. I am so sorry. I did not mean to bring you pain."

"It happened a long time ago. Keep talking," he said firmly.

"My father raised me. He was not always a coal baron. But he was always ambitious and always doing whatever it took to get ahead in the world. He said it was for me, but I always knew it was for himself. He sent me to the finest schools so that I would look and speak like Quality." Her fingers twisted in the soft, feathery squares of the coverlet. "He forced me to marry Edmund. Or rather, he explained to me why I was going to. Edmund is of the gentry. My children would inherit my father's wealth with Edmund's land. Then their children would marry into the aristocracy. My father has it all planned out." She gazed at nothing. "Had it all planned out."

Her thumbnail went through the silk covering of the coverlet and she began to pluck out the feathers. One by one, they fell to the floor. Guy did not think she even knew what she was doing. Her gaze was on something in the past.

"Then I lost them. Measles. Scarlet Fever. They were gone before I realized it. That was, oh, eleven, twelve months ago."

Fresh tears welled from her eyes to drip over softly.

The violent emotions of earlier had been drained from her.

"Edmund accused me of carelessness." Her jaw twitched. "It did not help that I had denied him my bed since Cedric's birth. There was no other heir." More feathers drifted to the floor. "My father was furious. He told me to reconcile with Edmund. To have another child." Her fingers shook so that the feathers drifted everywhere. "I could not." She looked up at him, her eyes huge in the pinched pallor of her face. "I know how important an heir is to a man, but Cedric was my son. My child. Not just someone to inherit my father's money and my husband's land. You understand, don't you?"

He nodded, unable to speak. If her father were here, this moment, he would murder the man for his brutality. He sat on the edge of the bed and pulled her close. All he could do was hold Felicia and try to comfort her. Frustration was an emotion he had not felt since Suzanne's death. It was not an emotion he enjoyed.

Guy lost track of how long he held her. He had not thought himself capable of giving just comfort to a woman who aroused him as this one did. Especially after last night. Yet, that was all he did. She was too vulnerable for anything else.

The fire popped and the mantel clock chimed. They seemed to rouse Felicia.

"Guy?"

"Hmm?" He was nearly asleep, content just to have her close.

"There is more."

Chapter Nine

Guy sighed. "There always is, Felicia." He felt her stiffen in his arms and regretted his unsympathetic words. "Tell me."

"I am—*was* on my way to London because Edmund is divorcing me."

Her words fell between them like weighted stones. For one instant, elation held him, then was gone. It did not matter. He was marrying Emily Duckworth. He needed an heir, just as her father and husband had needed one. Dispassionate and impersonal as that might sound to the woman responsible for bearing the child, that was a fundamental fact of life in his world.

A rebellious voice that he cynically attributed to his loins said that Felicia could give him an heir. The Lord only knew how much he wanted her.

He looked down at her face, raised so she could watch his expression as she told him her story. She was not beautiful. Emily Duckworth was more distinctive-looking. But Felicia had a delicacy about her that stirred him. And she had that glorious hair that lured his senses like a siren lured unwary seamen.

No. Felicia would never stop other men in their

tracks, but they would grow to love her when they came to know her. She was a gentle soul who had the spirit and strength of her convictions.

She also aroused him like no other woman ever had. But he could not, would not marry her. He needed an heir, and he would not impregnate a woman he cared greatly for. Never again.

"Say something, please," she whispered when he did not comment on her last words.

Guy's arms tightened around her. "On what grounds is he divorcing you?"

Her usually soft lips twisted into a hard smile. "My failure to provide an heir."

A sharp, short bark of laughter escaped Guy. The irony was exquisite. "As much as he might wish to divorce you for that, my dear, he cannot."

Her mouth twisted. "True. That is his real reason. But one cannot get a divorce because one's wife has failed to produce an heir, so Edmund has accused me of adultery."

A sharp twinge of anger was quickly followed by guilt. He might not have completed his lovemaking to Felicia, but he might just as well have. He did not think she was an adulteress before last night. But she did not remember and now was not the time to tell her.

"Your husband is the lowest form of life," he said, his voice cracking. "And why were you going to London? To fight it?"

"No. At first I was shocked and angry beyond bearing. Now I am glad. I want to be free of him." Her disillusionment and hurt tinged every word. "But he is determined to keep my jointure because I have failed to give him an heir. He is telling the courts that he is entitled to my money because of my infidelity." Her cheeks burned with indignation. "He knows very well that I have not been unfaithful. He is greedy. I need that jointure, or at the very least a part of it, more than he does. With it, I will be free of my father, as well."

Fresh guilt ate at Guy, but the last thing she needed to know right now was about last night. Yet, there was such yearning in her last words that Guy reacted without thought. "To hell with your jointure. I will give you enough money that neither one of those bastards will ever have any hold over you again."

She gaped at him.

He silently cursed himself. What was he doing? He had as good as asked her to become his mistress. But he did not stop.

"I will give you enough money that your jointure, whatever it is, will be as nothing." She looked stricken, as though he had wounded her. Then her face hardened, and her eyes glittered. "You don't have to do anything, Felicia. I am offering because I hate to see you in this situation because two men control your financial security." He smiled ruefully. "Bell would certainly applaud that reason."

She pushed hard against his chest so that he released her. "I cannot and will not take your money, Viscount Chillings. No matter what magnanimous reason you have for offering." Her voice was quiet and cold. "I would not accept your offer even if refusing it meant spending the rest of my life under Edmund's or my father's control."

He looked away from her at the fire, unwilling to decide if the knot in his stomach was from relief at her refusal or disappointment. "You are wise, Felicia. I spoke from anger at what those two men have done to you. They should be protecting you, not using you as

a pawn for their own ends.'' He looked back at her.
''But remember, the offer is always there if you have
need of it.''

The look in her eyes softened and she withdrew one
hand from the covers and cupped it around his cheek.
''You are generous, Guy. I should not have misjudged
you so.''

He said nothing. She had not misjudged him so
badly. He wanted her for a mistress, in his house, in
his bed, beneath him. Heaven help him, he just wanted
her.

A knock preceded Annabell. She stopped cold and
looked at them.

''What are you doing?'' she demanded in a harsh
whisper, glaring at her twin. ''What if someone besides
me came in?''

''Anyone else would wait to be asked in,'' Guy
drawled, but he knew she was right.

''Mrs Drummond would not and you know it,'' she
stated flatly. She reached them and studied Felicia. ''I
see you are feeling better.''

Felicia blushed from the roots of her hair to where
the pale flesh of her skin disappeared beneath the
covers. ''Much, thank you, Annabell.''

''Humph! No thanks to my brother, I am sure.''

''No, Annabell, your brother has helped me more
than I can say.'' Felicia's soft voice, firm in its conviction, caught and held Annabell's attention. ''I have
regained my memory.''

Annabell started. She glanced at Guy. ''When did it
happen?''

''When I woke up.''

It was a long, hard story for her to repeat. Some
things she left out. Annabell did not need to know

about her father's dynastic plans. That was too personal for anyone but Guy to know.

Hours later, Felicia watched Guy and Annabell leave. Even exhausted as she was, she could not sleep. She remembered everything: the children, Edmund, her father…Guy's lack of response to her declaration of love.

And why should he have responded? He did not love her, and he was engaged. She had known that from the first. He had not hidden it from her. Yet, she had fallen in love with him, nearly let him make love to her that evening in the games room.

And there were other images that refused to go away. Pictures of them here, doing things she could not believe. Making love.

She was crazy. Regaining her memory had made her crazier than before.

She tossed from side to side, unable to get comfortable, unable to stop thinking. The best thing was for her to leave as soon as possible. She had to get to London. She had to find a solicitor who would speak in her defence, since she could not do so herself, when Edmund accused her of being an adulteress and tried to keep her jointure. She had to have that money. She had to get away from her father and start a life of her own, and that money was her only chance.

And she was late. She should have been in London weeks ago.

There is always Guy's offer of money, a small voice insisted. Money with no strings attached. He could not—would not—marry her, but she sensed in her heart that he would make her his mistress if she would let him. She could not do that.

She would soon be a divorcée, an accused adulteress, a disgraced woman. That did not make her a fallen woman, and she would not become one. Not even for Guy.

Still, fury at the injustice of it all burned inside her. A woman had no rights. Edmund was accusing her of infidelity and as long as he found two witnesses he would be believed. She could not even testify in her own defence.

She turned to her side, then, unable to get comfortable, propped herself up on the pillows. The fire burned orange, its flames seeming like dancers leaping for the stars before falling back to earth. That was how she felt right now, wanting something she could never have.

Life was not easy. First the loss of her children… Her chest hurt to the point that drawing a breath was nearly impossible. She closed her eyes and forced her mind to keep thinking, willing away the emotional pain that nearly overwhelmed her. Then there was Edmund shaming her and dragging her reputation through the muck for his own ends. And now Guy. She loved him and it was too late. She was a woman with a reputation beyond the pale, and he was engaged to another woman. She did not think things could be worse.

With a sigh, she curled into a tight protective ball.

Felicia shifted the curtains just enough to see the gravelled drive way below. This was the last thing she should be doing, spying on Miss Duckworth's departure, but here she was. The other woman had only stayed one night. She had not met her, and her curiosity had got the better of her.

Guy walked beside Miss Duckworth with Annabell

on the other side. All three talked with much enthusiasm. Guy laughed at something his fiancée said. Felicia's nails dug into the thick velvet fabric of the curtain. Guy took the woman's hand and raised it to his lips. Felicia's nails ripped through the velvet. From this distance she could not see the expression on anyone's face.

She dropped the material and turned away.

It was time for her to leave. Past time.

A knock on the door made Felicia start guiltily. She had told no one of her intention to leave immediately and every creak or crack in the room made her think someone was coming to stop her. A ridiculous fear, considering that Guy had made it plain from the start that she was unwelcome.

"Who is it?" she finally asked.

"Mrs Drummond, Mrs Marbury."

Felicia gripped the leather straps of the portmanteau and considered what to do. If she let the housekeeper in, Guy would know her plans before she even finished packing. Not that it mattered. Her business in London was urgent and did not concern him.

She tossed her head, suddenly defiant. "Come in."

The older woman entered, took one look at what Felicia was doing, and gasped, one hand going to her mouth. "Never say you are leaving without a word to anyone, ma'am. His lordship will be that upset, he will."

Felicia's jaw clenched. "His lordship has other concerns." She forced her muscles to relax enough so she could smile. "What can I do for you?"

The housekeeper shook her head. "Never be asking what you can do for me, ma'am. I am here to see if

there is anything I can do for you.''. She moved closer
to the bed where Felicia stood. ''His lordship sent me.''

Felicia's first inclination was to say something unladylike, but that would not be fair. There was no reason to take out her sense of loss on this woman. Mrs
Drummond had always been more than kind to her.
Today the housekeeper looked particularly old, her
grey hair seemed dull and the lines around her eyes
and mouth were more pronounced. No, she did not deserve Felicia's hurt anger.

''Thank you, but I am fine. Please tell his lordship
so.''

''Yes, ma'am,'' the housekeeper said, casting one
last comprehensive look at the portmanteau and travelling case.

Felicia watched the other woman close the door before sinking down on to the chair by the bed, the same
chair Guy had sat in to watch over her. She had thought
the loss of her children was still more than she could
bear, and now she had this.

She was in love with a man who could never marry
her. He was engaged to another woman, an arrangement that no man with honour would break. She was
about to become a divorced woman, so that even if
Miss Duckworth broke off the engagement Guy still
could not marry her. No matter what, she could not
marry the man she loved.

She could become his mistress.

The thought was as insidious as it was tempting. It
was the only way she could see to be with him.

But she wanted more children. She wanted more
children so badly she ached from the need. She did not
want those children to be illegitimate.

No, she could not become his mistress. She had to find her own way in the world without him.

The door crashed open without any warning.

Felicia jumped to her feet, her heart skipping a beat. "What?"

Guy strode into the room, slamming the door with one violent push. "What are you doing?"

Heart still pounding, arms akimbo, she faced him. "Don't you believe in knocking?"

He reached her. "Don't you believe you owe me notification that you intend to leave my home and my protection?"

She could barely breathe around the tightness in her chest and her voice was squeaky. "Surely you jest? You have wanted me gone since the moment you brought me here."

He grabbed her upper arms and yanked her to him. She gasped in surprise.

"I...sto—"

His mouth crushed hers. The fury that drove him, communicated to her. Her body tingled and sparked as she responded to him.

His hands slid up her arms, cupped her neck in passing and burrowed into the depths of her hair. Shivers held her as she felt the thick strands come loose from their pins and tumble to her shoulders. They were heavy and pulled her head back. He took advantage and deepened the kiss.

Desire welled up in her, desire as she had never experienced it, not even with him. A desperate hunger seemed to drive him and made her respond against all her better judgment.

"I want you so badly I hurt," he said against her mouth, his normally smooth baritone a rasp.

She felt him against her, pushing and teasing even through the layers of her petticoat and skirt and his breeches. They were like two animals caught in a passion neither could control. Nor did she understand the intensity of her response.

"Don't leave," he said.

He lifted her into his arms and strode to the chair where he had held and comforted her just days before. He sank down, his lips never leaving hers. She clung to the lapels of his jacket, needing the security of his strength in her growing weakness.

Heat consumed her. The heat of the fire and the heat of her response to him filled her so that she did not realize he had undone the buttons of her dress and pulled the material from her shoulders until his mouth left hers and descended on her exposed flesh. She gasped as his tongue slid along the line of her collarbone until his mouth found the hollow at the base of her throat.

She gasped. "What are you doing?" A soft moan escaped her as his mouth found her breast. "What…?"

"I am making love to you," he murmured.

His words seared through her being. This was everything she wanted, but not enough. She wanted more.

Her body had a will of its own. Her nipple tightened and her stomach tensed. Her heart pounded.

But she had to stop this. She had to.

Felicia took a deep breath, pushing her breast deeper into Guy's waiting lips. She sucked in sharply as his teeth nipped her and a bolt of electricity shot to her loins.

"Oh, stop, please stop," she managed, wondering why her voice sounded so strange and distant, yet knowing why. She wanted to make love to him.

He lifted his head and his eyes, dark and stormy, looked at her. His cheeks were blade sharp. His mouth was swollen from consuming her. Slowly, she saw reason return to him. His dilated pupils no longer glittered with passion.

He stood and set her carefully from him. ''My apologies, Felicia. Mrs Marbury.''

She gulped hard, her throat feeling like it was closed. ''I...''

''There is nothing to say. I took liberties.'' He stared above her head. ''We are both committed elsewhere. I should have remembered that.''

He pivoted on his heel and left without a backward glance. Felicia crumbled to the floor. She buried her face in her hands.

She had to leave. There were no other choices. She loved him too much, while he only desired her.

The next morning, Felicia stood in the breakfast room gazing at the portrait of Guy's first wife while she waited for the travelling coach to be brought around. The other woman seemed to gaze down at her in mocking humour.

''She was a Beauty,'' Annabell said from behind.

Felicia whirled around, taken by surprise. ''Yes, she was,'' she managed to say calmly.

The last thing she wanted anyone to know was that her heart was breaking. That would be too humiliating, and she had already been humiliated enough by her unbridled response to Viscount Chillings's lovemaking.

Annabell gave her an oblique look. ''They were childhood sweethearts. Or rather, Suzanne was crazy about Guy from the moment she could walk well enough to follow him. He did not notice her until much later." She smiled. "I believe that is typical."

"I suppose," Felicia said.

She remembered how her daughter, Colleen, had followed her older brother Cedric like a puppy follows the master it adores. It was a bittersweet memory, no longer the painful wrench it had once been. It was a relief to remember the good things without feeling such pain that she wanted to remember nothing.

"Then Suzanne had her London Season," Annabell continued, drawing Felicia's thoughts back to the present. "She was the toast of the town. Every man courted her, even Prinny, although I dare say his intentions were far from honourable. Still, it was a great feather in her cap."

When Annabell paused, Felicia said, "I can see how that might have been."

She wanted the other woman to continue. She wanted to learn about this woman whom Guy had married. She wanted to learn about the younger Guy, to perhaps understand the present Guy better.

"Yes, well, Suzanne was still madly in love with Guy." Her eyes narrowed as she studied the portrait. "This truly is a good likeness of her. Guy finally saw that delicate beauty and began to pursue her. Or so I've always liked to think. But it might have been that he coveted what every man of his acquaintance coveted."

Felicia realized she must have made a sound of distress, for Annabell turned to her, concern writ across her features. She knew this all happened years before, but it might as well be this minute for her emotional response to the story. Still, she wanted to know what had happened. Felicia managed to force a smile.

"Please go on."

Annabell nodded. "He proposed, she accepted. They married and within the year Suzanne was breeding. Everyone was happy."

Felicia knew what happened next. "He never remarried."

"No. But he has never lacked for female company."

"That seems to be a universal trait," Felicia said, remembering Edmund.

"True." Annabell said. "He is only remarrying now to get an heir." Softly, she added, "I thought you should know that."

Before Felicia could say anything, Annabell turned away and sat at the breakfast table where she poured herself a cup of tea. She laced it liberally with cream and sugar.

"I would like to say that Suzanne would wish nothing but the best for Guy. I know she truly loved him as much as a young woman, fresh from the schoolroom, could love a man. But I am not sure." She drank the tea down and carefully laid the cup in the saucer. "She was over-possessive of him. I believe that had she lived, it would have driven a wedge between them. Guy goes where he will."

Their eyes met and Felicia understood what the other woman was telling her. "Thank you, Annabell. I shan't forget."

"Right," Annabell said, standing abruptly. "I believe the carriage is ready. That is why Guy sent me in here."

"Thank you all the more for risking his wrath to take the time to tell me," Felicia said with a smile.

"We must hurry. Guy has never liked to wait and we have left him cooling his heels quite a white."

There was a gleam in her eyes that did not speak of contrition.

"Not even when all he has to do is bid someone goodbye?"

Annabell gave her a funny look. "Don't you know?"

"Know what?" Felicia felt a sense of foreboding. "He is not supposed to come with me."

"I am coming as well. To chaperon."

Felicia came to a standstill, her hands clenched at her side. Her stomach roiled. "I told him I was going alone."

Annabell spread her hands wide to indicate that the situation had not been of her doing. "He is stubborn when he thinks he is doing the right thing. He always has been." She smiled wistfully. "I remember when one of the servants was accused of stealing some silver and Guy thought him innocent. He confronted our father over the issue and would not let the servant be punished. Impressed with Guy's determination, Father waited until the real culprit was found."

"Not many people would have defied their father for a servant," Felicia said.

Annabell started walking again. "No, and Oswald has been fiercely loyal ever since."

Nonplussed, Felicia blinked. The next thing she knew, Oswald was in front of her holding open the door. She smiled at him.

"Thank you for everything you have done," she said to the butler. "And please tell Mrs Drummond how much I appreciate her care of me."

He came as close to a smile as he could. "I believe she is here to say goodbye, madam."

Felicia turned around and there was the housekeeper,

tall, imposing and looking as though she really was sad to see Felicia go. ''Thank you, Mrs Drummond. Without your expert care, I doubt I would be able to leave now.''

The housekeeper beamed. ''I was that glad to help you, madam. And I hope your trip to London accomplishes everything you need.''

''Hurry up, will you?'' Guy's impatient voice called from outside. ''We haven't all day, and I want to be well on our way before we stop for the night.''

Mrs Drummond tsked. ''You had best hurry. He has spent his entire life trying to be patient. There are times when it is impossible.''

''Goodbye again,'' Felicia said, moving quickly outside.

The cold wind slapped her in the face and billowed out her cape. She looked at the cloud-covered sky and knew it would rain before evening. This did not look like a good day to travel, but there was nothing for it.

She stepped down to the gravel where Guy stood flicking his riding whip into his left palm, each contact making a sharp slap. A scowl told Felicia that he was in no mood for dallying.

''Viscount Chillings,'' she said, her voice as cold as the weather, ''I thought we had agreed that I was to travel alone? I do not need your protection, and had you told me this would happen, I would not need your carriage. I would have hired one as I did before.''

''And have the ham-fisted driver wreck you again?'' His tone brooked no argument. ''Annabell is already inside. I will help you up the steps.''

She eyed him with ill-concealed irritation. If she refused him, then it would be that much longer before she reached London.

As though he read her thoughts, he said, "If you refuse my protection, I shall see to it that you are hard-pressed to hire a carriage in town. I won't have you setting out alone again."

Her lips compressed into a tight line that kept back the scathing words she wanted to fling at him. Still, some slipped out. "You are not much better than the other men in my life. You think you know what is right for me and so you ignore my wishes."

His face darkened dangerously. "I think it in everyone's best interests that you get inside the carriage now."

He turned away and went to his horse, Dante, who stood nearby pawing the ground in his eagerness to be off. Guy jerked his head at a footman who rushed to Felicia. Chin high, knowing there was nothing else she could do that would not put her further behind schedule, Felicia allowed the young man to assist her.

Entering the carriage, she took the seat facing the back of the vehicle. Her fingers twisted tightly together inside the warmth of her muff.

"I thought I told you he is impossible to deal with when he thinks he is doing the proper thing," Annabell said mildly.

Felicia said with asperity, "So you did. I must not have listened very well."

Felicia was cold and hungry and tired when she felt the carriage slowing. Sitting up, she pulled aside the velvet curtain that had kept out the grey daylight and some of the cold. The Swan hotel proclaimed its ability to put up weary travellers and their mounts.

Annabell, who sat across from her, opened her eyes and yawned. "We must be at the Swan."

"How do you know?" Felicia asked. "You have not even looked outside."

Annabell rolled her eyes. "Guy always stops at the Swan. Always."

"Oh."

Felicia's stomach felt like a hollow pit. She knew almost nothing about the man she had fallen in love with. It was a sobering thought. Not that it mattered. She was never going to see him again after she arrived in London.

Guy opened the carriage door. There was frost on his moustache and a sprinkling of snow on the shoulders of his greatcoat.

"Come along, Bell," he said, offering his hand to his twin and helping her out. He turned to Felicia and asked softly, "How are you feeling?"

"Perfectly fine."

"Liar," he murmured. "You have circles under your eyes and your mouth has that pinched look I have come to associate with exhaustion." He took her hand before she could extend it and pulled her toward him. "Now, shall we start again? Unless you are still mad at me."

She gave him a rueful smile. "I am tired and very glad to be stopping for the night. Nor am I still angry with you. There is something about a jouncing carriage that puts everything else into perspective."

He helped her down the steps, giving her the strength she lacked. Before she could ease away from him, he slid his arm around her waist. Heat and security and desire welled up in her. Somehow she managed to resist her own urges.

"Please, Guy, let me go."

"You are on the verge of collapse," he stated the obvious, his voice hard. "You should have given yourself more time to recuperate before making this trip. Now I am taking care of you, whether you wish it or not.'' He edged her towards the entrance. ''And we have Bell. She will see to it that nothing happens between us, so you need not fear that.''

Felicia sighed. She knew she should continue to protest, but he was right about her being out of stamina. And, as he said, they had Annabell.

The innkeeper met them at the door, all smiles and profuse bows. ''My lord Chillings, welcome.''

''Glad to be here, Jim,'' Guy said. ''The weather isn't the best for travelling.''

''No, my lord.'' The innkeeper motioned to a boy. ''Take his lordship's things up to the first-floor room with the view.''

''I will need three rooms tonight,'' Guy said, still holding Felicia. ''And a private parlour.''

The innkeeper gave Felicia a discreet look before once more focusing on the viscount. ''Yes, my lord. The rooms will take a few minutes. But the parlour is ready. If you would follow me, please. I will have tea and coffee sent.''

They found Annabell already in the parlour, poking at the coals, trying to build up the fire. She turned when they entered.

''I vow, this place is nearly as cold as it is outside.'' Without waiting for an answer, she turned back to her task.

Guy stuck his head out the door and said, ''Innkeeper, we need a blanket and a hot water-bottle.''

The innkeeper, who had just reached the end of the hall, hurried back. ''Yes, my lord. Immediately.''

''And the makings for punch. And dinner.''

''Yes, my lord.''

Guy went back in the room and took off his coat, which he draped around Felicia, who sat in the chair closest to the fire. "I am sorry, but that is the best I can do until he returns."

"Thank you," Felicia murmured, burrowing into the heavy folds of cloth that were still warm from his body. They smelled of him too, a heady mix of lime and musk. She shivered.

"Are you still cold?" he asked, leaning over her so that his breath was a hot whisper against her cheek.

"No," she whispered, forcing herself to turn away from his concern. "No. If anything, I am the opposite."

Annabell snorted. "Leave her be, Guy."

He did not bother to acknowledge Annabell. Instead, he stepped away as though he had not just set her pulse pounding. Felicia resolutely turned her attention to the fire.

"It seems to be warmer than when we entered, Bell."

"Some."

There was a knock on the door.

"Come in," Guy said, moving to the mantel. He propped one Hessian-covered foot on the grate.

The innkeeper entered with a maid behind him. The servant carried a tray laden with a punch bowl, cups and the makings. She set her burden on the table the proprietor had pulled away from the wall and positioned between the several chairs and the fireplace.

"Thank you," Guy said in dismissal.

"Dinner will be along shortly," the landlord said. "Nothing fancy, my lord, but plenty of it. Roast beef with vegetables and Yorkshire pudding."

"That will be fine," Guy said.

The innkeeper bowed himself out.

Guy crossed to the table and started preparing the punch. Claret and brandy went in first, then a pinch of nutmeg, more sugar and some lemon juice. He swirled the mixture around before dipping a cup in and tasting it.

"I think more nutmeg," he murmured. "What do you think?" He handed the cup to Felicia.

She took the cup, careful not to touch his gloved fingers with her own. She was so strongly attracted to him that the gloves were no barrier to desire.

"Punch?" Annabell asked. "What happened to whisky?"

Guy shrugged and gave her a roguish smile. "I knew neither of you would drink it, and it is too cold for you to have only tea. This will warm you up better."

"Make us tipsy, more like," Annabell retorted, but she returned his smile.

Felicia sipped the concoction. "I believe it needs more nutmeg and lemon juice. But just a pinch of nutmeg."

He nodded and took the cup from her. He added the rest and stirred.

"Don't I get to sample it?" Annabell asked, her tone implying that she knew her taste was of little account with her twin.

"Of course." Guy produced another sample and handed it to her.

"Perfect," Annabell pronounced after finishing off the entire cup. "And exactly as you said, brother. It warms me to my toes."

Guy laughed. "Careful, or you will totter over into the fire."

He took back the cup and refilled it. After handing

it to Annabell, he tossed some toast into the bowl so it floated on top of the punch.

Felicia took the cup of punch Guy handed her. It warmed her fingers and the aroma of claret and brandy told her it would ease the tension that held her shoulders tight. She took a sip, and then another and another. Her coldness and sadness began to dissipate.

Another knock on the door and dinner was served.

Watching the meal being laid out, Felicia realized how hungry she was. Her stomach growled.

"Oops." She flushed and put her hand over her mouth.

Annabell laughed. "No more punch for you."

"What you need," Guy said, "is food."

The innkeeper and serving girl left and Guy started carving the roast beef. He put a helping of everything on her plate.

"I am not starved," Felicia protested. "That is far too much food, but I would like some more of that very delicious punch." She saw Guy and Annabell exchange amused glances. "Well, it is very good."

Guy dipped her another cup and sat it beside her plate.

Annabell said, "I think you need tea more than punch, Felicia." Suiting action to words, she poured Felicia a cup, adding plenty of cream and sugar.

"Thank you," Felicia said, intending to drink the punch first. The wine eased her emotional pain. The tea would not.

Everyone was served by the time Felicia finished her second cup of punch. Guy raised one black eyebrow but said nothing.

"We have a long day tomorrow and must be up

early,'' he said, eyeing Felicia as she raised her empty punch cup. ''I think not,'' he murmured.

Felicia felt like a small girl being told no more sweets. But she knew he was right. Drinking alcohol was no different from taking laudanum, and she had never taken the latter unless she really needed it.

She sighed and rose. ''You are right. This only numbs one's senses for a few hours and I am quite numb as it is.''

She made her way to the door where the maid waited to show them to their rooms.

After the maid had left, Felicia and Annabell helped each other undress, neither having a lady's maid. Felicia had left hers in her husband's house, determined that no servant hired by Edmund would spy on her. Annabell rarely travelled with a maid. It was easier since most servants did not want to go to the unusual and exotic places Annabell frequented.

As soon as Annabell left the room, Felicia crawled into bed. The punch had fuzzed her emotions and she fell instantly asleep.

Tomorrow was another day.

Chapter Ten

The travelling chaise pulled to a stop in front of an imposing Georgian townhouse. The fashionable Mayfair address spoke of money and position. Felicia gazed out of the carriage window and realized they were at Guy's London home. Guy opened the door and held out his hand to her.

Instead of putting her fingers in his, Felicia shook her head. "We have already discussed this, Lord Chillings." At her use of his title, he frowned. "I will not stay with you. Even with Annabell in attendance, it would not be the thing."

"Bell is plenty enough respectability. Aren't you?" He flashed his sister a look that said 'agree with me'.

Annabell looked from one to the other and shook her head. "Felicia is right, Guy. And you know it."

His scowl deepened, but he dropped his arm and stepped back. "Where will you stay?"

Felicia hugged her cape about her shoulders. She was sure her sudden sense of chill was due to the weather and nothing else. The inside of the vehicle was cold enough that the hot water-bottle was no longer hot.

"I shall stay with my father as I had always planned." Her voice cracked on the last word and did nothing to make her feel more confident of what lay ahead.

"You would do better in an hotel." Guy's words were as flat as his voice.

"Guy," Annabell remonstrated. "Do not make this more difficult than it is, and not in so public a place. Now step back and give the coachman the address. I shall accompany her so that you may be sure she is delivered safely."

Guy stepped back and closed the door. Bell was right and he knew it. His enacting such a scene in front of his townhouse was part and parcel with every other rash act he had committed with Felicia and because of her. But he would not let her go alone to her father after being weeks late. From what little she had said about the man, he did not imagine her welcome would be warm.

He mounted his gelding and gave directions to his coachman.

Felicia barely kept herself from sighing in disappointment as Guy closed the door. Annabell was right and had not told her brother anything that Felicia had not already said. Still, she felt bereft and vulnerable. Emotions she had felt for so much of her life and even more so in the last year.

"Thank you, Annabell," she said softly. "His accompanying me would only make a difficult situation nearly impossible."

"Don't fret," Annabell said stoutly, putting her gloved hands over Felicia's clenched ones. "I shall accompany you in. I have no fear of your father, having faced down more than one irate male who thought he could tell me to jump and that I would do so without further ado.''

Felicia smiled in spite of the growing tightness in her throat. ''I am sure you can do anything you set your mind to.''

''That is what I tell my brothers.''

They fell silent as the coach made its way through a labyrinth of streets. Her father was wealthier than many aristocrats, but he did not live in a fashionable part of London. He lived where the merchants did.

Felicia had never been to London before. Neither her father nor her husband had ever thought it necessary for her to accompany them. She was a country girl, educated at well-respected boarding schools in all the social niceties, but a country girl none the less.

Her eyes widened as she saw the sights. Elegant carriages, marked with the crests of their owners, passed them nonstop. A few hardy souls walked the West End streets, dressed in the height of perfection. Women wore warm capes and pelisses trimmed in fur. Jaunty bonnets, obviously designed by a milliner of the first stare, and delicate parasols protected them from the light drizzle. Gentlemen strolled along, their many-caped greatcoats buttoned securely against the cold breeze, their beaver hats sitting at rakish angles on top of their short-cropped hair.

Shop windows glowed so that the merchandise stood out like many-coloured jewels behind the glass. Peddlers pitched their wares everywhere. An urchin hawked roasted chestnuts.

Newcastle was considered a large industrial town, but it was as nothing compared to this. Doctor Johnson had been right, when he had said that to tire of London was to tire of life. She was enthralled.

A servant was lighting the gas lamp outside Felicia's father's residence when they pulled up. She did not recognize the man, and only knew this was where her father lived because of the address. Her stomach cramped and she wished for the umpteenth time that she did not have to be here. But unless she stayed in an hotel, this is where she had to reside.

If she was to have any chance of convincing Edmund to give her the jointure settled on her when they married, she would do well to have no breath of scandal attached to her name. Edmund knew very well that in order to prove her guilty of adultery he would have to bribe two people to testify to a lie. She had never been unfaithful. She would tell him that she would not naysay him if he returned the money that was rightfully hers.

She cut a quick glance at Annabell who sat across from her, her back straight and her face composed in the look of confidence she always wore. No, even with her presence, it would not do for her to be in Guy's London residence where all would know. Particularly since her father was also here.

Nor could she stay with her husband.

She pulled her cape closed, wishing it were armour and knowing that it would not even give her adequate protection against the storm moving in. The only defence she had against the fury she knew her father would direct at her was her determination not to be left destitute by this divorce and thus back on the mercy of her parent.

She picked up her case and moved to open the carriage door. Someone else opened it ahead of her. Guy blocked her exit.

"What are you doing here?"

He took her hand before she realized what he intended and pulled her out. "The obvious."

"I told you not to."

"You told me you were staying with your father. Bell told me not to come."

She stumbled on the coach's lowered stairs and would have fallen if he had not caught her. His arm went around her waist, burning like a brand. Her feet tangled in the hem of her cape and she clung to him. He was her safety and her love.

Then she was free.

He moved his arm away, keeping a firm grip on her lower arm. "Easy. I did not mean for you to trip like that."

"Yes," she managed to say around the sudden lump in her throat.

Much as she knew it was not wise, she was glad he was here. It would give her a few more minutes with him than she would have otherwise had. Soon they would part and she would not see him again.

"Can't you two keep away from each other?" Annabell asked drily, stepping around them.

Felicia shook her head to clear it of the pain of losing him shortly and the desire that his nearness always created. She felt her hair loosen from a pin.

Guy reached up and caught the errant strand. He ran it through his fingers, his expression saying that he felt the silken softness even through the fine kid leather of his gloves. Then he tucked it behind her ear, careful not to tip her bonnet.

"I am going inside with you, Felicia," he said softly, his tone implacable, his eyes unyielding. "I intend to meet your father."

She shook her head, not trusting herself to speak for

fear she would say what she should not, afraid she might thank him for this meddling. Another strand of hair came loose.

"You will be in complete dishevel if you continue that," he murmured.

The coldness left his eyes, replaced by the heat she remembered so well. Her knees turned to jelly and she would have sagged against him if he had not still gripped her arm tightly. Her gaze locked with his.

Desire and more flared in her. She loved this man. His offer of enough money to support her flitted through her thoughts, lodged in her conscious. She loved him, but she did not want to be his mistress. She would be second best in his life or worse. She would not be able to have the children she craved.

"This is not going to help me," she finally managed. "If you are with me, it will only make matters worse."

"Why?" His eyes, nearly black in the increasing dusk, pierced to her heart. "Why will my being here make it worse, Felicia?"

"Guy!" Annabell said sharply. "Enough."

Felicia blinked in surprise at Annabell's voice and then because she lost her balance when Guy released her. She wavered, but managed to stay standing.

"You are right," Guy said. "This is not the place to be doing this. Again." Disgust filled his voice.

He turned sharply on his heel and went to the door where he rapped smartly. Felicia waited behind him, feeling like all control of the situation had been stripped from her. She felt like a spectator, not the person whose future was being put in jeopardy by Guy's actions.

The door opened and a tall, imposing butler filled the entry. "Yes?"

The servant looked down his very long nose even though Guy was his equal in height. The butler's gaze travelled from Guy's mud-splattered Wellingtons up his road-stained trousers to his damp greatcoat. But his look of barely concealed contempt was reserved for Guy's unfashionable beard and moustache.

Guy returned the butler's perusal with the flick of a dismissive glance. "Tell your master that Viscount Chillings is here."

The butler's eyes widened a fraction before the same supercilious air settled once more over him like a mantle. His glance went to Felicia and Annabell. Just as Felicia did not recognize the servant, the servant did not recognize her.

"And Lady Fenwick-Clyde and Mrs Marbury."

The butler's gaze riveted on Felicia. He made a curt bow. "Please come inside, my lord. Ladies."

Annabell hung back. "If you are going inside, Guy, then I will stay in the carriage. Better yet, I will return home." She cast a regretful look at Felicia. "I am sure that Felicia feels one of us is more than enough. I had intended to stay with her for moral support." Her voice turned ironic. "I am sure you will provide more solid support."

Much as Felicia had come to like and admire Annabell, she could only feel relief at the other woman's decision. She did not want Annabell to be subjected to the scene she knew was coming. Her father was quick to lose his temper and even faster to start yelling. It would be bad enough with Guy here.

Knowing she would likely never see Annabell again, Felicia did not follow Guy immediately into the house. She turned to the other woman and held out her hand.

Annabell smiled at her before stepping forward and hugging her.

"I am way too forward," Annabell said, stepping back. "Guy never fails to tell me. But I have enjoyed meeting you and will miss you." Her eyes, so much like her brother's that they twisted Felicia's heart, turned serious. "Be careful and good luck."

"Thank you for everything," Felicia said. "I shall never forget you."

"Nor I you."

Without waiting to see Annabell get back into the coach, Felicia squared her shoulders and clenched her hands into fists inside her muff where no one could see. Thus fortified, she marched up the steps and through the door the butler still held open. There was no turning back.

The interior was dark with heavy wood panelling. Even the furniture was dark and heavy, nothing like Guy's country house had been. Felicia felt her spirits drag down. She instantly chided herself. She should not have expected anything different. Her father's house in the country where she had grown up had been like this. Her father was a driven man, not a happy man, and he surrounded himself with substantial things. From furniture to horses, he preferred large.

She followed the butler down the hall to the back of the house and into a small room with a smaller window that looked out on to a spit of garden. Nothing bloomed in the winter cold. Guy sat at his leisure in a chair drawn up to a small fire. He still had his coat and beaver hat on.

She shivered and gave Guy an apologetic smile. "My father believes in the saying 'waste not, want not'."

"That is how I have made my money, Felicia," her father's voice boomed from behind her.

She jerked and spun around. He stood in the doorway, his lips stretched in what he considered a smile. Tall and rotund, he was formidable. In shades of brown, he dressed in the style of an earlier age. He did not wear a wig, but his hair was long enough to be pulled into a queue instead of the current sporting Corinthian cut or, more to Beau Brummell's liking, the Brutus style.

"Father," she said, her voice breathless. She frowned. She sounded like a child caught with its hand in the biscuit barrel. She had nothing to feel guilty about. "Father," she began again, "I would like to introduce you to G— Viscount Chillings."

Her father's hard, brown eyes turned to Guy who stood now. "What are you doing here with my daughter? She is a married woman."

Guy's right hand fisted, then relaxed as he extended it. "Mrs Marbury has a great deal to tell you, sir. I merely escorted her here to ensure that she arrived on your doorstep safely."

Felicia looked from one man to the other. Guy's words were polite enough, but there was an air about him that spoke of danger, as though he were warning her father instead of trying to reassure him.

Nathan Dunston stepped to the Viscount. "Then thank you for your service, my lord."

Felicia flinched. Polite words with no genuine thanks behind them. This meeting was going exactly as she had anticipated. She moved forward so that both men looked at her.

She held her hand out to Guy. "Thank you so much for your care and concern, my lord. But I am tired after the journey.'' Her gaze held his, and she begged him with her eyes to understand and do nothing rash. ''I know you will understand when I ask you to leave.''

Guy flicked a freezing glance at her father before taking her proffered hand. Raising it to his lips, he murmured, ''I understand quite well, Mrs Marbury.'' He released her hand and moved back. He gave her father a curt bow. ''Good day, sir. I hope to have the pleasure of meeting you again.''

''And I, my lord,'' her father said, a challenge in his stance.

Felicia turned away, unable to watch the two of them any more. She was surprised at the relief she felt when she heard the door shut behind Guy. Her relief was short-lived. Immediately a sense of overwhelming loss, an emotional pain she was too familiar with, engulfed her. He had said he would call on her, but it was better for both of them if he did not.

''Well, gel, you came against my orders,'' her father said, his loud voice jarring through her tense nerves. ''Now you can just turn around and go home to New-castle.''

Felicia's neck muscles bunched into painful knots. She took a deep breath and then another. She had only defied her father twice in her life. The first time was when she would not give Edmund more children. The second was in coming here. To turn around and face him now was nearly more than her remaining strength could support. But she had to do so for her future.

But she moved slowly, not wanting to confront him for confrontation it would be. When she was completely turned, she forced herself to meet his angry gaze with her own, willing her eyes not to look scared.

''I am not going home, Father.''

She was pleased that there was no wobble in her voice. If there had been, he would hear it and use it against her as he had so many times in the past. Still, when his bushy grey brows drew into a furious line across his forehead, she could not stop herself from trembling. She hoped he did not see it.

"What did you say, daughter?" His voice boomed at her, his displeasure like a slap.

She licked her lips and cravenly wished that Guy had stayed. But there was nothing he could have done that would have changed this.

"I said that I am not returning home until after the hearings."

"You will do as I say or regret it."

He grabbed her upper arms and shook her until her hair tumbled from its pins and her already stiff neck hurt. She bit her bottom lip to keep from crying out. When he released her, she fell back against the windowsill. She licked her bleeding lip before speaking.

"Then I will go some place else, Father."

He sneered. "Go to your husband."

Slowly, anger began to replace her fear. He was goading her, belittling her. "You know Edmund will not have me any more than you will."

"If you had been a good wife this would not have happened."

"Bred for him like a mare?" The vulgar words spewed from her in a torrent she could not stop, did not want to stop. "Like you did Mother, until it killed her?" The old hurt and anger rode her.

"That is a woman's job. To have children. To give a man an heir." His face was puce, his brown eyes bulging. "Had you done so, Edmund would have an heir instead of getting one on another woman so that now he is trying to divorce you so he can marry her. Calling you an adulteress in the process. You'll be ruined, gel.''

''Let him,'' she said. ''I wish no part of him. I never did.''

''That was not your decision, just as this is not.''

''You cannot stop him. Or me,'' she added. ''All I want is to ensure that my jointure comes to me.''

''Get out.''

She notched her chin up, refusing to let the fury radiating from him scare her. Nor would she beg him to let her stay here. She would find some place. An hotel. There were reputable hotels where a woman alone could go.

She left without a backward glance. Standing on the doorstep, her case in one hand and portmanteau in the other, she gazed into grey fog. What had been a drizzle an hour ago was now a downpour. The feather in her bonnet hung limp and clung to her right cheek. Her half-boots were soaked through.

For a second her shoulders slumped. This past year had been so hard. And now this. But she was not going to give in.

''Felicia,'' Guy said, materializing in front of her, ''let me help you.''

''I thought you had gone,'' she said inanely.

She had thought he was gone and that, in spite of what he had said, she would never see him again. Even shivering from rain and wondering if her next breath would be liquid, she felt light hearted. With Guy beside her, anything was possible. He would care for her and keep her safe.

''Thank you,'' she murmured.

His smile seemed to break through the dreary

weather. "I had to make sure that if this happened I would be here to help you." He held his horse by the reins. "Where are you going now?"

Water ran down her face in tiny rivulets. "I don't know. An hotel. Surely there is one where a respectable woman can go alone."

"The Pulteney in Piccadilly. Tsar Alexander and his sister, the Grand Duchess, stayed there the summer before last."

She nodded and went down the steps to the street. "Could you, please, hire me a hackney?"

With his free hand, Guy took her portmanteau. "I have been out here for thirty minutes or more and have seen none. I think you would do better to mount my horse and let me lead you to a more fashionable part of town. We will be sure to find one there. Hopefully, not taken," he added.

"I can walk, but thank you."

"It is foul weather, Felicia, don't be stubborn."

"I am not." She wiped the rain from her brow with her handkerchief, only to have the water immediately replaced by more. "I can walk as quickly as your mount can take me with you leading it."

"You will tire quickly in this weather and carrying your case."

"And while we argue, both of us will get wetter. If that is possible," she added wryly.

"Were you this obstinate with your father?"

She gave him a resigned look. "Why do you think I am in this position? I refused to do as he said. He does not take defiance well."

Instead of saying something derogatory about her parent, Guy set the portmanteau down and shrugged out of his greatcoat. He moved to Felicia and draped the garment over her shoulders. The hem was a scant inch from the ground and the mud.

"This will help keep some of the water away and perhaps provide a modicum of warmth."

Her free hand gripped the coat's collar. "I cannot wear this. You have nothing."

"For once, do as you are told," he said, stepping away so she would have difficulty returning the garment. "Now come along. We have a distance to go."

She trudged after him.

After five minutes, he stopped and looked back. She trailed him, her right arm and shoulder pulled down by the case. His heavy coat did not help her, although it was keeping her drier and warmer than she would otherwise be.

"You look like a bedraggled kitten someone has dressed in ribbons and thrown into the rain."

She stopped before running into him and looked up so she could see him instead of the road that, in spite of being cobbled, had tiny rivers of mud running through it. He radiated exasperation.

"I have let you have your way, but that is over." His voice brooked no argument. "Put down your case. You are going on the horse. We will go much faster."

He was right and she knew it. Still... "It is not right that I should ride while you must walk."

"It is perfectly right. You will be able to carry the two cases. It will be easier on us both."

Before she could do anything, he took the case from her hand and set it down beside the portmanteau. Both pieces of luggage were going to be badly damaged. She sighed. That was the least of her problems. Then, while she was busy telling herself things could only get better, he grabbed her waist, his coat included, and lifted her to the saddle. Her rear end hit with a plop. She teetered precariously, holding tightly to his lower arms.

She looked down at him and the urge to slide off the horse and into his embrace was strong enough that not doing so made her shake. If only he could be the man she had married. If only he were not engaged. If only. If only.

"I am balanced now," she whispered, hoping the longing she felt for him did not show in her voice. "You can let me go."

He released her slowly. "Can you hold the luggage?"

She nodded. "I can try."

"It won't be easy. Sitting side saddle with no side saddle is something I could not do, let alone hold things."

She smiled. "You are being modest. Besides, men don't ride side saddle so they don't know how to do it." Still, it was hard with no horn for her to lock her leg around.

"True."

He picked up the pieces and handed them to her one at a time. As he had thought, it was next to impossible for her to hold both. She would be lucky to remain in the saddle holding nothing.

"Straddle him," Guy finally said. "The last thing we need is for you to fall off."

"I cannot do that." She felt every inch of her skin heat. "My skirts would come up to my calves."

"Probably higher," he said, his gaze going to where her clothing covered her legs. "You have lovely legs," he murmured so low she was not sure she heard him.

"What?" Embarrassment flooded her.

What had they done that he had seen her legs? To

her knowledge, she had never shown him. The time he had nearly seduced her on the billiard table, her legs had remained completely covered.

His gaze met hers. "You have beautiful legs."

"How…how do you know?"

He smiled, a smile full of knowing and promise and desire. "I have seen them, caressed them, got lost between them."

Heat, fast and furious, consumed her. "Never."

A fresh blast of wind drove rain into her face. She gasped. She had forgotten where they were, what the weather was like—everything. And, heaven help her, she knew nothing of what he spoke of.

"We must go," she said, her voice tight.

He nodded and the hunger that had sharpened the angles of his face receded. "Straddle him, as I said. If too much of your legs show, take my coat off and drape it over them. Although there will be bloody few people out in this to see you."

If straddling the horse was the only way to get him to stop looking at her like that, she would do so. It was awkward and unladylike, but with Guy's help to keep her steady, she managed. Her skirts rode up to her thighs, revealing her black silk stockings and satin garters. She saw him tense his hands, his gaze riveted by her exposed flesh.

"Guy," she said, painfully aware that she responded to him as he did her. "This is not the place. Or the time."

He looked up at her face, his eyes haunted. "It never is and never will be." He took a deep, shuddering breath. "Give me my coat. I will help you get it across your legs."

Somehow they managed. She did not know how,

when his touch heated her entire body even though the rain continued to pour down on them. This was madness. Her life had fallen to shambles a year ago, and now this.

For her own sanity, she had to be thankful they would never see each other once he got her to safety. Or that is what she told herself, as the horse followed slowly behind Guy and they made their way to Piccadilly.

Chapter Eleven

They arrived at the Pulteney Hotel without once seeing an available hackney. Felicia was wet and miserable, her bonnet a sodden mess. Guy did not look much better, but at least his hair did not hang down his back like drenched ropes.

She sighed and pushed a strand of hair off her face. She had been in worse situations. Guy was with her now, so embarrassing and uncomfortable as this was, she felt protected and safe. That was all she asked.

He turned to her and smiled. "We are here and not a minute too soon. We shall quickly have you dry and warm."

She returned his smile. She did not have a lot of clothing with her and hoped this hotel had a good staff.

Somehow she managed to get her left leg over the saddle and keep the greatcoat positioned so she could slide down to Guy's arms without showing her thighs. Unfortunately, her modesty had kept her from being as warm and dry as she might have been.

"Your lips are blue," he said severely, setting her carefully on her feet. "I knew this trip was premature. I will send my doctor to tend you."

"I am perfectly fine. A hot bath and plenty of hot tea will fix everything." She returned his scowl with one of her own, suddenly bone tired. "Stop fussing over me as though you have a right."

As soon as the words were out of her mouth, she wished she could take them back. He did not deserve such ingratitude from her. Nor did she like having said the words. They implied that perhaps he should have a say in what she did, that perhaps she wanted him to have a say.

She had told him once that she loved him. He had ignored her. She never intended to tell him again no matter what happened. They could never be together.

"I am sorry," she murmured. "You did not deserve that."

His face unreadable, he said, "No need to apologize. You were perfectly correct. I have no right to tell you what to do." He picked up her two pieces of luggage. "Having said that, will you please precede me into the hotel?"

She did so without a word.

The lobby was everything that is elegant. She felt like a fish out of water. The man behind the desk watched her enter with such a look of distaste on his long face that Felicia turned around, intending to leave. Guy was directly behind her, blocking her exit.

As though he sensed her unease, Guy lifted one black brow. She forced a feeble smile.

"I think this is not the place for me," she said, barely loud enough for her to hear, let alone him.

His attention shifted to the man behind the desk. At the man's supercilious look, Guy carefully set the luggage down, ignoring the puddles they made on the expensive carpet.

He strode up to the man. "I am Viscount Chillings, and I require a room for Mrs Marbury." When the man hesitated, Guy added in tones that would have frozen an inferno, *"Now."*

The clerk's eyes widened a fraction before he moved out from behind the desk and snapped his fingers. A young man, barely more than a boy, rushed up. "Take the lady's things to the second-floor room with the balcony. The one where her Royal Highness the Grand Duchess stays."

The boy gave Felicia a curious look before rushing to do as he was ordered. She swallowed a sigh of relief. For a moment she had thought the clerk would refuse Guy, and then she would be hard pressed to find another place to stay. Nor did she wish to go back out into the inclement weather. Had she been alone, the man would have turned her away without a second's hesitation. Now she was going to be in what were likely to be some of their best rooms.

"Come this way, please, my lord," the clerk said. "I am sure you and madam will be pleased with the accommodations."

In a voice laced with irony, Guy said, "I am sure we will." He motioned for Felicia to go ahead of him.

Felicia followed the clerk, feeling uncomfortable because she left a trail of water behind her. But after a quick look the clerk said nothing, so neither did she. They climbed the stairs silently.

They reached her rooms and Guy looked in. "This will do," he said. Turning to her, he asked, "Are you sure this is what you wish to do?"

She nodded, not at all sure, but not willing to tell him. This was all she could do except return to Edmund or to her father's home in Newcastle, which were not choices for her.

He turned to the clerk. "See that a hot bath is prepared immediately and that hot tea and dinner follow."

"Yes, Lord Chillings," the man said, his long nose all but twitching. He looked at Felicia. "When can we expect madam's maid?"

Felicia's gaze dropped.

"Mrs Marbury's maid will be here this evening," Guy said. "Until then, have one of the serving girls here help her."

Felicia said nothing, realizing that Guy intended to send someone from his own establishment. How many times would she regret not finding a maid to accompany her? But she had not wanted a woman on this trip who had been hired by her husband and whose loyalty belonged to him.

"Thank you," she murmured, remembering to add, "Lord Chillings."

"Take care," Guy said. "I will call on you tomorrow."

She nodded, her bonnet slipping forward, its ribbons finally giving up and coming undone. Guy caught the ruined confection as it fell from her head. He held it out to her.

Felicia took the hat from him. Their fingers brushed. All she wanted to do was rush into his arms. Instead, she stood like a statue, watching him walk away. When he was no longer in view, she entered the room and closed the door behind her.

Guy wished he could stay with her, but that was totally unacceptable unless he wanted to ruin her and he did not want to do that. So, he left.

He took long enough in the lobby to approach the

desk clerk. "If I hear that the slightest discourtesy has been given to Mrs Marbury, I will see that you and the Pulteney Hotel regret it."

The man nodded, his movement jerky. "Yes, Lord Chillings. There shall be none, my lord."

"See that there isn't."

The next day Felicia woke up tired and aching. Her throat felt as though she had screamed for the entire previous day without respite. All she wanted was to stay in bed and sleep. That was the last thing she could do.

She dragged herself out of bed and hoped her clothes had been dried and pressed during the night. This was the day she needed to call on her husband.

The light in the room was dim. A single candle sat on a nearby table. There was a fire in the grate. Felicia looked around dazed. She had not lit the candle or started the fire.

Movement in one of the corners caught her eye. A young woman stepped forward and curtseyed.

"Pardon me if I startled you, ma'am. His lordship sent me."

The woman, little more than a girl, was thin and anxious-looking. Her blonde hair was pulled back from a face with large blue eyes and a pointed chin. She looked vaguely familiar.

Felicia smiled at her. "What is your name?"

"Mary, ma'am." She bobbed another curtsy.

"You are from Lord Chillings's country estate, aren't you?"

She bobbed another curtsy. "Yes, ma'am. I came in the baggage carriage."

"No need to carry on so," Felicia said. "I am not some fancy lady."

"Yes, ma'am." She started to dip and caught herself. Instead, she twisted her hands in the folds of her immaculate white apron.

"Come along, Mary," Felicia said kindly. "I need to be somewhere soon, so must dress quickly. I am afraid I overslept."

"Yes, ma'am. Your clothing is in the wardrobe, ma'am. His lordship had it picked up last night. He had it dried and pressed and brought back here, ma'am."

"How considerate," Felicia murmured. And so like him.

She undid the ribbon at her throat and pulled the nightdress over her head. Before she got the fine muslin off, she felt Mary's hands fumble in an attempt to help her. After a little difficulty, Felicia was dressed.

"I am that sorry, ma'am," Mary said, bowing her head to look at her clasped hands. "I am not a lady's maid."

"You did just fine," Felicia said. "I am not used to having a fine French maid, so I am most comfortable with you. Give yourself time, Mary. We will get along well."

Watching the girl relax enough to smile, Felicia knew she had spoken the truth. She was a simple country girl herself, and would not know what to do if she had a fancy maid. It was better this way.

"You may have the morning to yourself, Mary."

"I will go with you, ma'am, if that is all right. His lordship said I was not to leave you."

The girl was wringing her hands again, obviously expecting Felicia to tell her no. Felicia's first inclination was to do just that, but she held her tongue. Much as she might be tempted to send the girl back to Guy after this much meddling, it would not bode well for the girl. And Guy was right. She did need a maid with her. Mary would lend her respectability.

"As you wish—or as Viscount Chillings wishes," Felicia said. "Let us get some tea and toast and then we will be on our way."

The maid bobbed another curtsy. Felicia shook her head, wondering how long it would take before Mary's eagerness began to be tiresome. But the girl was doing her best.

After a light repast, Felicia had a hackney cab waved down and set off on her visit. She had not seen Edmund in nearly a year. Not since the children… She pushed the memory away. She wished she did not need to see him now.

The coach pulled up at a very nice row house. It was not in the Mayfair area where Guy's London residence was, but it was still very attractive and respectable. Edmund had found enough money to set himself and his mistress up very well. Another thing she could use against him in court. He was supposed to be blameless.

Felicia got out of the coach followed by the faithful Mary. Together they mounted the steps. Felicia took a deep breath. Much as she did not wish for this meeting, she knew she had to go through with it. She lifted the knocker and rapped it smartly. It seemed a long, cold time before she heard footsteps.

An impeccable butler opened the door. He stood as tall as Felicia's chin and half again as round.

"Yes?" Somehow, he managed to look down his hooked nose at her.

Glad that her clothing had been dried, cleaned and

pressed, Felicia drew herself up so she was now a good foot taller than the servant. "I am Mrs Marbury, here to see Mr Marbury." She handed him her card.

He read the simple print. His eyes only widened a fraction. Otherwise, his features were completely impassive. He was indeed a good butler.

"If you will be so kind as to follow me, ma'am, I will inform the master that you are here."

Felicia stepped into the house. Her husband had spared no expense for his paramour. No wonder he now wanted to keep his unwanted wife's dowry. The interior was done in the popular Egyptian motif, almost flamboyant. Not Edmund's style at all. He was a country squire with a country squire's tastes.

She did not love Edmund, had never loved him, but she could not keep from feeling a pang of envy. He had never cared what she thought or desired. He had wanted her to bear an heir and leave him to his pursuits. And she had done so.

The butler indicated a chair in the hallway where Mary was to wait. The maid looked to refuse, but Felicia said, "It is all right, Mary. I will be fine."

The maid looked doubtful, but she sat where instructed. Next the butler ushered Felicia into a small dark room with no window and no fire. Felicia was grateful for her heavy pelisse and cape.

The room was an insult. She should have been shown into the drawing room or parlour. She told herself the slight did not matter. It was so typically Edmund and how he treated her.

It was not long before she heard voices raised in anger. One was her husband, the other…her father. Her father was here. This was going to be much worse than she had imagined. Her stomach twisted in dread.

The door banged open. Felicia flinched uncontrollably before getting herself in hand. There was nothing her father or husband could do to her that would hurt more or impact on her more than the loss of her children. The only person who could hurt her now was Guy.

She drew herself up and stepped towards them. "Good day, Father. Edmund."

Their looks of surprise that she dared to be the first to speak did wonders for her courage. She told herself she could survive this and, possibly, even come out of the discussion a winner.

"Felicia," her father nearly shouted. He turned to Edmund. "I thought you said she did not come to you yesterday."

Edmund eyed her with dislike. "She did not. This is a visit and nothing more, unless I am mistaken."

"Absolutely correct, Edmund," she said with more bravado than she felt. "I came to meet with you. I did not realize Father would be here."

"And why shouldn't I be, gel?" Even his thick, grey whiskers seemed to bristle.

She shrugged. "No reason. I just had not thought it."

Her father puffed up in his fury. "I came here to offer Edmund twice the amount of your dowry if he will stop this fool divorce." He glared at her, his face close enough that she could see the red veins in his eyes. "I told him you would give him an heir."

Her inclination was to step back, to cower under his attack. That was the last thing she should do. This was her future, not her father's—or Edmund's.

"Did he agree?" She looked at Edmund who appeared as angry as her father. "Because if he did, he will be disappointed. I will never, ever, give him another child. Never,'' she repeated for emphasis.

"Hah! I told you,'' Edmund said, satisfaction at being right mingling with the anger caused by her vehement rejection.

"Then make her, damn you,'' her father bellowed. "I will give you three times her dowry.''

"Father!''

"You are my property, gel. The law says so.'' He gave Edmund a sly look. "Or, more correctly, you belong to your husband. He can use you as he wishes and you have no say.''

Felicia blanched. Her father's words hurt more than she would let either man see.

In a bitter voice, she said, "Then it is fortunate for me that he has started divorce proceedings. If I understand correctly, he has found two witnesses to say I was unfaithful. I won't contest that if he will give me my jointure. Then the only thing left is for Parliament to approve after the courts.''

"Bah!'' Her father spat at the empty fire grate. "It is not final. Edmund can stop it.''

Edmund, a greedy gleam in his eyes, studied Felicia. She met his look defiantly.

"You would have to force me, Edmund,'' she said softly, her voice carrying with the force of her conviction. "You have a more willing woman now. One who already is with child. And if you ensure that I get my jointure, I won't contest your petition on the grounds that you are not blameless.''

The greed remained, but she knew him well enough to know her words had had the desired effect. "No, Dunston,'' he said to her father. "I don't think that even three times her dowry would be enough.'' His thin lips curved slyly. "If you gave me half your estate, I would consider it."

Her father blanched. Then he flushed a violent shade of red. She could imagine steam coming from his ears.

"You go too far, Marbury." He stormed from the room.

Felicia felt as though someone had pricked her with a pin and all the bravado that had sustained her was seeping out. She went to the nearest chair and sank down. But before she was fully recovered, Edmund spoke.

"Why are you here, Felicia? I had not thought to see you ever again."

She looked at her husband, truly looked at him for the first time since he entered the room. He was not a handsome man. Not much taller than she, he was slender and robust. His hair was a nondescript brown, cut in a fashionable Brutus. His eyes were also brown. His nose was a beak over lips that were well shaped but thin. His dress was casual, his coat looser than style dictated and his shirt points not high enough. But he was more than presentable.

Too bad he had not been a good husband and father. Although to do him justice, theirs had been a marriage of convenience. And as for the children, he had done by them the same that had been done by him.

"Well?" he asked, impatience showing in the set of his mouth.

"I came to ask you for my jointure. I—"

"No."

Felicia held down her anger at his interruption and refusal without hearing her side. This was so typical of him.

"I need it to live on, Edmund. Since you are divorcing me, my dowry is forfeit and Parliament has the choice of whether or not to give me my jointure. Surely you can afford to give me the jointure or a settlement.''

''No. I intend to use the money from your jointure to pay for the divorce. I have already spent a good portion of it going through the courts. The remainder and a significant amount of my rents this year will go for the Act of Parliament.''

She did not want to beg, but without the dowry she would be destitute. Nor did she want to threaten him, but as a divorced woman she would not even be able to get a job as a governess.

''For the children I gave you, Edmund.''

''For the heir you cost me? I think not.''

His words cut like a knife. He had always been able to hurt her more with words than another man might have with his fists.

''Then give me part of my jointure because while you can bribe two men to lie about me, you cannot keep my representative from telling the court that you are already living with your mistress.'' Satisfaction was a small comfort as she saw him go completely still, her words getting through to him. ''You are not blameless and the law states that you must be.''

His eyes narrowed. ''I see you have done some research. I will think about your request.''

He moved to the door. She remained sitting, unable to stand at the moment while she dealt with the fresh pain he had just inflicted. Not that anything she did mattered. He was done with this discussion and intended to end it like he had so many before by leaving. Still, he had listened to her last words. Perhaps she would have a chance.

She stayed in the dull, dim little room long enough

to regain her composure. As so often in the past, her pride was all she had. She did not intend the servants to see how Edmund's treatment of her hurt.

After several long minutes, she rose, knowing she should not feel disappointed or anything. She had not expected Edmund to agree, he never had. But she had had to try.

It was her father who had taken her unawares. He had always made it plain that his interest in her was to further his own plans. She had known he did not want this divorce, but she had never expected him to go to the lengths he was.

She left the room, not surprised that the butler was gone. Edmund's contempt for her would have been communicated to his staff.

The scuff of a shoe on the wooden floor drew her attention. A woman stood in the doorway of what must be the front parlour, a room Edmund's butler had not seen fit to take her to. The woman was blonde with striking blue eyes, pretty in a robust way. Felicia's gaze dropped. The woman was breeding.

Her heart squeezed—the pain was as sharp and fresh as though she had lost her children yesterday instead of nearly a year ago. It took all her concentration to keep tears of bereavement from filling her eyes. This was all so hard.

The woman stepped into the hall so that Felicia could not pass her without pushing her aside. Felicia stopped.

''Felicia Marbury,'' the woman said.

Her voice held a hint of brogue. Felicia had heard that Edmund's pregnant mistress was Irish.

''I am Felicia Marbury,'' Felicia answered, adding, ''for the present.''

The woman ran a speculative gaze over Felicia. "He said you were attractive, but cold as the fish in the sea."

Felicia flushed before feeling the blood drain from her face in anger. Edmund had discussed her with his mistress. Now he was divorcing her to marry this woman. What other insult had he heaped on her?

"You are fortunate. He has said nothing about you other than your condition and his intentions."

The woman smiled, showing a crooked front tooth. Her face lit up. She loved Edmund.

Amazed, Felicia moved past her husband's mistress and to the door. She glanced back at the woman. She could tell her husband's mistress that his case could be thrown out of court because she was pregnant. But she would not. There was no reason to hurt and worry the woman.

Best to leave. The sooner she was gone, the better. There was nothing for her here. Both Edmund and her father had made that plain. The woman had confirmed it.

Chapter Twelve

Felicia woke to her second day in London and the first day when the winter sun shone through the window. She heard Mary rustling around.

Rising up on one elbow she watched the maid. "Mary, what are some of the sights I might like seeing?"

Mary dropped the poker she had been using to stir the fire. "Lordy, ma'am, but you scared me. I thought you was sound asleep."

"I was. But now I am restless. I have two days before Edmund testifies in court." She threw back the covers and swung her feet off the bed. "I am ready to eat something and go out."

What she did not say was that she had to get out or go mad enough for Bedlam. She could not forget what her father had done yesterday. Nor could she work out what she was going to do without the money from her jointure—even a small portion would be enough. Strange as it felt, she might be better off if the courts refused to accept Edmund's petition because then he could not take it to Parliament for a divorce. In that case, he might insist that she move out of his country house so that he and his mistress could move in. That would not be as good as a divorce and her reputation would be sullied, but not ruined. And by the terms of their wedding agreement Edmund had to give her a certain amount of money as long as they were married.

But she would not be free. If she was free and Guy was not yet married, there might be a chance he would turn to her. She laughed, but it was mirthless and more like a cry from her heart. Guy would never break his engagement.

Guy did not love her.

Mary's voice drew her thoughts back. "What did you say?" she asked the maid.

The young woman gave her a quizzical look. "Tea and toast is on its way, ma'am." She picked up the poker and returned it to the fire set. "His lordship sent this message over earlier."

Felicia took the thick vellum writing paper that had been folded and sealed with wax. She read the contents and threw the note into the fire.

"Ma'am," Mary exclaimed.

Felicia gave the young woman a smile. "His lordship will be here in thirty minutes to take me for a ride in the park."

She should send a message right back, refusing. She did not want to. After yesterday and the abuse she had taken, she longed to be with someone who wanted to be with her. He might lust after her, not love her, but he enjoyed her company. There was a lot to be said for that.

And the thought of seeing him made her blood sing. She did not want to love Guy Chillings, but his constant pursuit of her made it hard to forget him. Her lips curled in self-derision. As though she would ever forget him. She might tell herself any number of Banbury tales, but in her heart she knew she would never, ever forget him, no matter what happened in the next couple of days.

She made her decision. It was just a few more days. After that she would leave London and never see him again. She was going driving.

"I don't have anything to wear," she muttered, forcing her mind to the present and more mundane concerns.

"Begging your pardon, ma'am, but I took the liberty of having the hotel clean your dress while you slept."

"You are a jewel," Felicia said. "I don't know how I got on without you. And I shall be sad to see you return to Lord Chillings's household."

The girl blushed. "Thank you, ma'am. No one's ever said such kind words to me. 'Ceptin' me mum."

"They are only the truth, Mary, and praise you deserve for your good service. Now, we must hurry. I would like a bite to eat before his lordship arrives."

Between the two of them, Felicia was dressed just as the toast and tea were delivered. She wolfed down the toast and gulped the tea, scalding her tongue in the process. She barely noticed, so strong was her desire to see Guy again.

She reached the lobby as he entered. She did not see the desk clerk frown as she went straight to Guy.

"Punctual as I have come to expect," he said, taking her outstretched hands.

She smiled up at him. "Mary is such a gift. I shall be sad to see her return to you."

He tucked her left hand into the crook of his elbow and escorted her outside. "She may stay with you as long as you wish."

She halted when she saw his vehicle. "Oh, my goodness. You cannot mean for us to ride in that?"

"I am considered a fair hand with the reins," he said, a slight chill in his voice.

"But it is so high."

"It is a high-perch phaeton, and I assure you that I have yet to turn one over."

She swallowed another protest. "Of course. I have no doubt."

He helped her on to the seat and tucked a blanket around her legs. There was no help for the rest of her body. She would freeze.

He hopped in and took up the reins. "You may let go their heads," he said to a diminutive tiger dressed in sage green livery with silver trim.

The young man jumped away and Felicia felt the horses step forward, eager to move. She took a deep breath and kept her eyes open, even though every sensibility urged her to close them. She did not want to see the ground rushing by so far beneath her.

"Stay here, Jem," Guy said. "Have something to eat and drink."

The tiger touched the brim of his hat before disappearing inside the Pulteney Hotel.

Felicia sat stiffly, her outside hand gripping the side of the carriage as though her life depended on how tightly she held on. The hand closest to Guy hung on to the front edge of the burgundy leather seat. She kept her head up and her eyes forward.

"You can relax," he said. "I promise not to turn us over. It is not as though we will be on bad roads. We are going for a drive through Hyde Park. If anyone sees how stiff you are, they will think I am making importunate comments."

She forced a smile to lips that felt numb.

He flicked the whip lightly and the horses jumped forward. She fell backward, a small squeak of alarm escaping her clenched teeth.

Guy slowed their movement. "Are you really that scared?"

"What a ninny you must think me," she said, her voice tight.

"Is it because of your accident?"

She had not even thought of that. "Absolutely not. It is just that we are so far from the ground. I have heard of high-perch phaetons, but never expected to see one, let alone ride in one."

"They can be dangerous driven by someone with ham-fists, which I am not. I assure you, the members of the Four-in-Hand club consider me skilled enough for this."

She risked a quick glance at him. His mouth curved up slightly at the corner. "I am sure you are."

She looked forward and gasped. A heavily laden wagon stood in the middle of the road. With a flick of his wrist, Guy had them around the seeming barricade. She swayed from side to side and renewed her grips.

The weather was much better and others were taking advantage of the unusual sunshine.

"Everyone is out," Guy said in explanation. "There will probably be people in Rotten Row as well."

Felicia recognized the derogatory term for Hyde Park.

Guy guided them smartly through the arch and into Hyde Park. There were several hardy walkers, a group of riders and a few other carriages. Nothing like the crowds that thronged the park during the summer Season.

Felicia looked around at the infamous Rotten Row. "Somehow I pictured this differently."

Guy smiled knowingly. "It is during the summer. The winter, even when Parliament is in session, is slow." He glanced at her briefly, before returning his attention to his driving. "And speaking of Parliament. When do you hear about your husband's court hearing?"

Felicia sighed, her breath forming steam in the cold air. "Not for two more days." She burrowed her hands deeper into her muff, more relaxed with Guy's driving. "That is when Edmund goes before the court."

Several riders approached them, two women and one man. Felicia felt a pang of discomfort when they matched their pace to the phaeton.

One of the women was Miss Duckworth. She nodded at both of them. "I see you are out for a drive, Chillings."

Her words spoke the obvious, but her eyes said more. She looked pointedly at Felicia.

"Miss Duckworth," Guy said smoothly, "let me introduce you to Mrs Marbury."

"Good morning, Mrs Marbury."

Felicia put on her most gracious face, but it was hard. Seeing the other woman reminded her of all the reasons why she should not be here. She was a married woman and Guy was engaged to this woman. The divorce Edmund was asking for only made matters worse.

Still, she tried to be pleasant. None of this was Miss Duckworth's fault. "The same to you, Miss Duckworth. It is a pleasure to meet you."

"This is the first fine day we have had in some time," Miss Duckworth said.

Guy slowed the carriage to a stop and the riders halted with him. "Mrs Marbury, may I introduce Miss Lucy, Miss Duckworth's younger sister."

Felicia nodded. "How do you do."

The other woman—or girl, more like—giggled. "I am very well indeed, Mrs Marbury. I do so love London." She grinned conspiratorially. "I am new to Society."

Miss Duckworth nearly groaned. "My sister is giddy with delight at being freed from the nursery."

Miss Lucy flushed scarlet and her full, red cupid-bow mouth pouted. "Now, Ducky, don't be dreadful."

Miss Duckworth gave her young sister a minatory look. "Then don't behave like a child."

Guy interrupted them. "And may I also present my brother, Dominic Chillings."

Felicia studied the younger man. He had a raffish air about him. His beaver was cocked at a jaunty angle over curls as black and glossy as the finest polished jet. His deep blue eyes sparked with mischief. Even his clothes were less than respectable. Oh, he was dressed in the height of fashion, but there was a sense of dishevelment in the looseness of his coat and the unpretentious twist of his cravat. Unless she missed the mark, he was a rake.

"Most pleased to meet you, Mrs Marbury."

He reached for her hand and before she realized what he was about, he raised it to his mouth. The grin he flashed was conspiratorial, definitely inviting.

She found herself grinning back without conscious volition. He was as charming as he was dangerous. Was he pursuing Miss Lucy? If so, she pitied Miss Duckworth the job of chaperon. Between the two of

them, Miss Duckworth would undoubtedly find herself
always a step behind.

Clouds scudded across the sky, obscuring the sun. A
breeze started. Cold penetrated Felicia's pelisse. She
was glad of the blanket over her legs.

Miss Duckworth looked up at the greying weather.
"We had best get home. It was nice to meet you, Mrs
Marbury. I hope you enjoy your stay in London. Chill-
ings."

"Miss Duckworth," Guy said, bowing lightly from
the waist. "Miss Lucy." He looked pointedly at his
brother. "I will see you later, Dominic."

"You can bet on that, brother," Dominic said, tip-
ping his hat to Felicia. "Mrs Marbury."

Felicia watched the three ride away before turning
to Guy. "I think I should go back to the Pulteney."

He expertly turned the phaeton and headed them
back the way they had come. "I will send my coachman around this evening. Annabell has asked if you
will dine with us."

Felicia hesitated. "Please give her my regrets."

He handled the team as smoothly as before, but Felicia could feel the tension in his thigh that touched
hers. "Why? Have you other plans?"

"No." She sighed and turned away from him. "I
don't know anyone in town. I just do not think it wise
for me to spend too much time with you. You are engaged. I am married."

"Do you really think anyone in the *ton* cares?" His
words dripped cynicism. "No, I take that back. Everyone would love to discuss us as the latest *on dit*, but
Annabell will be our chaperon so there will be nothing
to discuss."

She heard the sarcasm he did nothing to hide. She

knew he was correct as far as it went. "What if rumour starts that I stayed at your estate alone with you?"

"That would be a different situation."

"I thought so," she said drily. "Nor would it be nice to put Miss Duckworth through the scandal."

"Do you really care?" he asked, his lip curled sardonically. When she did not immediately reply, he glanced at her. "I believe you do."

"I don't wish to hurt anyone. Particularly a woman who has done nothing to deserve being hurt." She clenched her hands inside her muff. "I know how devastating it is to be in pain from something over which you had no control. I don't ever wish to be the cause of pain to another."

Fresh memories welled up of Cedric and Colleen playing in the garden or fishing, catching nothing but enjoying themselves immensely. Then she remembered them as she had last seen them.

"No," she whispered, "I would not wish pain on anyone."

Guy laid a gloved hand on her arm. "Let it go, Felicia. There is nothing you can do. You have your entire life ahead of you."

"Yes. I know."

She could not share her fears for the future with him. He would offer her money again. She did not want that.

He pulled up in front of the Pulteney Hotel. The tiger who had stayed behind immediately appeared and went to the head of the horses. Guy tossed down the reins and jumped lightly to the ground. He circled the phaeton and held up his arms for Felicia. She looked down at him.

The sharp angles of his face, softened by his beard, were dearer to her than anything else in her life. Yet, she could not have him. Her chest tightened and her stomach twisted. She would leave London as soon as the court made its decision. It would be better for all of them.

"Well?"

She put her hands lightly on his shoulders as he gripped her waist and swung her down. For a brief time, she felt giddy with pleasure. He was so close she could smell his lime and musk and see the fine lines around his eyes. He was so close that if she tilted her face up her lips would touch his.

She looked away. "Thank you for taking me. I enjoyed it much more than I would have enjoyed staying in the hotel."

"Look at me," he said, his tone brooking no denial.

She bit her lower lip but did as he wished. "What?"

"I will send my coachman for you."

"I…" She pushed away from him, regretting her freedom the second his hands fell away from her. "I don't think that is a good idea."

"To hell with what you think." His voice was implacable. "My coachman will be here. I will be with him. Don't make me come and fetch you."

She moved away from him, saying over her shoulder, "I will consider it. Thank you and goodbye."

Guy watched her enter the hotel and saw the desk clerk come forward to meet her. Only then did he get back in the phaeton.

"Stand away, Jem."

The tiger stepped back, seeing that the Viscount had the reins before moving quickly to the back and hopping on to his perch. They set off at a smart pace.

With only half his mind on his driving, Guy thought about their situation. He wanted her more than he had ever wanted a woman. He laughed, a harsh bark. He wanted her and he could not have her.

His stomach tightened with desire and anger. He put them both aside as best he could while his loins ached and his jaw was so tense it twitched. It was better this way. If he could have her, he did not know how long he could trust himself not to take her completely and risk getting her pregnant with his child. For if she came to him, it would not be for convenience.

He pulled the phaeton to a stop in front of his London townhouse, handed the reins to the tiger and leaped out. Knowing that Jem would take care of the horses, he strode into the house and stopped in his tracks. His brother and sister stood in the hall, arguing. The butler looked on with a worried frown.

"What is going on?" Guy moved to them.

"We were discussing Mrs Mar—"

"Hush," Annabell said. She turned to Guy. "Miss Duckworth is here."

Guy stopped the expletive that came to his lips. "How long?"

Dominic shrugged. "Ten minutes at the most. She must have taken Lucy home and then come straight here." He eyed his brother. "Not that I blame her. Don't you think you were doing it up too nicely taking Mrs Marbury around Rotten Row?"

Guy thought of a scathing retort and swallowed it. Dominic was right. "I did as I wished. I would do it again." His words and the look in his eyes told them not to pursue this topic.

"As you will," Dominic said. He focused on his sister. "You and I have a discussion to finish, Bell."

She grimaced. "You are the pot calling the kettle black, Dominic."

"I am your brother."

"Go somewhere private to finish your discussion," Guy said, irritable because he knew that he must meet with Miss Duckworth, and he knew what she was here for. "Where is my guest?"

The butler answered without a second's hesitation. "In the front parlour, my lord."

"Good luck," Annabell said softly.

"Be careful," Dominic said, his eyes alight with a knowing glint. "Single women who call on bachelors are up to no good."

"That has been my experience." Guy left them to their argument and entered the room where his fiancée waited.

Miss Duckworth sat, back ramrod straight, in the chair nearest the fire. The weather had got colder. She rose and came to meet him.

"Miss Duckworth," Guy said. "What can I do for you?" He raised one brow to let her know that her presence was very unusual.

Her gaze held his. "We need to talk, my lord."

"As you wish," he murmured. He moved past her to the chairs where she had been. "Won't you be seated?"

She sank on to her original seat. "Not to beat around the bush, Chillings, for we are both busy people."

"Please don't," he murmured, stopping before he said something more sarcastic than she deserved.

"I have two reasons for being here." She raised two fingers for emphasis. "First is your brother, Dominic Mandrake Chillings."

"Really?"

"Yes, really. You may stare me down all you want, Chillings, but that will not erase the fact that he is paying marked attention to my younger sister, Lucy. She is barely out of the schoolroom and your brother is a libertine.''

Inwardly, Guy groaned. ''Are you saying that Dominic's attentions are unwelcome?''

''By me. Lucy is too flighty and immature to realize that he is only amusing himself at her expense.'' She sat straighter. ''As the responsible member of my family, I am asking you, as the head of your family, to speak with him. It must stop.''

''You are right, of course.'' And she was. Dominic was dallying where he had no business. ''I will speak with him.'' And hope it does some good, he added silently. He rubbed his beard with one finger. ''And what is your second reason?''

Her peaches-and-cream complexion deepened. ''The second is about us. That is, you and Mrs Marbury.'' She took a deep breath and faced him squarely. ''If you wish to end our engagement, I will understand.''

''Do you mistake me for a man without honour, Miss Duckworth?'' he asked, his voice cold enough to freeze water.

Her face stiffened. ''No, my lord. I take you for a man who is showing a marked interest in a woman who is not his wife or fiancée, and who, in fact, is married to another man.''

He was furious with her, but he was more angry with himself because she was right. ''If you wish to call off our engagement, Miss Duckworth, I will understand. Otherwise, I believe this discussion is over.''

He watched her for several long moments. Emotions moved over her features. He did not think pain was one of them.

Finally she spoke. ''As we said before, ours will be

a marriage of convenience, Chillings. You are marrying me for an heir and I am marrying you because my father and brother's gambling debts are beyond our financial ability to pay. In short, we are both marrying for family. I don't fancy myself in love with you, so that will be fine. But my pride bids me tell you that if you should decide our agreement is something you no longer wish, I will accept ending our engagement.''

He was tempted. Very tempted. But he needed an heir, and he needed one from a woman he did not care greatly for. He liked and respected Miss Duckworth, but she did not make his blood boil so that his body wanted to do things to her that his mind knew were wrong. Miss Duckworth was the perfect wife for his needs.

"If that time should arise, you will be the first to know," he said firmly. "But as you say, we are both entering this marriage for reasons other than our own happiness. Therefore, we must both accept that there will be times and actions that we are not pleased about.''

She nodded, a slight grimace twisting her lips. "You are entirely correct, Chillings. My pride bids me to break our engagement now, my family's needs tell me I cannot." She stood. "Thank you, Chillings.''

"You are more than welcome," he murmured to her retreating back.

The door closed behind her, and he went to a side table where a decanter of whisky sat. He poured himself a strong helping and drank it down, staring outside without seeing anything.

She had given him a way out of their engagement. Felicia would be a divorced woman soon. He could marry her.

He shook his head and poured another glass. No, he could not wed Felicia. He needed an heir. That was the only reason he was marrying now. And he needed a wife he did not love.

Suzanne's death had nearly ruined him. He had blamed himself for years afterwards. Even now, this moment, a small part of him still blamed himself for it. It did not matter that women died in childbirth, that it was one of the hazards they all faced. He had felt responsible for her premature death.

Guy sighed and turned away from the window. He had loved Suzanne as a big brother loves a sister, but he had not realized that when he married her. He had not truly realized that until Felicia.

He had felt desire for Suzanne, but it had been born more of necessity than passion. While with Felicia, it was nearly impossible for him to keep his hands and body from her. He wanted her day and night, like an ache that never ended.

But he could not, would not, marry her.

He had to do something to stop this road of thought. He would speak with Dominic while he was here. That would take his mind off Felicia. He strode from the room.

He found Bell and Dominic in the library, as he had expected. Both turned in surprise when he entered.

"You are not needed here," Annabell said.

"You can side with me," Dominic said at the same time.

"I am here to speak with you, Dominic, not get into the middle of your argument." He stopped in front of them and looked from one to the other. "Although, perhaps you need a referee."

Annabell snorted. "Nothing of the sort. Dominic is out of line and knows it. Our discussion is over."

"Not by a long shot," Dominic said. "And Guy will support me in this."

"I will?"

"Absolutely," Dominic said. "This Roman excavation she is so set on doing is on Fitzsimmon's property. Totally unacceptable."

"Which you already knew," Annabell retorted.

"I did not think you would actually do this," Dominic said, fists on hips.

"And?" Guy knew Dominic's reasons, but goaded him anyway. Perhaps if he vocalized his objections and then was reminded of what he was doing to Lucy Duckworth, the lesson would sink in.

"And? He is a notorious rake. No woman is safe from him." He shot his sister a severe look. "Not even a bluestocking widow."

"How dare you," Annabell blustered. "You make me sound as though I am ripe for the picking, and Fitzsimmon will be the one to harvest me."

Dominic shrugged.

Guy decided it was time to intervene. "Bell is old enough to take care of herself, Dominic. Something that cannot be said for every woman."

As though he sensed more than Guy said, Dominic bristled. "So you say. Bell is my sister and it is my duty to protect her."

"From men like yourself?"

"Low blow," Dominic said.

"Is it?" Guy asked. "Miss Duckworth was here on behalf of her young sister."

Dominic had the grace to look chagrined. "What about Miss Lucy?"

"Miss Duckworth feels your attentions are too marked and not welcomed."

"Ah hah," Annabell said. "I thought you were coming it too brown over Fitzsimmon."

"Not half enough," Dominic shot back. "As for Miss Lucy, at least she is an amusing chit. Not like Mistress Sourpuss."

"Sourpuss?" Guy and Annabell said.

"Sourpuss," Dominic repeated. He turned back to Annabell. "Mark my words, Bell, you will rue the day you tangled with Fitzsimmon."

She sighed dramatically. "As though I am not all of three and thirty, financially independent and unattractive to men. You worry too much."

For one brief moment, Dominic met her eyes without anger or humour. "I hope so."

"Bell must go her own way," Guy said.

Dominic rounded on him. "And what about you, brother? Was Miss Sourpuss's visit only about my unwanted attentions?"

Guy took a step back from their triangle.

"I thought not," Dominic said. "She did not like your drive in the park with the lovely Mrs Marbury."

Annabell laid a hand on Guy's arm. "Be careful, Guy. Felicia is a married woman about to go through divorce proceedings. The last thing you want is for your name to be linked with hers. Or for Miss Duckworth to cry off your engagement."

"Heaven forbid," Dominic said.

Guy moved away from Bell's touch. She was right and he knew it. That still did not make it any easier to reject Felicia.

"I have invited her to dinner tonight."

"What? Who?" Dominic asked. "Mrs Marbury?"

"Surely not," Annabell said.

"Surely I have," he said. "I told her you would be our chaperon, Bell."

She rolled her eyes skywards. "As Dominic said, heaven help you. For you don't help yourself."

Chapter Thirteen

With growing dismay, Felicia listened to Edmund. He had made an unannounced visit to her here at the Pulteney.

"Furthermore—" he stopped pacing and faced her "—you were in Hyde Park with him today."

She nodded. "We were in a high-perch phaeton. There is no impropriety in that."

Thank goodness he did not know she had stayed at Guy's country seat for over a week unchaperoned. Her mouth twisted. If he had cared about her enough to inquire about when she left Newcastle, he would know her trip took nearly three weeks longer than it should have. It was bad enough that he was prepared to pay two male servants from his own country home to testify against her in court, lying about her supposed infidelity. What would he do if he knew about Guy, demand the Viscount to testify? She could not allow that.

He glared at her. "Your father persists in offering me large sums of money if I will stop the divorce proceedings."

He stopped speaking, waiting for her to say something. There was nothing she could say. A month ago she would have agreed with her father, if for no other reason than the disgrace of being divorced. Now she wanted one, no matter what it did to her reputation. Edmund had gone too far.

"I know," she said. "If you remember I was here when he offered you up to three times my dowry."

"Well, he has been back." He paused to let her suffer in ignorance. "He has agreed that, if I stop divorce proceedings, he will see that I am given the revenues from half of his holdings."

She gasped. She could not help it. Her father, who was tighter with his money than the Prince Regent's stays, had agreed to that?

"What did you say?" She was almost scared to ask. Edmund had married her for money in the first place.

"I told him I need an heir."

Her fingers twisted in the folds of her skirt. "Your mistress is breeding."

He nodded, satisfaction easing the thin line of his mouth. "But she does not bring me any money."

Felicia's heart skipped a beat. "Nor do I," she said softly.

He advanced on her. "Your father told me to make you give me an heir."

She blanched. "You would have to use force."

He inched closer. She moved to put a chair between them. He had never hurt her, but she did not want him near her. As it was, she could smell the faint sourness of him, a distasteful contrast to Guy's clean lime and seductive musk.

"Something I would not do even for the amount of money your father is talking about." Disgust dripped from every word. "However, I told your father that I would give you one more chance. You have refused."

She gaped at him. "What about your mistress? Would you have cast her off?"

He shrugged and ran his gaze over her. "You could give me the heir I need if you had a mind to it. And you would bring more money. A country estate always needs money."

Her lip curled. "I think it best if you go now."

"One more thing," he said, stuffing his hands into the pockets of his coat. "Your father told me you left Newcastle over three weeks ago."

Her eyes widened. Satisfaction softened his face and she knew she had given herself away. "My carriage had an accident."

"He also said you arrived at his house escorted by Viscount Chillings."

Each word fell with the bruising intensity of a stone lobbed to hurt. Even if he did not say another word, she knew her father had told him everything he needed to know in order to ensure that he got the divorce. Not only would Edmund drag her name through the muck, he would pull Guy in with her. It was her father's way of trying to force her to stay with Edmund.

"Where is this leading?" she demanded, her voice more forceful than she felt. But she had a sick feeling in the pit of her stomach that she knew exactly where this was going.

He pulled his hands from his pockets and picked up his beaver hat, which sat on a table. A small, detached portion of Felicia's mind registered that Edmund wore his beaver like a plodding man forging ahead. Guy wore his with dash. The Viscount was the type of man who made the hats so fashionable.

Edmund fixed the beaver on his head. "Since you will not bear me an heir, I am forced to present Viscount Chillings as an accomplice in your adultery. This way I will be sure to be awarded a divorce and your dowry to pay for the expense I have incurred. I hope to retain your jointure as well.''

She had known this was coming, but it still felt like he had knocked the air from her lungs and left her helpless. She gripped the back of the chair until her knuckles turned white. She told herself she should not be surprised.

She took a deep breath. ''You have not been blameless, Edmund, and I believe in order to get approval from the courts for divorce, you must be unsullied.''

He scowled. ''Are you threatening me?''

''No,'' she finally said.

Nor was she. It went against everything she was to use this against him even though he deserved it.

''That is good,'' he said. ''For I would just send her out of town until this is over. No one would bother to track her down.''

He was probably right. She was the only one with any interest in the condition of his mistress, and she would not push this further. It was not in her to do so.

''Please don't drag Viscount Chillings into this, Edmund.''

She hated begging him for anything, but this was not about just her. Guy was involved. Testifying in court like this would ruin his good name. Miss Duckworth would be sure to break their engagement.

Edmund gave her a smile that was more like a sneer. ''Afraid you will lose your dowry? Well, it was never yours after you married me. And your jointure is something I agreed to give you, but I will do everything in my power to keep it now.''

She looked at him, noting the closeness of his eyes

and the way his nose turned red at the tip when he was upset. She knew it would do her no good to appeal to his noble side. He did not have one. But she had to try.

"The Viscount is engaged. If you drag him in to testify, it might ruin his future marriage."

Edmund's sneer widened. "He should have considered that before making you his mistress."

"How dare you." He had gone too far. She whipped around the chair that separated them and slapped him hard. Her fingers left a red imprint on his ruddy cheek. "I am not his mistress."

Edmund put one hand up to his face and the look he gave her was deadly. "A momentary fling."

"Neither," she stated. "We have done nothing. Nothing. How can you even say that we have? I am married. He is engaged."

"A Banbury tale."

Before she could respond, Edmund stormed from the room. She sank into the chair. This was horrible. Guy was going to be dragged through the mud for something he had not done. They had never been lovers. She would remember something as momentous as that. Surely.

She flushed. They had wanted to make love that night on the billiard table. But they had not. Yet... She had a sense of more between them, as though, perhaps, they had made love.

She shook her head. Clearly she was upset about the situation to even think they might have done more than she could remember.

She could stay with Edmund, give him an heir and everything would be fine, except her heart. She would be with a man she did not love or even like or respect.

But it was not as though by staying with Edmund she gave up Guy. Guy would never be hers, no matter what she did.

What was she going to do? She had to stop seeing Guy. Somehow she had to control her response to him and refuse him no matter what her heart wanted. She had to, for both their sakes. Not that it would change Edmund's plan. Not that she would keep her dowry. But perhaps if nothing happened in London that could be brought out in court they would be all right. No one knew for certain that she had spent one unchaperoned week under his roof.

That would have to do. For now.

Guy entered the lobby of the Pulteney Hotel. The clerk was by his side instantly.

"How may I help you, my lord?"

"Please inform Mrs Marbury that I am here."

The man gave him a funny look, but hurried away. The unease that Guy had managed to keep in check since Miss Duckworth's afternoon visit returned. He had learned while Wellington's aide to trust his instinct. Something was wrong.

The clerk returned. "Mrs Marbury sends her regrets, my lord."

"She does?" he said dangerously.

The clerk nodded, his Adam's apple bobbing. "Yes, my lord."

Guy headed for the stairs.

"My lord," the clerk said, his voice hesitant.

Guy wheeled around. "What?"

The clerk licked his lips. "She had a male visitor this afternoon. He was with her for quite some time."

Guy's eyes narrowed. "What are you implying?"

The man took a hasty step back. "Nothing, my lord. Merely telling you what I know. Nothing else. My lord."

"See to it that you keep your mouth shut."

The clerk jerked his head up and down. "Yes, my lord. I won't say a word."

Something was very wrong. Guy took the stairs two at a time. He reached Felicia's door in seconds and wondered if he was too late.

The girl he had sent over to care for Felicia answered his knock. She bobbed a curtsy, her eyes wide with fear.

"I am here to see Mrs Marbury," Guy said, stepping forward with the intention of going inside.

The maid held her ground. "I am that sorry, my lord, but she don't wish to see anyone."

The girl twisted her apron until Guy thought she would rip the material. He scowled at her. Eyes downcast, she did not budge. He had to admire her courage. Evidently she had developed a loyalty to Felicia. It spoke well of Felicia.

He reined in his anger. "Mary—that is your name?" She nodded. "You should go downstairs and get something to eat. Mrs Marbury and I have something to discuss."

Her mouth crumpled. "I'm that sorry, my lord, but I can't let you in." Her voice lowered. "I can't, my lord."

Guy's patience ran out. "Get out of my way, Mary. I won't harm your mistress, but I will speak with her."

Felicia's voice came faintly to them. "Do as his lordship says, Mary. It is not fair that you should take the brunt of his anger when I am the one who is the cause."

The maid cast a frightened glance back at her mistress. Guy shifted so she could get out the door. What she saw must have reassured her because she slipped between him and the wall and out into the hall. She gave him one scowling look before scurrying to the stairs.

Guy stepped through the doorway. "She is devoted to you."

Felicia stepped from the shadows by the window. "She is very loyal. I could not have asked for better. Thank you."

She looked haggard. Something had happened. The urge to go to her, enfold her in his arms and kiss her until nothing else mattered raged through him. He nearly groaned aloud at the need he had to fight so desperately.

Finally, when he was sure his ardour would not show in his voice, he asked, "What has happened?"

"You should not be here," she said, her voice barely above a whisper.

"Is it because of the man who visited you earlier?"

He could not stop the cold blade of anger that entered his voice. Jealousy was an emotion he had no experience of. She started, but there was a sadness about her that tore at him.

"Yes. It was Edmund."

"Ah," he said.

He wanted to go to her, but dared not for fear of what he would do. He wanted to erase the hurt look about her eyes and replace it with one of satiation. He wanted to lay her on the bed and make love to her until they both forgot about the rest of the world.

She gave him a wan smile. "My husband." She moved to the side table where a decanter sat. She poured a glass of something red. "Sherry," she said. "Would you care for some?"

"I think not."

She sipped the sweet wine. "I had never had it until this afternoon." She twisted around until he faced him again. "Edmund is going to force you to testify in court." She took a deep, sighing breath. "He is going to accuse you of being my lover. He is going to drag your name through the mud on a lie so that he can be assured of getting my dowry." Her mouth turned sour. "Your testimony is infinitely better than that of two servants."

He went to her, unable to see her suffer and not comfort her. She backed away, using the full glass as a shield.

"I am so sorry." Her voice trembled. "I don't know how he can do so dishonourable a thing as lie about what has happened between you and me." Her hands shook so that sherry slopped over the edge. "I know we nearly became lovers that one night, before my accident. But we did not. Now you are going to pay for something we have not even done."

She turned away, her head bowed, the glass forgotten. He took it from her fingers before she dropped it and set it on the table.

"Felicia," he said gently, "look at me."

She shook her head. "Go away, Guy. There is nothing we can do—or you can do." She took a great shuddering breath. "I can stay with Edmund and give him a child. My father offered him more money than he can refuse." She turned to Guy, her eyes glistening with unshed tears. "But I cannot bear the thought of him even touching me, let alone kissing me and…and doing other things to me."

He gathered her into his arms even though her fingers splayed against his chest in an effort to stop him. He gripped her chin and forced her to look at him when she would have buried her face where he could not see her.

"Felicia, don't. Don't ever think of being with Edmund again."

Jealousy ripped through him even as his arousal tightened his loins to painful intensity. The picture of Edmund touching her as he had touched her was more than he could tolerate.

He lowered his face to hers. "Don't ever think of another man."

He crushed her mouth with his, driving away all his anger and jealousy in one searing union. Her lips opened to his and he plunged in, willing to drown in the passion she offered so willingly.

Driven by the need to make her forget Edmund, he lifted her into his arms and took her to the bed. His lips never left hers as his fingers moved nimbly down her back, undoing the multitude of tiny buttons that held her bodice on. He slid the black fabric from her shoulders as she lifted to give him better access.

Her arms wrapped around his neck, keeping him close as her clothing peeled away. "If he is going to ruin you, then let us at least experience the joy he is accusing us of."

Guy lifted his head to look at her. "Do you truly mean that?"

"Yes," she whispered, raising her lips for his kiss. "Yes, with all my heart."

Guy felt a pang of guilt. It was obvious she did not remember what they had done the night she lay cold and delirious. He had not told her.

Then her arms brought him down to her and everything else fled except the feel of her body pressed hot and urgent against his. Her breasts, covered only by her chemise, felt full and soft beneath his chest and sent hot tingles through him.

Minutes later, she lay naked and he stood by the side of the bed, caught up in her beauty. She smiled at him with her arms held up to welcome him. He discarded his clothes without thought. Something ripped, but he did not slow down.

Then he was beside her, her right thigh running the length of his left thigh. His nerves sparked. He leaned over her until his mouth found hers. He slid his fingers into the luxuriant length of her hair and revelled in the supple silk.

He held the back of her head as he teased her with his tongue. She responded to him like a woman too long unloved.

"Oh, Guy," she murmured. "This feels right."

He opened his eyes to look down at her. She was flushed and her mouth trembled with passion. "Yes," he finally whispered. "Perfect."

And heaven help him, it was. She was everything he wanted.

She arched her back until they were chest to chest and he was lost. When her hands slid down the ridges of muscle along his spine and her fingers hooked into his hips and pulled him to her, he went. And when her thighs opened for him, he entered.

Exquisite pleasure. Exquisite pain.

They were joined. He gasped and felt her stiffen beneath him. Slowly, afraid to break the bonds of delight that connected them, Guy began to move. She encouraged him with her hips, her hands and her lips. He tried harder.

He opened his eyes, wanting to see her face in these moments of passionate intimacy. Her eyes were half-closed, her pupils large enough that he could see his own reflection in them. Her lips were parted and plump. She smiled up at him just as he felt her spasm.

Her eyes widened. She gasped. He pushed.

Then she was over and he was so close it hurt.

His back bowed. Sensation shot down his legs. Instinctively his hips bucked. He was nearly…

He gasped just as he pulled free.

Later, she lay in his arms, her legs tangled with his. Guy rested his forehead on hers and breathed deeply of the lavender scent that clung to her, mixed now with their lovemaking.

She ran her fingers down his ribs. ''Guy, why won't you—I mean, you did not…''

He looked down at her, saw the unease in her eyes even as he felt the tension begin to mount in her body beneath his. ''I won't do that to you. I won't get you with child.''

''But it is only one time.''

He closed his eyes, unwilling to see the emotions moving over her face. ''It is the second time, Felicia.''

She stiffened beneath him, her legs gripping him tightly where he lay cradled between her thighs. In spite of everything that was going on, he hardened. She drove him crazy without even trying. Why? He did not know, he only responded.

''What do you mean? Look at me!''

He opened his eyes and met her accusation with a

calmness his body did not feel. "When you were sick. You begged me to warm you, to love you. I did."

She shoved him—hard. He allowed her to push him off. He lay on his back, oblivious of his nakedness, one knee drawn up, one arm flung across his eyes.

"We have done this before." It was a flat statement.

He nodded, not bothering to speak. There was nothing else to say. He felt her sit up and then get out of the bed. He heard her fumbling and figured she was putting on a robe.

"So, Edmund is right."

"Yes, Felicia." He did not bother to keep the tiredness from his voice. He opened his eyes and stared straight at her. "We both wanted it, Felicia. Just as we both wanted what just happened."

"I am your mistress," she said, her voice barely above a whisper. Her eyes closed and he barely heard her next words. "My imagination was right."

"I would not go that far," he said. "I have not set you up in your own establishment. We do not do this on a regular basis. But Edmund has every right to call me to testify."

Her fingers knotted into the sash around her waist. "When were you going to tell me?"

He got out of bed and gathered his clothes before putting them on. "I tried telling you once, but being in the frozen rain after being turned out of your father's house was not the right time." He shrugged. "I don't know when I would have told you, just that I would have." He stilled, his fingers on the buttons of his trousers. "You have to believe that, Felicia."

He could see her indecision in the angle of her head

and the pinched look around her mouth. Then she nodded.

"I do, but we are ruined."

He finished dressing. "We were ruined anyway."

Chapter Fourteen

Felicia woke up the next day with a splitting headache. Her mouth tasted like dried ashes, and her limbs felt as though she had been stretched out of alignment. Yet, a strange lethargy held her, a sense of complete satiation.

Then she remembered—everything. Her entire body throbbed. She had to stop what was happening between them, for it was plain that Guy had no intention of doing so.

"Ma'am." Mary's meek voice intruded on Felicia's memories.

"Yes," she managed to say in a normal voice.

"A man is here. A big man. He says he is your father."

What more could happen? Felicia thought. First last night and its revelations and now her father fast on the footsteps of Edmund's threat and Guy's lovemaking. She was not sure she could continue to be strong enough to see this through. But she had no choice. She had to stay in London until she knew whether the courts would agree to a divorce so that Edmund could go to Parliament.

Then she would have to find a way to make her living. She had no skills other than those a housekeeper or governess might use. And she would not take anything from Guy. Especially now. She might have made love with him—twice—but she would not become his mistress.

"Felicia, you in there, gel?" her father's voice boomed through the door separating her sleeping room from the parlour.

She dragged herself from bed. "I am coming, Father."

Mary helped her to hastily don her clothing and pin up her hair. She took a quick look in the mirror. She was presentable.

Smoothing her skirt as she went, she entered the front room where her father paced. She could tell he was angry. Her first reaction was apprehension, but she drew herself up. She was no longer the little girl who cringed every time her father lost his temper.

"What do you want, Father?"

He stopped in his tracks and scowled at her. "What do you mean, turning Marbury down again?"

"He was quick to tell you," she said derisively. "But I am not surprised."

Her father's scowl deepened until his bushy brows were one thick bar across his forehead. "He was right to tell me. You are going back to him, gel, make no mistake."

"No, I am not."

Even as she defied him, she took a step back. Refusing to do as he ordered left a strange sensation in the pit of her stomach.

He towered over her. "You will regret that decision."

"I don't think so," she said, forcing all the conviction she felt into her voice. "Edmund only wants one thing from me. Two, now that you have offered him so much financial incentive. I want nothing from him. We are better apart."

"You will be ruined," her father stated. "A divorced woman. No other man will have you."

His face edged forward, as though he were trying to get a better look at her. It made her feel uneasy. Her father had never cared what she looked like or what she felt.

She made herself shrug. "I can live with that, Father. All I want is my dowry back."

"You won't get that, gel. Not now." There was a strange light in his eyes that told her there was more to come. "Edmund says he's going to have that Viscount brought forward. Says you have committed adultery with the man." His small brown eyes bored into her. "Is it true?"

Felicia was not a liar and much as she wanted to deny Edmund's accusation, she could not. Instead she turned away. Better to refuse to answer.

"Tell me, gel."

The force of her father's voice nearly had her speaking. She had thought defying him before was hard. This was next to impossible, but she could not admit to anything.

"If it is true, it will come out at the hearing," her father said.

She shuddered as dread took her. She and Guy would both be shamed. But the alternative… She shook her head.

"Don't shake your head at me, gel. If it is true, I

will see that the man weds you.'' Her father laughed, not a nice sound but one full of power.

She whirled around. ''You would not dare.''

''Watch me, gel. Just watch me.''

She stood paralyzed as he left. Things were going too fast, changing too rapidly, and none of them for the better. She had to warn Guy of this latest development. He did not deserve this. All this had come about because he'd rescued her from a carriage accident, and now his reputation was about to be ruined.

She sank to a chair and dropped her head to her hands. Her neck and back ached. Her entire body ached. Her temples throbbed. She knew it was all because of frustration and fear over what might happen next.

If only she had not fallen in love with Guy. If only he had not made love to her. They should have never met. Their lives were being tangled in knots by one another.

Felicia felt tears welling up and could do nothing to stop them. She had become a watering pot.

Felicia stopped pacing when she heard the knock. Guy must be here. Thank goodness he had come promptly. Mary answered the door and the next thing Felicia knew, Guy was striding across the room to her.

''Felicia,'' he said, grasping her hands. ''Whatever is the matter that you send me a message saying I must come immediately?''

''Oh, Guy,'' she said. ''It is my father.'' His fingers tightened until she squeaked. ''He was here this morning. He is threatening to force you to marry me because I won't go back to Edmund. He means to ruin you.''

Guy laughed. ''He is full of himself.''

She pulled her hands free only to start wringing them. "He is rich. He can do anything he wants. He always has."

"Felicia," Guy said firmly, "you are overreacting. Your father cannot make me do something I don't wish to do."

"You don't know that," she said, turning away and going to the window. She looked out on the street, seeing the carriages and people passing by. "He can do a lot of damage."

Guy shook his head in amazement. "Not to me, Felicia." He crossed to her, stopping without touching her. "You think he is all powerful because he has controlled your life and your decisions. He is not."

"He said he will ruin you." She turned to him. "I have thought seriously of going back to Edmund. That would make Father happy. You would be safe from his threats."

"Don't you dare." He grabbed her upper arms and shook her gently. "If you do that, I will call out that miserable excuse of a husband you have. That will take care of everything. You will be a widow and beyond your father's touch."

"Guy!" She stared at him, nearly not recognizing the man she had fallen in love with because of the fury that contorted his features. "You cannot do that."

He released her and stepped back. "Then do not make stupid statements. You are not going back to Edmund and your father can do nothing to harm me." A dangerous gleam entered his eyes. "Just let your father try and see how he likes it when someone who is stronger and more influential than he makes him do what he does not want to do."

"But what of your testimony? Father and Edmund

both have assured me you will be called on to—'' It was so hard to say the words, even though the act had been the easiest and most pleasurable thing she had ever done. ''To tell about our liaison. That will ruin you in the eyes of Society.''

He shrugged. ''Let it. I have been a marginal participant for years. If I never came to London except to sit in the Lords, it would not bother me. It is you who will be truly hurt by my testimony.''

She took a deep breath. ''Miss Duckworth might break your engagement.''

It was out. Just saying the words exhausted her. She knew that no matter what happened, he would not marry her. But…but if Miss Duckworth called off, he could.

He looked at her, his face devoid of emotion. She had no idea what was going through his mind.

When he finally spoke, his voice was calm and matter-of-fact. ''Miss Duckworth will do as she thinks best.''

No hint that he might want Miss Duckworth to break their engagement. No intimation that he might, just might, want to marry her.

Felicia took a deep breath and willed herself to speak as dispassionately as he had. ''As we all will.''

He quirked one brow and took a step toward her. She warned him off with her eyes. He did not come closer. Instead he made a curt bow.

''I had best go.''

She nodded, doing nothing to stop him. She turned back to the window so she would not see him leave. If only he had desired to marry her given the chance, but no. He did not.

Sometimes life was so hard, so disappointing. She

lifted her head, even though her chest hurt abominably. There was nothing she could do except keep going and hope that her dowry would be returned to her. When the petition reached Parliament they appointed a Lady's Friend and a gentleman from Parliament who would represent her when the divorce petition was presented. Otherwise, there would be no one to speak on her behalf. Then she would leave London and Guy behind. He would become her past just as so much this last year was now her past.

If everything became too complicated, she could go back to Edmund. There was safety in that decision. One could live with a broken heart. She had done so all this year. One could not live without food and shelter.

Guy left the Pulteney. He had not told Felicia he was due at the law courts shortly to testify. She was troubled enough without knowing how close everything was to blowing up in their faces. He signalled his tiger to follow him with the phaeton. He was feeling too reckless to drive at the moment.

He entered the building, with its dark panelling and smell of beeswax. The hearing was to be held in a small room for privacy. He entered and looked around. Edmund Marbury was already here. He knew some of the other men.

One lord came over and shook Guy's hand. "Didn't expect to see you involved in this, Chillings. Dominic, possibly. Rum business."

Guy shrugged and resisted the urge to cut the man for his derogatory reference to Dominic. "It happens to the best of us."

There was no time for social niceties. The hearing started.

Edmund Marbury spoke first. ''She has been my wife for ten years. She bore me two children, one a boy. Through her negligence as a mother, they both died just a year ago. But that is not the reason I want a divorce,'' he said with feigned contrition. ''She has been unfaithful. This man here…'' he waved his hand at a man who was obviously a servant ''…saw her at the Pulteney with Viscount Chillings. Also, I have named the Viscount as my wife's accomplice.''

The urge to throttle the man and the determination needed not to do so turned Guy's stomach. The most cynical part of him noted that Marbury no longer intended to use the two male servants from his country estate. He had caught a bigger fish.

Guy glanced around at the others to see how they reacted to the statement. No one blinked an eye. The man wanted a divorce and he was paying thousands of pounds to get it. They would give it to him, unless Guy missed his reading of their countenances.

Then it was his turn. He could lie. Deny that he had even touched Felicia. No one here could prove differently. The servant's testimony would be damaging, but alone it might not stand. It would be his word against Marbury's. The men here would believe him. Then he would have to live with his act of dishonour.

In his thirty-three years, he had only told one lie and Mrs Drummond had blistered his bottom and sent him to bed without supper. He had been five and it had been to protect Bell who had really been the one to climb down the apple tree outside the nursery window. Even thinking of not telling the truth closed his throat.

But the truth would ensure that Marbury got his divorce. It would ruin Felicia. No man would marry her. By law, her dowry would not go back to her. She would be completely dependent on what the final decision makers gave her for funds. Usually something, but it did not have to be much. Nor would she be able to work for money. No respectable household would hire her. She might get work as a maid for someone in the deep country who had no ties to London, a well-to-do farmer or clerk. Or even factory work. Both would be condemning a woman of her intelligence to a life of bare existence.

Then there was his situation. His reputation would be ruined. There was every possibility Miss Duckworth would call off. Then he would be without a wife to provide him with an heir.

It would be better for everyone if he lied.

He made eye contact with everyone in the room, lingering on Marbury, before he spoke. Felicia's soon-to-be ex-husband gloated, he was that sure of success. No matter what the cost, Guy could not lie, but he could make very clear where the blame lay.

He stood and started speaking. "Mrs Marbury came to my country estate after I found her in a coach wreckage. She was hurt. When she woke, she did not remember who she was. She thought she was a widow. I thought she was a widow." He told about the ice-skating accident and Felicia's subsequent fever and delirium. Now came the moment of truth. "While she was unaware of what was really going on, I seduced her."

Everyone stilled. Hands that had been fiddling with a pen, sheet of paper, or just twiddling, stopped. One man had been fidgeting in his chair. He froze. Marbury was stunned, his mouth hanging open like a beached fish.

No one had really expected Guy to confess to adultery. They had definitely not expected him to confess to taking advantage of a woman who did not know what she was doing. He was doubly ruined.

The Lord Chancellor rose before Guy could say anything else. Almost as though he wanted to forestall Guy from saying anything further that might be damning.

"Thank you, Lord Chillings. That will be all."

Guy stood and without another word, left. He had done what he could for Felicia. Somehow, he did not think it was enough.

Chapter Fifteen

Felicia set down the cup of tea and took the note from Mary. Her hands shook as she ripped open the envelope. Edmund's scrawl covered the enclosed sheet of paper. *The divorce petition has passed the courts. Only a matter of time before it goes to Parliament. Your dowry is mine.* The fine vellum fell from her nerveless fingers.

She was as good as a divorcée. The courts had approved, there was no reason for Parliament not to agree.

Emotions overwhelmed her. On one level she was ecstatic about the news. On another she was sad. She had spent the last ten years of her life with Edmund, had borne him two children. Still, she was glad for her freedom.

Drained and exhausted, she let her head fall back onto the chair. She plucked the handkerchief from its place up her sleeve and blew her nose. She felt almost anticlimactic.

It was time for her to go home, except that home was Edmund's country estate. Well, she would go there and pack her belongings. She had some money left from the quarterly allowance Edmund had given her. She doubted he would give her more now. With any luck, Parliament would make Edmund give her a stipend of some sort, possibly her marriage jointure. But that was in the future. One thing at a time.

She rose. ''Mary,'' she called.

The maid came scurrying from the bedroom. ''Yes, ma'am?''

''Pack my things. We are leaving in the morning.'' Felicia stopped as she realized what she had said. ''I will be leaving in the morning, Mary. You will return to Viscount Chillings.''

''Never say so, ma'am.'' The maid's mobile face twisted in sadness.

Yet another loss, Felicia thought, her emotional exhaustion weighing on her like a ton of coal. ''I wish I could take you with me, Mary, but I cannot. I don't even know how I shall care for myself. I have not means to care for another person. I am truly sorry. I will miss you.''

The maid wrung her hands, her eyes wide and dazed. ''Yes, ma'am. If it ain't too presumptuous, ma'am, did you get yer divorce? Is that why you be leaving?''

''I will. It is almost guaranteed. That is why I am leaving. I am done with my reason for coming to London. The sooner I leave, the better for all of us.''

She had to turn away from Mary's anguished face. The servant only reflected back what she, Felicia, felt in her heart. It was better this way. She had failed to convince Edmund to give her support. She knew what Parliament would decide. There was no reason to linger.

Not even for Guy. In truth, it would be better for

him if she left. He had his own life to lead and he had made it obvious that his future did not include her.

Felicia took a deep, shuddering breath. "I am going for a walk." She needed to get out of the hotel. She felt contained and claustrophobic.

"Yes, ma'am."

Mary went into the sleeping area and returned with Felicia's pelisse and cape, which she helped Felicia don. The maid then shrugged into her own outerwear.

Felicia looked at her. "I am going by myself."

"Ma'am?"

"By myself," Felicia repeated. "I need to be alone."

"Beggin' your pardon, ma'am, but his lordship said I was to go everywhere you went." The girl flushed and her gaze dropped to the floor.

"His lordship is not my keeper, Mary. I am going alone." She realized how harsh her voice had been and forced herself to smile gently at the maid. "I will be all right."

The maid watched her leave, helpless frustration writ on her countenance. Felicia could sympathize. That was exactly how she had felt about everything this past year.

Passing through the lobby, she nodded briefly at the desk clerk, the same one who had been on duty when she had checked in two days before. It seemed an eternity ago. He made her a brief bow and his gaze went to the stairs she had just descended.

Felicia knew he was looking for her maid. Out of sheer perversity, she said, "I am going out on my own."

A frown marred his previously impassive features.

"I am sure that madam knows what is best." His tone implied just the opposite.

"Yes, I do," Felicia said, the perversity still riding her.

She stepped outside into a blistering wind. Lifting her head proudly, she set off at a brisk pace towards Hyde Park. It would be dark soon, but she had plenty of time to walk there, go down some of the paths and return to the Pulteney without mishap.

She had many plans to make. Somehow she had to get out of London, but this time she would go by mail coach. As it was, she could barely afford that.

She grinned. She would have her bill for the Pulteney sent to Edmund. He was such a stickler that, hopping mad as he would be, he would pay the price. Besides, she had incurred the expense while his wife. He was legally responsible.

That was the only bright spot in her future.

Guy set the newspaper down with a snap. They had printed a lurid story of how he had been called to testify before a private hearing, telling how he had committed adultery with the soon to be ex-wife of Edmund Marbury. Failure to produce an heir was an underlying cause, but infidelity was the reason for the petition.

Marbury had promised to drag his name through the mud, and he had done so with a vengeance. Guy could have no more lied under oath than he could have kept from making love to Felicia. It was his bad luck that she was married to a man of Marbury's stamp.

Not only was his reputation ruined along with Felicia's, but he could expect a visit from Miss Duckworth shortly. Probably tomorrow, if not later today.

He stood and strode to the window, his Hessians

clicking sharply even through the thick Aubusson carpet. He yanked open the heavy green velvet curtains and stared out at the overcast day. Night would fall soon. One of the servants lit the gas-fed light in front of the house so that it cast a yellow glow into the gathering mist.

A small, slim figure hurried past, head bent. The servant he had sent to Felicia. Something was wrong or she would not be here. His heart skipped a beat.

He turned to the library door and waited, his patience a hard-won thread that threatened to break. At the first knock, he said, "Come in."

Oswald came in and said, "The girl, Mary, wishes to speak with you, my lord."

"It is fine, Oswald," he responded to the butler's look of disapproval. "Send her in."

"Yes, my lord."

Mary entered with her head down and her hands clasped tightly in front of her. Even though every nerve screamed for him to demand that she tell him why she was here, he did not. The girl was already afraid.

"I am glad you came, Mary," he said gently. "This is what we arranged."

She nodded. "Yes, my lord."

"So, tell me," he said, trying to keep his fierce need to know from making his voice harsh and scaring the girl. It would do no good and probably make her stumble around and take longer telling him.

"Mrs Marbury. She received a letter this afternoon. She threw it in the fire immediately she read it. Tomorrow she leaves town." Her voice broke. "She won't take me."

Leaving town? She must have got word about the court's decision. It had to be in favour of her husband.

As though it could have been anything else, given the reason Marbury was seeking a divorce.

"Thank you for coming so promptly, Mary. I will see that she does not leave without you." The girl looked up, her face alight with hope. "I promise."

"Thank you, my lord. Thank you so much. She means that much to me. She is kind." The words tumbled from the servant's lips.

Guy smiled, although he wanted the girl to leave. But he did not want to send her away until he was sure there was nothing else.

"Is there anything else I need to know?" He spoke calmly when he felt anything but.

"Yes,'m, my lord. I don't rightly know as it matters, but Mrs Marbury went out by herself. She would not take me."

"What?" Guy surged forward and it was all he could do not to shake the chit. "When? Where did she go? Why did you not follow her?"

Her eyes widened and she edged away from him. "She told me not to. She said she wanted to be alone, that she would not be gone long. She was going to a park. I came here."

He tamped down on his irritation. The girl had done her best, there was no sense in punishing her or making her feel worse than she already did.

"You did right, Mary. You may go now. Cook will see that you get something warm to eat and drink and a footman will take you back to the Pulteney. It is getting dark."

He turned his back to her, listening for the sound of the door closing behind her. Felicia was going to a park, probably Hyde Park since that was where he had taken her. Surely she would be back at the hotel by now, but he would make sure.

He strode from the room, calling, "Oswald, have the phaeton brought round. Jeffries," he yelled for his valet, "I need my greatcoat."

Five minutes later the carriage waited with two fresh horses and Jeffries helped him into his coat. The valet handed him his beaver and cane.

"Thank you," Guy said, already forgetting everyone but Felicia.

It was a quick trip to the hotel. The tiger jumped down and went to the horses' heads. Guy leaped gracefully to the ground.

"Walk them until I return, Jem."

"Of course, my lord," the tiger said, affronted that his master had even felt it necessary to tell him what to do.

Guy heard the tiger's tone and looked over his shoulder as he strode into the lobby. "I know you will do so, Jem, without my telling you. Habit."

And worry about Felicia and what foolhardy plans she was making. The desk clerk saw him immediately. A long-suffering look came over the man's face, but he smiled and came out from behind the desk.

"My lord, how may I help you?"

Guy glanced at him and kept going towards the stairs. "I am calling on Mrs Marbury."

"Mrs Marbury is not here, my lord."

Guy stopped. "Damnation." He whirled around. "Are you telling me she has not come back from her walk?"

"Yes, my lord."

"I am going after her. If she returns before I do, tell

her to stay here. I will be back." He glared at the other man, who remained impassive. "Do you understand?"

"I will tell her that you wish her to remain here, my lord, but I cannot make her do so against her will." He was stiff as a poker and about as emotional.

"See that you do," Guy said, scowling.

He strode from the building and signalled to the tiger who had walked the horses down the road. Determined to waste no more time, Guy lengthened his stride and went to them. He jumped into the phaeton before the tiger managed to stop the horses.

"We are for Hyde Park," he said, setting the carriage in motion.

"Yes, my lord," the tiger said, just barely catching hold of his perch in the back and leaping on to it.

Guy drove at a fast clip. Dusk had already set in. Most of the street lamps were lit, their golden glow a haze in the gathering mists. It was a bone-chilling damp that went through layers of clothing as though they were non-existent. Felicia should not be out in this weather.

Guy increased his speed.

He thought he saw a lone figure up ahead. He strained to see better, but all he could make out was something billowing out that must be a cape. Very likely a female, then.

Even as he caught sight of the walker, he heard a group of men, their voices raised in merriment—and inebriation, if their slurring and vulgar language were any indication. They were cultured. Young bucks on the town early.

Nearing, he heard a woman's voice—Felicia's voice—say, "Excuse me, please."

There was an absentmindedness in her tone that told

Guy she was thinking of something besides the group of young men who blocked her way. He spurred his horses on.

One of the men, his words less than distinct, said, "Excused all you want, mistress. Demme if we don't."

His cronies laughed.

Another one said, "You are about late without an escort."

Guy bristled at the leering note in the man's voice. He pulled the phaeton to a rocking stop and sprang down. He'd be damned if any man made importunate remarks to Felicia.

"You are in my way," Felicia said, her tone forceful now as though she finally realized the situation she was in.

"Not without a little sport," the first said.

Guy saw the group of drunken bucks close around Felicia. He was just in time.

"The only sport we will have here," he said dangerously, taking hold of the shoulder of one of the men and flinging him backwards, "is when we see how well you bounce."

The other man whirled around. "Just havin' some innocent fun. She's alone. Must be looking."

"You are mistaken," Guy said, his voice deathly cold.

"Guy," Felicia said, relief seeping from her words.

"Come away, Felicia," Guy said, keeping his attention on the two men.

The one he had flung to the ground now stood, brushing off his trousers. "No cause for violence," he said. "We did not know she was taken."

It was all Guy could do not to give the lout a facer.

''You should know not to accost any woman. A gentleman protects ladies. He does not molest them.''

''Well—'' one of them sputtered.

Guy turned his back on them, judging them harmless when confronted by a man. He took Felicia's arm and hurried her to the phaeton where he helped her up. He quickly joined her and set the horses in motion with a light flick of the whip.

''Thank you,'' Felicia said a little bit breathlessly. ''I never thought something like that might happen.''

''You did not *think*,'' Guy said harshly, his relief at finding her unharmed making him sharp. ''You had no business being out alone. It is not done in daylight, let alone at dusk and night. This is not the country.''

''I did not expect to be gone so long,'' she said, drawing away from him.

''That is no excuse.''

His tone brooked no argument and she gave none. Neither one spoke.

With a supple movement of wrists, he guided the horses down the streets and around the corners while his mind was on Felicia. More aptly, his thoughts were on his worry for her and subsequent relief on finding her.

They arrived at the Pulteney Hotel before he realized it. He gave the reins to the tiger and went around the carriage to help her down. She ignored his hand and managed to clamber down without catching her skirts or falling.

She stalked by him, head high. He let her go. To stop her now would only cause a scene and the two of them were already providing more than enough fuel for the gossips' fire.

Instead, he followed her, fully intending to accom-

pany her up to her room and see that she was safely
behind the door. When he had learned she was out
alone and then found her in a situation that might have
harmed her if he had not shown, his only thought had
been to protect her.

"I am perfectly capable of going on by myself from
here, Lord Chillings." She gave him a look over her
shoulder that would have made a less determined man
leave.

He studied her, noting the mutinous look on her face.
Her cheeks were red from the cold or her anger, probably both. Her glorious hair was dishevelled, looking
as though a lover had run his fingers through the long
strands and then haphazardly pinned them up in an
effort to restore her look of respectability. He nearly
groaned aloud as desire rose hot and heavy in him.
Instead, he pivoted on his heel to leave.

"As you wish," he said, his voice heavy with sarcasm that he made no effort to soften.

He heard her soft gasp behind him but ignored it.
She had told him to go, and this time he would. She
was safe, and he needed to think, something he would
not do if he stayed here.

It was a matter of moments before he was once more
in the phaeton. Too irritated to go home, he directed
the horses towards Brook's.

He entered the club and handed his hat and coat to
the waiting butler. "Bring me a bottle of port." He
took a step forward before adding, "Make that two."

The servant nodded and left to do Guy's bidding.
Guy found a large leather chair in a dark corner and
flung himself into it. The last thing he felt like was
company.

The servant quickly delivered the two bottles and

poured Guy a glass of the dark red wine before leaving. Guy drained the glass and wondered if he should have ordered whisky. He would get that next.

The mood he was in, two bottles of port would not be nearly enough. He was furious with Felicia, but he was more angry with himself and the way he forgot everything but her. He had never been this way.

"Another night of inebriation, brother?"

Guy looked up to see Dominic. The younger man was immaculately dressed in evening wear. He had to admit that his brother cut a dashing figure.

"And what about you, Dominic? You don't normally haunt Brook's."

"Well," Dominic drawled, pulling up a chair and straddling it with his hands crossed on the back. "I just left Almack's and decided I was not ready to go home."

Guy's eyebrows lifted. "You? At the Marriage Mart? Whatever for?"

"Escorting Miss Lucy Duckworth." His voice lowered and he said in tones of disgust, "And the Sourpuss. She is like a burr on a horse's backside."

In spite of himself, Guy chuckled. "I fear she will pay me another visit tomorrow." He sighed, the humour gone, and poured another glass. "And she will be perfectly right to be upset."

"She ain't the only one," Dominic said. "Best check the Betting Book."

Guy groaned. "An entry about yesterday's proceedings?"

Dominic nodded.

Guy remembered only too well what entries in the Betting Book had caused his friends the Duke of Braborne and the Earls of Ravensford and Perth to do.

Marry their ladies. He was not eager to see what the entry about him said. It could be scathing in the extreme.

He levered himself up. "I suppose it will do no good to ignore it."

"Probably not," Dominic said, following him. "But I don't think you will call anyone out either. Big enough scandal as it is."

Guy shot him an irritated glance. "That bad?"

Dominic shrugged. "See for yourself."

It was a matter of minutes to the book. Guy emptied his glass of wine before opening the cover.

Viscount C. Engaged to one, fornicating with another. A monkey that he marries neither.

Guy closed the book very carefully, his glance going around the crowded room. Some of the men scattered around at tables and lounging in chairs watched him back. Others paid him no mind, whether from respect for his privacy or embarrassment over what they knew he would find in the book.

"Time I left, Dominic," He did not realize he used his brother's full name, something he only did when he was beyond anger.

"Right," Dominic said.

Guy took his coat, hat and cane from the waiting doorman and strode into the night, oblivious to his tiger standing ready with the phaeton.

"Pace us," Dominic said to the servant, for it was obvious Guy was beyond being aware of anything but his anger.

Haze hung over the streets, making it difficult to see more than a length ahead. Cold permeated everything, and ice was beginning to form.

"That entry was not made in jest or goodwill," Guy

said through clenched teeth. "Nothing like what Perth did."

Dominic nodded. "No. It was meant to hurt." He looked at his brother out of the corner of his eye. "I didn't know you had an enemy."

"Everyone has people who don't like them." He slapped his cane against his thigh in rhythm with his pace. "Very likely it is someone who thinks he is about to come into five hundred pounds. Bastard."

Dominic said nothing for some time. "What are you going to do?" he finally asked.

"What can I do? I am guilty of the charges. I even confessed before all the world because I could not bring myself to lie, no matter who the truth might hurt."

"You always were too honourable," Dominic said with only a hint of teasing in his voice. "I thank everything sacred that I am not like you in that aspect."

"And I can almost agree with you after that entry," Guy said wryly.

They walked on. The only sounds were those of the horse's hooves clopping behind them. It had started to drizzle minutes earlier, and still neither of them noticed.

"You are in for a hell of a day tomorrow, I wager." Dominic said.

Guy shrugged, the capes on his greatcoat lifting in the wind. "Unfortunately, nothing I don't deserve."

"What are you going to do about the Sourpuss?" Dominic asked, his voice curiously flat.

"Miss Duckworth?" Guy asked, intentionally using her proper name.

Dominic sighed gustily, his breath billowing out in frosty smoke. "Yes, her."

"I am going to let her berate me."

"Are you going to break off your engagement?"

"A gentleman does not cry off, Dominic," Guy said firmly.

"In your position, it might actually be better for her if you did."

"I can't argue that." Guy gave Dominic a curious look, noting his brother's fixed interest on the ground. "Why do you care? Afraid that if the family connection is severed you will be unable to court the fair Miss Lucy?"

"It would make it difficult if none of us were any longer welcomed in the Duckworth establishment."

"That has never stopped you before."

"True." Dominic seemed to perk up at the thought and started whistling a jaunty tune more often heard in pubs.

"We are here," Guy said, surprised at how quickly they had walked home.

"It is too early for me, brother. I have a gaming hell to supervise, so I'll be on my way since you seem to have everything under control."

"Take the phaeton," Guy said, signalling to Jem. "The weather is too nasty to be out and about. Not that an open carriage will be much better, but it will be faster."

"I wish you had thought of that thirty minutes ago," Dominic said, leaping into the carriage and waving with the whip.

Guy watched Dominic tool off down the road.

Tomorrow was going to be hellish. He had made a botch of everything. But worse, by his lack of control, he had ruined Felicia. Not only was she now a divorced woman, no longer acceptable to Polite Society, she was a confessed adulteress. People would not invite her to their home, nor would they hire her to care for their children or themselves.

Lord Holland had married his lady, but that had always been his intention. He, Guy, could not marry Felicia even if he wished. He was engaged, and as dishonourably as he had behaved towards Felicia, he could not compound his trespasses by jilting Miss Duckworth. He had given his word to Miss Duckworth.

Lord, but his passions had made a damned mess of everything.

Guy groaned aloud as he mounted the stairs to his front door. Felicia had been delirious that first time. He should have never got into bed with her and then he surely should never have made love to her. That experience had opened the floodgates of his passion, and he had never been able to get enough of her since.

He went through the door Oswald held open.

"Good evening, my lord," the butler said.

Guy nodded and continued to the library. What was he to do? He had ruined Felicia and could not marry her himself. He was engaged. Even if he were not, he could not marry her. He could not keep his hands off her or his body from wanting her. If he married her, he would have her pregnant within a fortnight, even though that was the last thing he would want to do. He knew he would.

He crossed to a side table and poured himself a tumbler of whisky. He had started this night determined to get drunk and forget all his worries. So far, he had been unsuccessful. But no more.

Tomorrow he had some hard decisions to make.

Chapter Sixteen

Guy studied himself critically. "I shall have a number of visitors today, Jeffries."

The valet twitched Guy's shirt points so they stood a little straighter. "Beau Brummell himself would approve of you, my lord."

Guy took the cravat Jeffries held out to him and carefully wrapped it around his collar. When he was satisfied, he slowly lowered his chin to set the crease. The Chillings's Crease was perfect.

"Very nice, my lord."

"Thank you," Guy said with only a touch of irony. He held out his arms and Jeffries helped him into a bottle-green coat perfectly tailored by Weston. "I shan't disgrace you. At least not in my clothing," he finished.

"You are a credit to my skills, my lord."

A knock on the door told Guy that his first visitor was here. He did not need Oswald to tell him Miss Duckworth was in the front drawing room. He had fully expected her to show as early as decently possible.

"Come in, Oswald."

The butler entered and held out a silver tray with a card. "You have a visitor, my lord." He raised one expressive grey brow.

"Miss Duckworth," Guy stated without looking at the card.

"Ahem, would that it were, my lord. This is a gentleman caller, or so he styles himself. A Mr Dunston." He sniffed. "He says he has urgent business with you."

Felicia's father. He had not expected this. But with hindsight, he should have.

"See that he is treated with all respect." When Oswald did all but look down his nose, he added, "He is Mrs Marbury's father."

If Oswald could look shocked, he did. His eyes widened a fraction and his shoulders drew up. But he said nothing scathing.

"Yes, my lord."

Guy watched Oswald walk stiffly to the door and leave. He wished he was sending the butler to deny Dunston's request for a meeting, but he could not. Felicia's father was here because Guy had admitted to adultery with the man's daughter. This promised to be a very awkward visit.

Guy headed out. The sooner he got the accusations and recriminations over with, the better. He still had to deal with Miss Duckworth when she arrived. After that, he had to go to the Pulteney and reason with Felicia.

He found Felicia's father where Oswald had put him, in the front drawing room. The man probably did not even know the honour accorded him. Oswald always put tradesmen in the small, dark antechamber nearer the back of the house. It was the butler's opinion that tradesmen did not visit lords.

"How do you do," Guy said, striding into the room. "I see you have been offered refreshments."

Dunston rose from the chair where he had been eating cakes. "Very nice, too."

"I am glad," Guy said. There was no sense in wasting time on polite nothings. "What can I do for you?"

Dunston took another bite of cake and studied Guy. His stare was an impertinence, but Guy admitted that the man had a right to be angry. The testimony had not been pretty.

"I'm sure your lordship knows why I am here."

"I have a good idea."

"You admitted yourself that you have been Felicia's lover. Bad enough her husband was divorcing her, you had to go and ruin all her chances of possibly making a good remarriage."

Guy kept quiet. There was nothing to say. But he felt the tension creeping into his shoulders and making them ache.

"It is your duty to make reparation." It was a statement that was more of a command.

Guy's sense of guilt evaporated to be replaced by mounting irritation. "To whom?"

"To me. To Felicia." Dunston smiled, but it was only a stretching of his lips while his eyes looked greedy.

"And what do you suggest?" Guy asked, his voice deadly calm.

"Marriage."

Guy managed not to say anything. Felicia had mentioned that her father was talking marriage, but he had never really thought the man was serious. Money and lots of it would have been more in keeping with his impression of Felicia's father. And money he could have given her.

"Marriage is out of the question," he said, his face drawn into sharp angles. "I am engaged."

"Break it," Dunston countered, his round face hardening. "You ruined my daughter, Viscount Chillings. I know you lords don't believe in paying the piper for your indiscretions, but this time I mean to see that you do. And the only acceptable payment is marriage."

Guy's eyes narrowed. "Does Felicia know you are here?"

"Ain't her business. She's about to be a single woman again. I am her father. I decide what she does, not her." He scowled and stuffed his beefy hands into the pockets of his old-fashioned breeches. "Ain't like she's a respectable widow with a jointure, her dead husband's name and mother of his children. She's disgraced. She's mine again. She's marrying you."

Guy drew himself up so that he looked down on Dunston. "You are despicable. But that is neither here nor there. I am not free to marry your daughter."

Dunston stepped up until he was chest to chest with Guy. "I mean to change that."

The urge to give the man a facer was nearly greater than his personal acknowledgment that Dunston had a right to be here demanding marriage for his daughter. Guy was not sure what angered him more, the fact that this man was toe to toe with him or the knowledge that he could not marry Felicia.

Guy did not step back as he stared into Dunston's close-set brown eyes. "Leave my fiancée out of this."

"I will do as I think necessary," Dunston stated.

With grim haughtiness, Guy said, "You have overstayed your welcome."

"Throw me out," Dunston challenged.

"I would throttle you if doing so would not send me to prison," Guy murmured, his voice low and colder than the outside weather. "Get out."

A knock on the door interrupted them.

"My lord," Oswald said entering without waiting for a reply. He stopped and looked at Guy. "You have a visitor."

Guy never took his eyes off Felicia's father. "Oswald, escort Mr Dunston out. Use a pistol to encourage him if needed."

"Yes, my lord," Oswald said with relish.

Guy glanced at his butler. "Bloodthirsty? I am surprised." He turned back to his adversary. "You heard my butler, Dunston. I have another guest. You are *de trop*."

Knowing that Oswald would see their unwelcome guest out, no matter what it took, Guy left. Miss Duckworth would be in the library. That was Oswald's second-favourite place to put people.

He paused outside the room long enough to adjust his coat so it lay more smoothly across his shoulders. Oswald had not named this visitor, but Miss Duckworth was the only one left except for Felicia, and she would not come to him.

He waved off the footman who waited to knock and announce him. He opened the door and walked in. She stood at a bookcase, looking over the titles.

"Miss Duckworth," he said.

"Chillings," she replied without looking in his direction. "So good of you to see me yet again on such short notice."

There was an edge to her voice, from tiredness or ire, Guy could not tell. He did not know her well enough. Although he expected it was due to the situation he had landed her in. Betrothal to a man with his reputation could not be easy for a very proper woman.

"Please have a seat. Oswald will serve tea shortly. He is busy at the moment." He waved to a small grouping of chairs and tables.

She shook her head and finally turned to face him. "No, thank you. I won't be staying long." She pulled open the reticule that dangled from her wrist and fished something out. "I have come to return this."

The engagement ring he had given her sparkled on her palm. He had not expected this, but yet again, was not totally surprised. He had added insult to injury with his testimony.

"I see," he murmured. "You don't have to do this, you know."

She smiled sadly at him. "Oh, but I do. While ours was to be a marriage of convenience and neither one of us was in love with someone else, it was fine. But now, things have changed drastically."

Her wording was a little discommoding. "How do you mean?"

"Come along, Chillings. You are in love with Mrs Marbury, or as close to that emotion as you are capable of."

He drew back in affront. "I beg your pardon, Miss Duckworth. My attachment to Mrs Marbury is private."

Her mouth twisted wryly. "Very private indeed."

"My testimony was behind closed doors and supposed to have been confidential. Someone obviously felt he could derive some benefit by leaking the information to the press. I am sorry for that. I never intended to embarrass you like that."

She turned away again, her hands clasped behind her back. "As to that, I cannot say. The damage is done." She whirled back around and thrust out her fist. "Will you take this, or should I leave it on a table?"

He sighed. "On a table."

She did, the ring tinkling as it hit the polished wood and rocked from side to side. The centre diamond glittered like ice.

"I wish you only the best," she said, angling so that she would walk past him with more than enough distance separating them.

"Miss Duckworth," he said, causing her to pause. "I will send a notice to *The Times*."

"Of course."

She left without a backward glance. Guy stood where he was for several minutes, wondering if what he felt was joy at being freed from an engagement that had been getting more and more burdensome or disappointment that she had released him.

Now he truly could marry Felicia.

It was not a totally joyful realization. Wedding her was fraught with too many possibilities, not all of them pleasant or happy.

He crossed to the table where the ring lay and picked the piece up. The large centre diamond was flawless as were the smaller circling stones. He had gone to a jeweller with the intent to have them make a new ring for Miss Duckworth, but they had had this one already done. He had purchased it without a second's thought.

His family's traditional engagement ring was in a safe in this very room. He took the set wherever he went. His mother had given it to him when he asked Suzanne to marry him, thus when his parents had drowned the ring had been on Suzanne's finger.

He went to the fireplace and ran his fingers along the trim that went down the right side until they found the spot. A soft click and part of the wall opened. Behind was a lead-lined safe. He opened it and reached inside.

He pulled out a velvet bag and put the diamond ring into the safe. He sat in a chair and emptied the contents of the bag. A blood-red ruby, large as a thumbnail and set in platinum, fell into his palm. A thin band with channel-set rubies followed. The Chillings engagement and marriage rings.

He sat looking at them for a long time.

Felicia held tightly to the mail coach's strap. They were travelling the York Road, and she had got up at five-thirty in order to do so. The hackney she had ordered the day before had, thankfully, been waiting for her as she said farewell to a tearful Mary. She had been in this smelly coach since she boarded it at six-thirty at the George and Blue Boar in Holborn. She was more than ready to get out of it.

There were eight of them and they were squeezed in like fish wrapped tight, heads and tails touching. Most of them smelled worse than sardines. Felicia took as shallow a breath as she could and pressed her nose to the window.

The sun was well up and they had already changed horses several times. Hopefully, they would stop for lunch soon. She had had nothing to eat today and very little yesterday. She had been too upset over everything that had happened.

With luck, she would reach Edmund's country home before word of the divorce did. Although in all fairness to Edmund, his servants would not kick her out or refuse to allow her in to pack her belongings. She just did not want to go through the mix of stares, conjecture and pity that would be directed her way.

The coach hit a particularly bad rut and everyone went up in the air. Felicia came down with a hard thump and hoped her luggage was still strapped to the top.

Over the babble of her fellow passengers, she heard the crack of a whip. The carriage sped up.

"What is going on?" bellowed one of the male passengers, his ample form taking up more than his share of the seat. He stuck his head out of the window nearest him, having to lean over a woman who frowned fiercely. "Coachman, what are you about?"

Another man on the opposite side, who sat near the roadside window, stuck his head out. "Damn. The fool driver is racing a high-perch phaeton driven by some town swell. We are all in for it now."

The woman who was being squashed by the fat man, who still had his head out the window beside her, rolled her eyes. "Heaven help us. Plenty of innocent people have perished in mail-coach accidents caused by this very thing."

Another woman, thin, angular and plainly dressed, closed her eyes. Her lips moved with a fervency that spoke of prayer.

Felicia groaned in unison with the coach's springs and clung tighter to the strap. The vehicle rocked from side to side, the passengers hanging on for dear life. Heaven help the people on the roof. They would all be lucky to get out of this with only a few bruises.

Bang!

A gun. Someone was firing a gun. What was going on?

As suddenly as they had begun their mad dash, it ended. The coach started slowing down. They hit a rock or hole or something and she herd a crack. But they still moved forward until, finally, they stopped.

"You've no call to be firing at us." The driver's angry voice carried. "I thought you was wantin' to race, what with coming up on me all asudden like and trying to pass, nearly forcing me into the ditch."

"Count yourself lucky that I don't turn you in for reckless driving," another man said angrily in a deep, melting baritone.

Guy.

Felicia caught her breath. Her heart seemed to stop before starting again at a painfully fast pace.

The door farthest from her banged open, and Guy peered inside. "Felicia."

She stared at him. "I... Go away, Guy. Leave me alone. I won't become your mistress."

The prim woman gasped. "Well, I never. And on the King's road."

One of the men snickered.

Felicia came to a belated awareness of the people around her. In her shock at seeing Guy, she had forgotten she sat in a crowded carriage.

The door closed and Felicia sighed in relief. He was going to let her go. Yet, even though she knew this was the only way it could be, her relief quickly disappeared. Knowing what was right and reasonable was a far, painful cry from what she longed for.

She heard activity on the roof and shortly after a piece of luggage thumped to the ground. Suspicion began to grow.

Before she could step outside to see if it was her portmanteau on the ground, the door nearest her opened. Guy stood there. He reached in, grabbed her and hauled her outside.

Her momentum carried her into his chest. She looked up and his face was right there. She could see the individual hairs of his beard and the fine lines around his eyes.

"You are coming back to London," he said, his tone brooking no argument.

She squirmed against his hold, but quickly realized he was not going to let go. She stopped moving, but held herself stiffly and as far from him as she could, which was not far. She could smell the lime and musk that was so essentially him.

"And do what?"

He took a deep breath and his eyes closed. He looked like a man faced with a life and death decision. His eyes opened and he looked down at her.

"Marry me."

"What?" Startlement followed by pain followed by anger gave her strength. She wrenched herself from his hold. "Your jest is cruel."

He shook his head, making no move to grab her. "It is no jest. Miss Duckworth broke our engagement today."

"She… Over your testimony," Felicia said, all the fury draining from her. She was the cause of his misfortune. "I am sorry."

"Don't be. I am the one at fault, not you."

He rubbed at his beard, a habit she now knew that showed he was upset over something or thinking deeply. He did not touch her, but his gaze held her as surely as his arms could have.

"That does not mean you have to marry me."

He sighed. "No, it does not. I need a marriage of convenience and a wife to give me an heir."

"A marriage of convenience," she echoed faintly.

He did not offer love. But then he never had. She bit her lower lip. He was offering her security, which was nothing to disdain. But no love.

"Come away, Felicia." He finally reached for her arm. "This is not the place to discuss this."

She followed him without thinking. Her portmanteau was being loaded on his phaeton. Her travelling case was on the front seat. The other passengers in the mail coach had their heads out of the window, watching. The driver was on the ground, fists on his hips, frowning.

"You shoulda said you was after a female, gov'nor."

Guy flipped him a coin that flashed golden in the meager sunlight. "I did not have the opportunity," he said drily.

"Right-o." The driver deftly caught the piece of gold and pocketed it in one smooth gesture. That accomplished, he climbed back into the driver's seat. "Ever'one get ready. We're off." His whip cracked and the carriage set off one person lighter.

Felicia stared after the coach. What was she doing? But she knew. Guy might be offering a marriage of convenience with no love, but she was sorely tempted to accept. She loved him with enough passion for the both of them. It might be enough. It might have to be—for now.

Chapter Seventeen

Felicia's teeth chattered in spite of the blanket over her lap and the one around her shoulders. Her feet, in their half-boots, were like blocks of ice.

She took a surreptitious look at Guy. He had to be colder than she because he had already been driving this open carriage for hours.

As though sensing her study, he glanced at her. "I have changed my mind, we are going to The Folly. It is actually closer than going all the way back to London. A serious consideration in this weather."

"Ah," she murmured, "I shall be able to feel my feet soon."

His mouth twisted in a wry grin. "I was more concerned with catching up to you than in practicality. A closed carriage would have been better, but not as fast. I am sorry for the resultant discomfort."

She kept her gaze straight ahead. She had to know why he had made this decision, even though she was sure that she would not like his answer. Some things were better left unknown and this was probably one of them, but she could not marry him under the current conditions.

"Why did you come after me?" she finally managed to ask, her hands gripping the seat of the phaeton until she thought they would snap.

"I told you." His tone was clipped and no nonsense.

"Even though Miss Duckworth has broken your engagement, that does not make it necessary for you to marry me. Any woman would be glad to wed you and give you an heir."

His eyes narrowed as though what she had said angered him. "I am not marrying you to have an heir."

"But…"

Irritation radiated from every part of him. "I am marrying you because it is the right thing, the honourable thing to do."

His words hit a chord and she responded tartly, "Then don't bother. For I won't marry someone whose only reason is *honour*. You can just turn this carriage around and catch up with the mail coach, for I am not going anywhere with you."

His mouth tightened and his words were clipped. "You are coming to The Folly. As soon as your divorce is final, you will marry me. I have the Special Licence in my pocket."

"What? You are certainly confident."

His lips curled. "You have given me every indication that I am not repulsive to you."

She flushed and for the first time since clambering aboard the phaeton, she was warm. "Not very gentlemanly."

He flicked his whip over the lead horse's head. "As I told you long ago, I do what I must."

"And so do I. You can take me where you will, but you cannot force me to marry you."

"This is a pointless conversation."

She immediately bristled. "I don't agree." They entered a town before she could fully berate him. "Ah," she said as they pulled into the courtyard of a hotel. "The Swan. Annabell said you always stop here."

He glanced at her. "We cannot get to The Folly today, just as we could not get to London. Dark will be here shortly and, in this weather, we are better off here."

The fact that he was right did nothing to make her less disgruntled. He was being high-handed and autocratic. Traits she had nearly forgotten he had.

Ostlers grabbed the reins as the tiger jumped down to help. Guy climbed out and went around to help Felicia, but the mood she was in, she was already putting a foot on the ground. The innkeeper rushed out to greet them and stopped dead.

He bowed. "My lord Chillings." He turned to Felicia, "And madam." His gaze went beyond her as though he looked for someone else.

It was obvious he remembered her.

"We need two rooms," Guy said. He glanced at Felicia. "Dinner in our rooms."

A servant came out and Guy directed the boy to Felicia's luggage. It was then she realized Guy did not have any. She gave him a questioning look.

He shrugged. "I was in a hurry. I can make do. I've done so under worse conditions than these."

They followed the innkeeper inside to warmth and the smells of dinner. Instead of going to the private parlour, they went directly to their rooms. Felicia realized with a start that Guy's room was directly across the hall from hers. Embarrassment was her first reaction. The innkeeper, not seeing Annabell this time, had decided she and Guy were intimate.

She cast one fulminating look at Guy and went into her room. Her luggage was already here and she quickly got dressed for bed. The day had been long and all she wanted was food and sleep.

Tomorrow she would deal with Lord Chillings. She was not going to his estate to await his pleasure on marrying her.

Felicia descended the inn's stairs the next morning feeling human. Her clothing had been brushed and pressed while she slept. She had had plenty of tea and toast and was ready to face Guy. To her chagrin, she found him outside, impatiently waiting for her.

"We have a long way to go," he said in greeting.

The same boy who had carried her bags upstairs the night before scurried around her and deposited her luggage in the phaeton. Guy tossed him a coin for his effort. Felicia frowned.

"I am positive I can catch a coach from here to my destination, my lord," she said, staring defiantly at him.

He glanced at her. "I am sure you could. But you are not. Now get up."

She ground her teeth. "I think not," she muttered.

He stalked up to her. "If you persist in this, you will cause a scene. Believe me, they will remember it when word reaches them of my testimony, as it will. You and I are the latest scandal."

His words took the fire out of her. He was right. A fight here would just be more trouble. She shook off his helping hand and climbed in on her own, only catching her skirt once. The boy handed up the blankets, which she draped around herself. This promised to be another very cold ride.

Fortunately, it was not raining. The roads would have been quagmires. As it was, the ruts were still deep and in their way just as bad because the ground was frozen. They moved slowly and steadily in spite of the conditions.

Felicia, determined to work things through before they reached The Folly, said firmly, "I am not marrying you under the circumstances."

He did not even bother to look at her. "What will you do? You have no money, and I doubt your father will take you in."

"I will become a governess," she said with more bravado than sense.

He laughed, curt and harsh. "I doubt that. No one will hire you after the divorce and my testimony. You should know that someone leaked to the press what I said, nearly to the word. We are both doubly ruined."

The breath caught in her throat. "I did not know that."

"I did not think you did."

She stared at nothing. "Well," she finally said, "I did not really think anyone would hire me. I will just have to think of something else. There must be something. I am a good seamstress. I could do that."

He snorted. "Now you are grasping at straws. Face facts, Felicia, you have to marry me. You have no other options unless you wish to starve."

She closed her eyes and wished she could as easily close her ears to his words. Her voice shook. "I can go back to my father. He won't like it, but he cannot turn me out."

"He can and he will," Guy said, his voice laced with anger. "I can guarantee you that he will."

"How?" Much as she hated saying or even thinking

the next words, she did. "If I agree to remarry at his choosing, he will be furious with me now, but he will take me in. I am a commodity to him."

"And who could he find to marry you?"

"I don't know, but I imagine that if he offers enough money, someone will take me off his hands. Edmund would have done so if I had agreed to give him more children."

By the time the words were out of her mouth, she felt totally defeated. Everything she had hoped to gain by going to London was ashes.

"Have you spoken to your father?" Guy asked, a funny note in his voice. "Since the testimony?"

She shook her head. "No. I left."

He did not speak for some time. "Then you don't know that your father has already picked your new husband."

She jerked. "What? How could he?" An awful suspicion caught her. "How do you know?"

"Because Dunston told me."

"You?" she asked, aghast, her voice barely loud enough to hear.

"Yes."

She collapsed back in the seat. "He has gone too far," she said. Then another thought hit that brought with it more pain. "That is why you asked me to marry you."

He did not answer.

She turned away, wishing she could jump out of the carriage and never have to face this man again. Through no fault of his, he had been dragged into the sordid details of her life. And now her father had tried to make him marry her.

When she thought she could speak without sobbing, she said, "I am sorry. Truly sorry."

"Don't be," he said curtly. "Your father cannot make me offer marriage unless I wish it. I have offered."

Felicia sat, dazed and hurt. She did not know what to answer. She wanted to marry him. Had wanted to do so since the moment she saw him, coming towards her bed, when she did not even know who she was.

"Why?" she finally asked.

He shrugged, the capes of his greatcoat filling with the breeze. "Not for an heir."

"Why?" she asked again, wanting him to say something she knew he would not, yet unable to resist the need to try and make him say he loved her.

"Honour, as I already said."

His gloved hands tightened on the reins and the horses shied just a little. He was too good a driver to lose control.

"Honour and nothing else?"

With an abrupt twist of the wrist, he pulled the phaeton to the side of the narrow road and stopped. Still gripping the reins in one hand, he reached for her with the other. Hope rose in Felicia's heart.

He pulled her to him. His mouth descended on hers. "Passion, Felicia, passion such as I have never known before."

His kiss was brutal, consuming and arousing. She sank into sensations. Still, a part of her cried. Passion, not love. It had never been love for him. But at least he felt something for her, a powerful emotion that might become love—some day.

He finally released her and Felicia swayed. Fortunately, he kept hold of her arm, or she would have fallen backwards and tumbled to the ground. Her mind still whirled.

"That is why I am marrying you, Felicia," he said, his deep voice a harsh rasp.

She lifted her gloved fingers to her swollen lips, her eyes, wide, watched him. Surely passion such as theirs was a start. Love would follow.

"I accept," she said softly.

"You won't regret it, Felicia," he said. "I promise you that."

She nodded. There were no words she could say because she could not tell him her hope.

It was late afternoon with dusk rapidly approaching when they pulled into the circular driveway of The Folly. Oswald was still in London, so a footman met them. Felicia soon found herself in her old suite, where she collapsed on to the bed. She felt as though she had come home after a long and perilous journey.

She fell instantly asleep, feeling safe.

Felicia started awake.

Sitting up, she realized she had fallen asleep on top of the bed still in her travelling clothes. There was a fire in the grate that sent tendrils of warmth her way.

Movement caught her eye. Guy.

He had pulled the slipper chair near the bed and sat there watching her. He had changed into his robe.

"I did not mean to wake you," he said. "But it's probably best. You did not look comfortable, just exhausted."

She stood, feeling much less vulnerable on her feet than lying across her bed. "Why are you here?"

He got to his feet and dug a small velvet box from his pocket. "To give you this."

She took the container.

"Open it," he said when all she did was look at it.

"A ring?"

He nodded. "The Chillings engagement ring."

Shivers chased down her spine. With fingers suddenly clumsy, she fumbled open the top. Inside was a magnificent ruby ring.

"This is beautiful," she said softly. "I cannot wear this. What if I lost it?"

"You said you would marry me," he replied. "Or have you changed your mind again?"

She shook her head. "No. Only I would feel uncomfortable wearing something this valuable."

He shrugged and stuffed his hands into the robe's pockets. "All the Chillings's brides wear it. It has not been lost for over a hundred years."

She looked from the ring to him. "You did not give this to Miss Duckworth. I would have seen it if you had."

He turned his back to her and went to the fireplace. "No, I did not. The arrangement between her and me was too impersonal. I might have given it to her later."

"Did Suzanne wear this?"

As soon as the words were out of her mouth, Felicia regretted them. This was none of her business.

"Yes. She loved the ring."

Felicia nodded. "I can see why."

"Put it on," he said harshly.

She stared at the piece of jewellery. Surely he cared for her. Surely he felt more than passion. He had only given this ring to one other woman, and he had loved her.

Slowly, her fingers shaking, she took the ring from the box. She set the box on the table and slid the ring on to her finger. It fitted perfectly. She heard him release his breath.

"For a minute, I thought you would not do it," he said.

She held her hand up so she could admire the ruby. It flashed like blood in the light from the fire. "It is lovely."

"Burmese. A Burmese ruby," he murmured. "They are the finest."

Still looking at the ring, she said, "You loved Suzanne a great deal."

He started. "Where did that come from? We were talking about the ruby."

"Yes, I know," she murmured. "But she was the last to wear it. Putting it on reminded me of her."

He pushed off from the mantel and headed to her. He caught her chin in his hand and lifted it so that she looked at him.

"What Suzanne and I had was different from what you and I share."

She gave a tiny, brittle laugh. "You had love."

His eyes widened before narrowing. "Yes. On my part it was more the love of an older brother for a woman he had watched grow up. Oh, I won't lie to you, Felicia. We obviously consummated our marriage, but what I felt for her was nothing like what rages through me when I am near you—or even when I am not." His lips twisted into a self-derogatory smile.

She watched him, waiting and hoping he would say something about love. Yet knowing he would not. He did not surprise her.

Finally, he released her and stepped away. She did nothing to stop him.

"I am leaving tomorrow," he said. "Oswald and Mrs Drummond should arrive. As will Mary."

"You are leaving?" she managed to say around the lump in her throat. "Why?"

He studied her. "Surely you know."

She shook her head. "No, I don't. You have never fled from me before."

"I was never engaged to marry you before. I was never so afraid of losing control with you before."

His vehemence surprised her. "I don't understand."

He scowled and rubbed his long fingers through his beard. "I don't want to get you pregnant, Felicia. I don't want to lose you like I did Suzanne."

She moved towards him, but he spun on his heel and left. It was as though he truly feared what he might do. She did not understand any of this, and he had not given her an opportunity to talk with him about it.

She could follow him. She knew where his rooms were, but what then?

She did not know. She felt totally helpless when she should feel completely happy.

She hoped more than anything that this marriage would not turn out as badly as her first. Surely not. She loved Guy desperately. He desired her. It was a start. It had to be for it was all she had.

Chapter Eighteen

The Folly, six months later...

Felicia stood dressed in lavender trimmed with Brussels lace. Annabell stood as her bridesmaid. The minister who presided over the small family chapel read the marriage ceremony. At first the minister had hesitated, but his living was given to him by Guy and the Special Licence entitled the possessor to be married anywhere, any time, by anyone.

Guy stood dressed in grey with a heavily embroidered waistcoat and matching satin breeches and silk stockings. Dominic stood as his groomsman.

The four of them, Oswald, Mrs Drummond and Mary were the only ones present. Felicia had not asked her father.

Felicia watched her future husband's face. He looked solemn, not joyful or even glad. For the hundredth time since he had collected her from the mail coach, she wondered if she had done the right thing in accepting his offer. It was too late now.

She turned her attention back to the minister. He

droned on until reaching the part where he asked, "Do you, Felicia Anne Marbury, take this man as your lawfully wedded husband, to have and to hold in sickness and in health until death do you part?"

She looked at Guy who was watching her with a quiet intensity that made her nerves jump. "Yes," she whispered.

The minister said, "Do you, Guy William Chillings, take this woman as your lawfully wedded wife, to have and to hold in sickness and in health until death do you part?"

"I do," Guy said firmly, his voice carrying in the stone interior of the chapel.

"The ring."

Dominic stepped forward with a gold band inlaid with channel-set rubies. Guy took it, never taking his eyes from Felicia. She held her hand out, and he slid the circle over her finger until it lay next to the engagement ring with its flawless ruby.

"I pronounce you man and wife." The minister beamed at them. "You may kiss the bride," he prompted.

Guy looked to her for permission. She managed a tiny smile which he took as welcome.

His mouth moved on hers like a butterfly, then he was gone. Brief as the encounter had been, she felt as though he had ravished her. She tingled everywhere.

It was also the first time he had touched her since he put the engagement ring on her finger six months before. She had decided that not only was theirs to be a marriage of convenience, but that he no longer desired her. It was as though his proposal killed whatever else he might have felt for her. She had spent the last six months living at The Folly with Guy never coming to stay at his own home. Still, rumours had reached her that the ladies of the *ton* shunned him. The members of that elite group would never accept her. Even after she and Guy wed, she would not be acceptable to the sticklers.

She felt Annabell's fingers on the small of her back and realized belatedly that Guy had turned to go, his elbow crooked for her to tuck her hand into. She did so, feeling awkward and gauche. Together, they walked sedately down the aisle to the outside door. They passed through the portal into fresh air.

Even the sun smiled down on them. The daffodils were in full bloom, their butter-yellow and pale white clusters the harbingers of the summer to come.

Neither spoke as they made their way down the paved path to the main house. Behind them Annabell and Dominic conversed in hushed tones. Felicia caught mention of a man named Fitzsimmon, but nothing more.

The servants awaited them at the entrance, lined in order of precedence. Felicia nodded and shook hands with every one, right down to the lowest scullery maid.

Very few people came to the after-wedding breakfast. Not many had been invited.

Dominic rose and lifted his champagne glass. "To the happy couple. May they live long and prosper." Everyone clapped and drank their fine French wine.

Annabell rose. "May they be fruitful." Laughs accompanied this toast. "For Dominic and I are not interested in taking over this elephant," she finished, waving her arm to encompass The Folly. "This is Guy's passion and should go to the heirs of his body."

Felicia blushed at such bold speaking. Fortunately all she had to do was smile at their guests.

Guy stood. "Thank you all for being here. Please enjoy yourselves."

He held out his hand to Felicia, who took it and rose to stand beside him. His fingers were warm and strong around hers. She needed to know that he was here. All through the past months she had wondered why he had really stayed away. Together they left the dining room. In the foyer, he released her.

"Mrs Drummond has arranged for your things to be moved into the suite adjacent to mine. The rooms were my mother's. If there is anything you want changed, by all means tell Mrs Drummond."

She nodded.

He gave her a curt bow and turned away. "Guy," she said hastily, "where are you going?"

Even as she said the words, she regretted them. After he took her off the mail coach and sent her here to live without him, everything had changed between them. And not for the better. Now, he had married her after six months of not even writing to her. Why did she think he would give her an explanation? He had not sent even a note during the last half-year. It had been as though she had ceased to exist for him. Then, suddenly, he was here with Annabell and Dominic, saying it was time to marry.

"Out." His tone brooked no argument. Nor did he bother to look at her.

She watched him go, and blinked rapidly to try and stop the moisture from becoming tears. This was her wedding day, not a funeral.

But it was hard.

* * *

Felicia dismissed Mary. "You may go, Mary. And don't bother tomorrow morning. I intend to sleep late after today."

"Yes, my lady." Mary bobbed a curtsy, her face flaming.

Felicia's mouth twisted. Mary thought her mistress and master were going to make love all night. Nothing could be further from the truth. Much as Felicia might wish it otherwise.

Resigned to a wedding night spent alone while her groom was goodness only knew where, Felicia picked up Jane Austen's latest book and sat by the fire. She huddled under a cashmere blanket and the heavy wool of her robe.

She was well into the story when she heard a soft knock coming from the door that connected with Guy's room. She twisted around in time to see him enter, leaving the door open behind him as though he intended to leave in just a minute.

"Felicia," he said, "may I come in?"

She nodded. "You are the master of the house."

Her words were loaded with bitter irony. He was the master and he had made it abundantly clear that she might be the mistress legally, but any woman could fill her position in his life. He might just as well have wedded Miss Duckworth for all the passion there was in this marriage.

He moved closer so the light from the fire and the brace of candles she had lighted to read by showed him better. He wore the same dressing gown he had worn her first night here, when he had interrogated her mercilessly. A glowing white linen shirt, open at the neck, filled in the V formed by the robe crossing his chest. Black satin trousers showed beneath the robe's hem.

And like that night so long ago, she found her pulse

speeding up. He was not a classically handsome man, but the angle of his jaw, the slant of his nose, the full sensuality of his mouth all combined to make her want him with an unrelenting ache.

Would that he felt the same about her—still.

"I wanted to give you this," he said, holding out a velvet case. "It is traditionally given to the Chillings brides on their wedding night."

"Another gift of jewellery?" she asked, not trying to hide her bitter sarcasm.

"Just open it, Felicia," he said.

She did so. This time her fingers did not shake as they had when she had opened the box with the engagement ring. Inside was a pearl and emerald choker. Nestled in the strands of pearls were matching ear drops.

"Oh," she breathed. "It is even more beautiful than in the picture."

"I was going to give it to you to wear at the wedding," he said, stepping forward and taking it from the box. "But it did not go with the lavender you were wearing."

"No." She finally smiled. "It would not."

"Turn around," he said, "and I will hook it."

She did so without thought. It was such a stunning piece of jewellery and it did not have the same emotional impact as the engagement ring had had for her.

His fingers played along her nape as he fastened the necklace. His breath brushed her sensitive skin. Was she the only one feeling this deep need?

"There," he said finally, his voice a rasp.

When he did not step away from her, she turned, her shoulder touching his chest in the process. Completely facing him, she stopped. Inches separated them, but it could be miles. She did not reach for him, only looked at him.

Guy's jaw hardened. "Don't look at me like that."

She notched her chin up. "Like what?"

His hands clenched at his sides. "Like you want me to make love to you."

She flushed, but did not turn away. "We are married."

His Adam's apple moved as he swallowed. "Convenience."

"Ah, yes," she said, sarcasm dripping from every word. "You do seem to have a fondness for convenience."

"And what do you suggest I do, Felicia?" he said coldly, pointedly. "Make love to you, get you pregnant with my child and then watch you die bearing that child?"

If he had hit her, she could not have been as surprised. "That is a macabre chain of events," she said carefully.

She was beginning to understand his behaviour, or so she hoped. If his real reason for avoiding her these past months was fear she would die birthing his heir, then there was hope for them. He had to care for her.

He smoothed down his beard with one long finger. "It is a very possible scenario."

"Why?" she asked softly. "Because that is how you lost Suzanne?"

He nodded. "It is not uncommon."

"You need an heir."

He shrugged, turned and walked away from her. "Dominic can provide one. Even Bell can if Dominic does not. We Chillings are fortunate in that regard."

"I see," Felicia said, taking a step towards him,

careful not to be too aggressive. "You have no intention of making love to me because you do not want
me to die in childbirth."

He tensed. "Yes," he said, his voice full of pain.

She shook her head slowly and took another step
toward him. "I have already had two children, Guy.
My chances of dying like Suzanne are very slim." Her
mouth quirked just a little. "If I were a gambler, I
would put odds on my survival."

"What kind of odds?" he asked, watching her with
eyes full of hunger.

"Ninety-nine to one," she murmured, drawing
closer.

"You exaggerate."

"Perhaps, but none the less they are very good."
She paused when there was only a foot separating
them. "And you need an heir. Why should you put
that burden on Dominic or Annabell, for I would wager
they do not want it?"

His mouth twisted. "You know them well."

"Guy," she said softly, coaxing him with her tone,
"do not push me away because you are afraid. I am
not, and it is my life."

Instead of closing the distance between them, she
reached up and undid the bow that held her nightdress
closed at the neck. Guy's gaze darted to the hollow at
the base of her throat. She could not stop the smile that
curved her lips.

Moving slowly, wondering if other women did this
sort of thing and not caring one way or the other, she
lifted the fine muslin over her head. She wore nothing
underneath.

He took a step back, but his gaze roved hungrily up

and down her body. His robe parted where his response to her protruded. Her smile widened.

She pulled out the ribbon holding her hair in a braid and started combing her fingers through the length. "Would you help me?" she asked, knowing how much he liked her hair.

He gulped.

She closed the distance between them. "You might as well, Guy, for I intend to have you. We are married now. You must do your husbandly duties."

His reaction was swift and fierce, as though a dam had broken inside him. He grabbed her to his chest and devoured her lips. The dread of his rejection that she had held at bay slipped away. She wrapped her arms around his neck and held tightly.

The fine silver thread on his robe pricked at the tender flesh of her bosom. It was shockingly arousing while his mouth was on hers and his maleness pressed to the juncture of her thighs. When he lowered his mouth to her bosom, bowing her back so that his loins pressed into hers and his teeth caught her nipple, Felicia exploded.

She gasped with surprise and pleasure.

He released her only to gather her into his arms and carry her to the bed. She lay there watching as he pulled his robe off, then his shirt and then his trousers. He never took his gaze off her, and then he was beside her, stroking her, stoking her desire once more.

She rose to meet him, her mouth grazing over every part of him. Her hands explored him as intimately as was possible. His breathing became ragged.

He was above her, then below her. She straddled his hips, her eyes never leaving his. She saw surprise move over him as she caught him in one hand and slowly guided him inside her. She did not stop her downward movement until he was deeply buried.

She bit her lower lip at the intense pleasure. He remained perfectly still, as though to move would shatter everything. She began the age-old rhythm.

His hands went to her hips and guided her, speeding them up, then slowing them down. It was sheer bliss.

His fingers tightened on her skin and he lifted her up. Suddenly aware of what he intended, she shook her head.

"No."

She gripped his wrists and took him by surprise. She pulled his hands from her and sank down, deeply, irrevocably. She gasped. His moan joined hers as he bucked, taking them both over the edge.

She collapsed on top of him, still holding him tightly inside her body. She never wanted to let him go.

He took the decision away from her. This time when he lifted her, she let him. She sank down on to the bed beside him.

"Why, Felicia?" He lay on his back, one leg bent at the knee, one arm flung over his eyes.

"Because I love you. Because I could not stand to be married to you, to see you every day and not make love with you. It would have killed me more surely than giving you a child."

"It was only once. I can hope that nothing will come of it."

She sat bolt upright and then straddled him. "I intend to pursue you morning, noon and all night."

She rotated her hips, a fleeting sense of embarrassment at her boldness heating her already warm skin. She pushed the hesitation away. She was fighting for her happiness.

She moved again, an invitation so erotic that Guy instantly accepted before he even knew what was happening. She rode him to ground until both of them panted in exhaustion and release.

"You cannot keep away from me forever, Guy," she said.

"You are a determined woman, Felicia."

His chest rose and fell as he took gulping breaths of air. His entire body felt like he had been well used. Satisfaction curved his lips.

She leaned over him, her mouth finding his nipple while her fingers went lower. It was minutes only before, still inside her, he found his pleasure yet again.

"It has now been three times," she said, her lips swollen and her eyes dilated with desire. "Do you think we can make it four?"

He groaned. "Felicia, I am not a stud."

Her smile was seduction itself. "I think we can remedy that, my love."

He gasped as she lifted off him only to take him into her mouth. It was long, agonizingly pleasurable minutes before he was able to think coherently again.

"Enough," he panted.

"Promise me you will never deny me or yourself again, Guy?" Her fingers took the place of her mouth.

"Gads," he moaned. "I don't…know….how much…more I can…take…"

"Promise?"

"I…"

"Guy," she said, "I am not a hothouse flower to be cosseted and left to live a sterile life. I love you. I want to bear your children. I will bear them, will you or nill you."

He looked at the determination written over her face

and knew she spoke the truth. She knew the power she wielded over him and she would not hesitate to use it. His good intentions would be as naught when she began to caress him.

With the little energy he had left, he caught her face in his hands and kissed her. "You are stubborn, my love. Stubborn. I pray to God that you are as strong as you claim, for you have made it abundantly clear that I cannot resist you when you set your mind to having me."

She returned his kiss with ardour. "I love you, Guy William Chillings. Our children will love you."

Epilogue

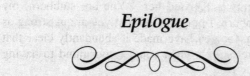

The Folly, nine months later...

"Guy. Guy," Felicia said, pushing her husband in the ribs in an attempt to wake him.

They lay in his large four-poster bed where they had slept every night since their wedding. The fire was dead and the room was freezing.

"Guy," Felicia tried again, poking him harder this time.

"Wha—?" He raised up to one elbow. "Is it...?"

"Yes," she said, joy filling her voice. "I...oh, that was particularly strong."

"Right." Naked as the day he was born, he jumped from the bed and groped in the dark for his robe. He pulled its warmth on and yelled, "Jeffries."

Felicia, both amused and exhausted from the last nine months and knowing the next hours were going to be trying, laughed. "Guy, I have done this twice before. Calm down."

"Jeffries," he yelled again.

Felicia angled herself into a sitting position and

rested. "Guy, please help me up. It will be easier and quicker if I can walk some."

He rushed to her side. "Don't get up, Fel. I need to light a lamp. The doctor did not say anything about walking. Stay there," he said more forcefully when she tried to stand on her own.

"Jeffries," he yelled again. "Drat the man. Where is he when I need him?"

"Sleeping, Guy," Felicia said patiently. "I need Mrs Drummond. Please fetch her."

"I cannot leave you," he said stubbornly. "Jeffries will fetch her."

"Jeffries isn't here to get her, Guy. You are."

He rubbed his beard. "Promise me you won't get up."

"I won't promise you anything, Guy. You need to trust my judgement. I know what I am doing."

He scowled. The yellow glow from the gas lamp he had lit showed him her grimace of pain. "All right. Stay here."

She smiled. "There is nowhere I can go in this condition," she said, humour lacing her words.

He cast one last anxious glance at her and raced from the room. Felicia's smile disappeared as another cramp spasmed through her abdomen. She had never told Guy that her last delivery had been long and difficult. It would have done no good and worried him to the point that he would have been impossible to deal with through the pregnancy. But Mrs Drummond knew and had found a very good midwife.

She struggled to her feet and took slow, deep breaths in an effort to control the pain. Her water broke.

"My lady," Mrs Drummond said, coming through

the door with Guy close behind. "I have sent for Mrs Jones."

"I have sent for the doctor," Guy added.

"Thank you, both of you. *Oh!*" Felicia gasped.

Mrs Drummond turned back to Guy. "It is time you left, my lord. This is women's work."

Guy's mouth tightened.

Felicia waddled over to him and put a hand on his arm. "It is going to be fine, my love. A woman knows these things."

He stared at her, his pupils dilated. "I will be right outside." He grabbed her by the upper arms and pulled her to him, burying his face in the crook of her neck. "I love you so much, Fel. Don't leave me."

She slid her arms around his waist and turned her head so that her lips brushed his cheek. "Never, my love. Everything is going to be fine. I promise."

He took a deep, shuddering breath and released her. With infinite tenderness, he smoothed the loose tangles of hair back from her face and hooked them behind her ears. Just hours before he had lost himself in its luxuriant length.

"I love you," he murmured, kissing her lightly on the lips.

She nodded, tears at his tenderness and concern blurring her vision. She heard the door close behind him. Then Mrs Drummond was at her side.

Guy paced the hallway.

Annabell stuck her head out of the bedroom. "Guy, go to the library. You are not doing any good torturing yourself like this, and you already look awful."

He turned a haggard face to her. His hair was unkempt. He was still in his house robe with nothing on beneath. He was a mess.

"No. I'm not leaving until I see my wife and child safe and healthy."

She shook her head. A moan of pain came from inside. "I must go. This shouldn't be much longer, Guy."

The door slammed shut.

Guy stood still looking at the place where Bell's head had been. This should be going very fast. Mrs Drummond had assured him that Felicia would have no trouble. Felicia had assured him.

He was glad Bell had come to stay with them this last month. She had been a good companion for Felicia and a rock of strength for him. She remembered Suzanne's lying-in and oftentimes understood his fear where no one else could. Felicia had been so positive that everything would be fine. He had learned that about her these last months.

When he first met her, she had been recovering from grief. As their marriage and their bond had strengthened, her naturally positive outlook on life had surfaced. She had brought him great happiness. He could not lose her now. He could not.

He turned to go down the opposite length of the hall. Ten paces later, he heard the door open.

"Guy," Bell said.

He whirled around, dread turning his stomach to mush.

"Guy," Bell said, "you have a healthy son." Her smile broke through. "And an exhausted, but otherwise fine, wife."

His entire body slumped with relief, followed by an energy he had thought long gone in the wake of the last hours. He sprinted to the door and into the room. He sensed Bell and Mrs Drummond leaving, but he did not say anything to them. He couldn't. His entire focus was on his wife.

Felicia lay propped on a mountain of pillows, her hair spread around her like a copper-shot satin skirt. Her face was white from exhaustion and her eyes bruised, but she smiled.

"Guy—my love—" she said softly, "you have an heir."

He closed the ground between them and took her hand and raised it to his lips. "More importantly, I have you safe."

Snuggled into the curve of her arm, his face nuzzled to her breast, was his son. A tuft of dark hair sprouted from the baby's head. Joy and amazement filled Guy.

"He has blue eyes," Felicia said softly. "But that may change. All babies have blue eyes."

He looked at her, not understanding the importance of this. "He is perfect no matter what colour his eyes. He is ours."

She continued to smile, but he could see she needed rest. He circled to the other side of the bed and got in next to his wife and son. Careful not to squash the baby, he gathered mother and child into his arms.

Felicia sighed and laid her head on Guy's shoulder. "You see," she said, her voice drifting. "I told you not to worry, that everything would be fine. I was right."

He stroked her hair, his fascinated gaze on his son's face. "Yes."

"And the next one will be easier still," she murmured, falling into sleep.

Love such as he had never thought possible filled Guy. He looked in wonderment at his family. Miracles did happen.

* * * * *

LIVE THE EMOTION

Modern Romance™
...seduction and
passion guaranteed

Tender Romance™
...love affairs that
last a lifetime

Medical Romance™
...medical drama
on the pulse

Historical Romance™
...rich, vivid and
passionate

Sensual Romance™
...sassy, sexy and
seductive

Blaze Romance™
...the temperature's
rising

27 new titles every month.

Live the emotion

MILLS & BOON®

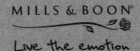

MILLS & BOON®

Live the emotion

Historical Romance™

THE UNKNOWN WIFE by Mary Brendan

A single night's passionate encounter has come back to haunt
Colonel Etienne Hauke. He has a son by a disgraced Society
beauty who demands that he make an honest woman of her!
Isabel must marry her charming seducer for the sake of her child
– though she determines it will be a marriage in name only…

A DAMNABLE ROGUE by Anne Herries

Forced into earning a living, Emma Sommerton was thankful that
an old schoolfriend wanted a companion. Little did she realise
that she would be put at the mercy of the Marquis of Lytham!
Angered at his intention to make her his mistress, she was
amazed when her love for this rogue prompted her to accept…

THE OVERLORD'S BRIDE
by Margaret Moore

Early Medieval England

The wife of Raymond D'Estienne, Lord Kirkheathe, was dead,
and rumour tarred his reputation. Now Elizabeth Perronet
found herself his new bride – astounded at the feelings he
provoked in her. Raymond believed all women were traitors –
what was he to make of Elizabeth, fresh from the convent and
determined to change his life!

On sale 2nd January 2004

*Available at most branches of WHSmith, Tesco, Martins, Borders,
Eason, Sainsbury's and all good paperback bookshops.*

1203/04

The *Midnight* Hour

Celebrate the New Year...
with a gorgeous new man!

Kate Walker   Kate Hoffmann   Lilian Darcy

On sale 2nd January 2004

Available at most branches of WHSmith, Tesco, Martins, Borders,
Eason, Sainsbury's and all good paperback bookshops.

0104/24/MB84

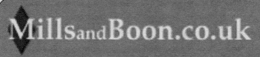

FREE
2 BOOKS
AND A SURPRISE GIFT!

We would like to take this opportunity to thank you for reading this Mills & Boon® book by offering you the chance to take TWO more specially selected titles from the Historical Romance™ series absolutely FREE! We're also making this offer to introduce you to the benefits of the Reader Service™ —

- ★ FREE home delivery
- ★ FREE monthly Newsletter
- ★ FREE gifts and competitions
- ★ Exclusive Reader Service discount
- ★ Books available before they're in the shops

Accepting these FREE books and gift places you under no obligation to buy; you may cancel at any time, even after receiving your free shipment. Simply complete your details below and return the entire page to the address below. *You don't even need a stamp!*

YES! Please send me 2 free Historical Romance books and a surprise gift. I understand that unless you hear from me, I will receive 4 superb new titles every month for just £3.49 each, postage and packing free. I am under no obligation to purchase any books and may cancel my subscription at any time. The free books and gift will be mine to keep in any case.

H3ZEC

Ms/Mrs/Miss/Mr ....Initials ....

BLOCK CAPITALS PLEASE

Surname ....

Address ....

....

....Postcode ....

Send this whole page to:
UK: FREEPOST CN81, Croydon, CR9 3WZ
EIRE: PO Box 4546, Kilcock, County Kildare (stamp required)

Offer valid in UK and Eire only and not available to current Reader Service subscribers to this series. We reserve the right to refuse an application and applicants must be aged 18 years or over. Only one application per household. Terms and prices subject to change without notice. Offer expires 31st March 2004. As a result of this application, you may receive offers from Harlequin Mills & Boon and other carefully selected companies. If you would prefer not to share in this opportunity please write to The Data Manager at the address above.

Mills & Boon® is a registered trademark owned by Harlequin Mills & Boon Limited.
Historical Romance™ is being used as a trademark.